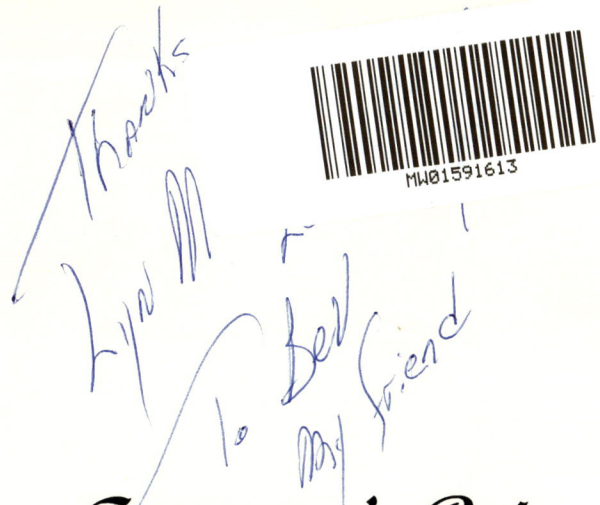

Thanks
Lyn M

To Ben
my friend

Tomorrow's Rain

By

Lyn Miller LaCoursiere

Comments from readers:

You did it Mom. I'm proud of you!
----Jeff Loven /Cities GREATEST one-man band!

I had a hard time putting your book down. I was actually sad it ended, as I WAS GETTING SO ATTACHED TO LINDY!
----MariLou Anderson /Well known teacher

I loved it, and I am looking forward to the next one!
----Julie Larsen /top Remax realtor

A REMARKABLE USE OF PROSE. Well written and suspenseful. Hard to put the book down!
----Karen Siegfried /Retired and loving it!

CHARMING, WITTY AND INTRIGUING! Red enjoyed it and is waiting for the next one!
----Judy Ann Anderson /Arizona's newest residents

When will we hear more about Tanner Burke?
-----Billy Loven/CEO and president

Good job. KEEP ON WRITING!
----Del Loven/Director of Myers School of Art

Now who is SHE really?
----Val Thayer/Cole, Kaden and Trey's Grandma

Books by Lyn Miller LaCoursiere

Nightmares and Dreams

Tomorrow's Rain

A Note from the Author

If you read *Nightmares and Dreams,* you have met Lindy Lewis. You know her troubles begin after she loses her husband, when she burns the mansion they had lovingly renovated and that the driving-force was her discovery of carpenter ants feasting away on her precious domain.

Actually, some of this is true, only I found the ants dining voraciously on the garage walls and the wooden fences my husband had built around our yard. I was truly horrified at the scene as I watched the huge creatures prodding along with pieces of my property stuffed in their proboscis. And, as a child, I do recall hearing my father declare, "Burn them, it's the only way!"

Years ago, when I started what has evolved into this series, I needed an incident for the story and chose the actual discovery of the ants and their disturbing destruction for the beginning. And, of course, I embellished.

Writing can be a lonely business and sometimes hours and even days can fly by as ideas and dialogue ramble around in your head occupying and demanding space. Lindy's tumultuous adventures and travels are the result of that process. So, my dear readers, as you continue to accompany her on her journey seeking peace and contentment, I trust you will enjoy *Tomorrow's Rain.* I am truly blessed by your generous, loving support!

You can e-mail me at lindylewis1@msn.com or please visit my web-site at Mystery Novels Lyn Miller Lacoursiere.com.

Acknowledgements

Over time with help of friends in my
critiquing group I'm learning how to further develop
my ability to tell a story.
Hats off to all of you in your own endeavors.
Thanks to Mary for her patient technical
advise along the way.
And also a special thank you to my granddaughter
Danielle for her final assistance!

This book is dedicated
to my children;
Del, Bill, Jeff and Val
And their
lovely families!

-1-

Speeding out of Birch Lake, a small town in the north and with no destination in mind, her emotions deep and troubled, Lindy Lewis drove through the day and well into the night. When her eyelids drooped and the loud booming horn of a semi-truck suddenly startled her wide awake, she managed to swerve out of its path just in time. Realizing for everyone's safety she had to get off the freeway, checked into the first hotel she found along the way.

Using a favorite nom-de-plume, she signed in as Lola Lang and informed the clerk she would stay several nights and paid in cash. The first thing she did after locating her room was hide the box which held her most treasured possession, then ran a tub of hot water and finally sank into its soothing embrace. So much had happened her head was in a whirl.

***

It had been over a year since her troubles had begun and her secure world had come crashing down. Loaded with bills after her husband's illness and his sudden death, and then the discovery of a horrid infestation of ants that were in the last phase of destruction to her beautiful home, she had burned the marauders. When the house had lain in a pile of charred ashes on the ground too, she'd collected the cool million dollars insurance. And believing she could find happiness again now that she was rich, had traveled far and wide, changed her name and appearance numerous times and almost found that perfect place. Then she had met Mario D'Agustino, and witnessed the handsome playboy murder another man in cold blood in Hilton Head, South Carolina. When she'd rushed back to Reed Conners for his legal help and protection, he'd straightened out her involvement and believed all her promises. But today, just this morning she had left his bed and his town.

She sighed and sank lower in the bath tub, terribly sad. She wondered now if she had been too hasty when she'd made that decision. But, her dream about what a future might have been like with him had totally shaken her.

She swiped at a stray tear and raised a foot out of the water as she contemplated the events of the last days, then amidst all her troubles saw she needed a pedicure and a manicure!

The next day as she sat in a coffee shop and munched on a sandwich after hours at a spa, her heart beat thundered in her chest as a woman waved at her from across the room.

"Miss Lang, I saw you check into the hotel last night." she said as she came over to where Lindy was seated. "Do you mind if I join you for a few minutes," she asked in a heavily accented voice.

Lindy warily sucked in a breath as the woman pulled out a chair and sat down. "I see you've been shopping," the stranger commented looking at Lindy's packages.

Lindy's thoughts raced. Who is this woman? And, how does she know my name? But taken aback by her bold intrusion, she remained silent.

"My name is Solvieg, Solly for short." Plump lips piled up over her even white teeth.

Lindy busied herself lighting a cigarette, then blew out a cloud of smoke as she studied her. Had Mario's people found her?

Out of curiosity and stalling for time she asked, "Solvieg, that's Scandinavian, are you new in this country?"

Solly shook her head. "Oh no, I've lived here for years. But how about you, are you going somewhere special?"

Lindy straightened in her chair on guard at Solly's obvious interest. A tingle of alarm shot down her back. Actually she didn't know where she was going. Had just been intent on traveling fast and far and now randomly picked a place and said, "Savannah, Georgia."

"Really," Solly exclaimed, "have you been there before?"

"I've just traveled through." Lindy took another drag of her cigarette. Now, why is she so interested in where I'm going? But deciding to play along and see what developed she added, "From what I've seen it's a lovely place."

Solly seemed about to say something then glanced at her watch and said, "Oh cripes Lola, I've got to leave, but why don't we meet later in the lounge at the hotel and have a cocktail?"

Lindy agreed. "Around eight works for me," she replied.

Solly stood up and hurried off leaving a trail of Ciara perfume in her wake. But as Lindy finished her sandwich and sipped the last of the soft drink she thought, just what is this woman's agenda? A little niggling worry nipped at her thoughts that maybe she should get back on the road, right now!

But several hours later, after deciding she needed to find out more about this woman Lindy waited in the hotel lounge, and soon Solly's fragrance preceded her as she entered the bar. Wearing an ankle length beige outfit, jewelry adorned her ears and a necklace draped over a full bosom. Her green eyes were lined in brown which accentuated her fair skin and blonde hair.

Lindy took a swallow of her Manhattan and sat back. And remembering a phrase she'd heard somewhere about "keeping friends close but your enemies closer," she smiled at her new found acquaintance, intent on finding out just what she was up to. If she might really be one of Mario's minions!

Smiling warily she asked, "What do you drink Solly?"

Solly sat down at the bar and put her elbows on the mahogany surface. "A martini," she told the bartender who stood waiting.

"Hmm, I love those too," Lindy said, "But lately brandy seems to work." She put a cigarette into the elegant silver holder that she used for special occasions and lit up. Solly opened her purse and took out a foreign looking package and put a skinny brown cigarillo between her lips. After getting settled with their drinks Solly said, "Lola I'm sorry, sometimes I just come on too strong. It's just that I get so darn lonesome in this country!"

"Don't you have family?" Lindy asked as she blew smoke towards the ceiling.

Solly pressed her lips together. "Oh sure," she said, "but they live in Europe. I haven't been home for years." Her handsome face saddened as she went on to say that she was divorced and had one son who was terribly busy.

As the two women sat together that night sipping their cocktails and sharing parts of their lives, Solly said, "Lindy, I would love to join you in Savannah." Then confessed, "I'm just a lonely middle aged woman who makes beds here in the hotel and I need a friend!"

And two weeks later, needing a friend herself, Lindy called her and invited her to join her in beautiful Savannah. And, together they toured the city, enjoyed the restaurants and shops.

And just a few days after Solly's arrival, after a late night out, Lindy rolled over in her four-poster bed, irritated by an intrusion. Someone was yelling something. Then she heard the voice again, this time shrill and filled with alarm.

"Lola, for cripes sake, get out, the house is burning!" a woman yelled.

Lindy pulled the comforter closer and snuggled. Who was yelling and who the hell was Lola?

Finally settled in her new home, a place to start over in, in this town of southern history and romance, she dreamed of frilly curtains, moss laden oak trees, floating long skirts and large garden hats.

So lovely, she murmured and relaxed with a stretch, then suddenly realized she had to struggle to get a breath! She threw the covers off and jumped up. And to her horror saw it was not the morning sun blazing in through her windows, but flames darting in and out under her door lighting up her room. As she gaped horrified at what was happening black smoke began to creep towards her. Realizing escape was impossible through the flaming exit, she ran to the French door that led out to a balcony. Although her bedroom was on the second floor with a long way down to the ground, she had no choice but to jump. Broken bones were better than the alternative.

When she turned the doorknob, it wouldn't open. She kicked and pushed with all her might, but it was sealed shut. It wouldn't budge, which was odd, it had opened freely just days before when she had shown Solly around the house. Now the place seemed to twist and groan, and Lord, she was trapped in it!

Grabbing a blanket to cover herself, her only chance to get out, after all would be to run through the flames to get downstairs. But when she opened the bedroom door the fire exploded and the force knocked her to the floor. Instantly the ceiling burst into flames and she lay momentarily stunned. Then she saw the box under the bed. She moaned, aghast at her momentary forgetfulness and on her hands and knees inched her way over and managed to grasp it. Fiercely determined now to get out and clinging to her fortune, she crawled back to the French door. Struggling to stand up, she kicked at it with her last breath. This time it let loose and suddenly she was outside. Scrambling over the railing she dropped to the ground clutching the only possession she had in the world. But as the flames devoured her second home in Savannah, even though her new friend had surely saved her from dying, Solly's sudden appearance in her life caused suspicions to again cascade through her thoughts!

- 2-

Reed Conners awoke with a start. He sat up, disoriented in the strange surroundings. As he ran a hand through his hair, he remembered his home on the lake had been smashed to hell in an ice storm and he was staying at a motel. He turned expecting to see Lindy's head on the next pillow, but the bed was empty with only a dent in the starched white case, the blankets mussed at the corner. Assuming she was in the bathroom, checking his watch he saw they had four hours before they had to catch the plane in Brainerd that would take them to South Carolina.

His body ached from the long drive back home from Dallas after giving up the search for her. Then arriving home and first seeing his house standing forlorn and devastated by the ice storm that had come through the area earlier, and the surprise of seeing her standing in his front yard. He shook his head, after all he'd gone through there she stood; she'd come back to Birch Lake desperately seeking his help.

He threw the covers off and reached for his jeans on the floor where they'd tossed their clothes the night before as they had clung together. They'd spent the day with a judge from a neighboring town who was a fishing buddy and things were looking up. Now as soon as Lindy returned the insurance money to his company he could close the case and get on with his life. He had paid her fine of a whopping fifty thousand dollars with his own money, but she had promised to pay it back and declared she was through running. He was feeling good and believed they'd have time now to work things out! As he gathered up their clothes spread around the bedroom and small living room a chuckle rumbled in his throat at what the folks in his town called a suite. He had to smile then, they were his people, his town and he loved it.

The living room and the tiny kitchen crammed into a corner had a homey look even though it was outdated. Brown paneled walls accentuated with slightly yellowed wallpaper. A fifties style couch with sharp angles sloped down to a slight sag in the middle. A television stood on a table that held shelves of paper back books, most likely accumulated from former tourists who had read their romances and mysteries while vacationing in the north. Two Danish chairs with blonde wooden arms and legs, blue covered seats stood side by side facing the TV. Blooming violets sat on tables in fat pots and brightened the rooms.

Getting restless, Reed ran a hand through his ruffled sandy hair and knocked on the bathroom door.

"Lindy, are you about ready?" he asked. It was awfully quiet in there and when he didn't get a response he repeated, "Lindy, are you ready?" Still nothing! He opened the door and to his surprise saw an empty room. What the hell? He went over to the window and looked outside then and when he saw his Corvette was gone too, he muttered goddamn!

He opened the door and stood in the crisp morning air. The streets were empty except for the usual early locals who gathered at the Woodsmen Cafe across the street. He recognized Joe Johnson's pick-up and Sandy Harrison's Cadillac.

He turned on the television, then showered and grabbed some black jeans and pulled a white sweater over his head as he walked back into the living room. He yanked the door open again and looked outside.

A thread of uneasiness began in his stomach when he checked his watch and saw they had about three hours until their flight left, and it was an hour's drive to the airport.

He forced himself to stay calm, sat down on the couch, lit a cigarette and inhaled deeply. The news came on the television; and the announcer told of the unrest in the world. Of storms paralyzing some of the northern plains and stranding travelers in airports on their way home for the Thanksgiving holidays.

Goddamn, he mumbled again and jumped up. What the hell was Lindy doing? He opened the door again and checked the one and only street for traffic. Still nothing! Damn that woman. Didn't she understand the importance of their trip to South Carolina? He swiped a hand over his face, ran it through his hair. The telephone rang then jolting his nerves further. His western boots dug into the carpet as he hurried to answer shaking his head impatiently.

Abby, a neighbor who lived next to him at the lake was on the line and said, "Reed, we've been looking all over outside for you, the workmen are here and want to start on your house!" Then added, "Your car is here!"

"What? My car is there?" Reed repeated confounded.

"Yes, but the black one is gone."

Reed's face paled. He pressed the telephone receiver closer to his ear as a chill spread up his spine. "Gone?" he replied still thunderstruck.

"Is everything okay Reed?" she asked.

"Yeah-- nothing for you folks to worry about Abby. I'll be right over."

"Okay, Joe will tell the guys to start then."

Reed hung up the phone, disbelief written on his face. Sweat shimmered on hisforehead.

It could only mean one thing. Lindy had run again! "Apparently last night didn't mean anything to her," he mumbled and wrenched the door open. He inhaled the cold crisp air and tried to calm down. Light snow covered the ground now and heavy gray clouds hung suspended. The aroma of bacon cooking from the Woodsmen Cafe across the street tantalized his churning stomach.

As a man pushing fifty, Reed Conners had retired from his successful law practice, sold his ranch and moved to his cabin by a lake in northern Minnesota. He'd remodeled and finished his home into a spacious showplace. Just to keep in touch, he'd renewed his detective license and worked part-time as an investigator for a large insurance company in Minneapolis. That was how his and Lindy's path had crossed again. First Federated Insurance was his company, the same one that had paid her a million dollars for the loss of her home from a fire, then later charged her with fraud and demanded the money back! Today they had reservations to fly to Hilton Head to pick up the money which she declared was safely tucked away in a bank.

The phone rang again as he stood in the doorway. It had to be her with some kind of story!

"Yah," he barked.

"Jesus, what bit you in the ass?" Reed recognized Ed Anderson's voice, his boss from the insurance company. Not wasting time Ed said, "Reed, I'll need

you to stay on here in Minneapolis for awhile longer
after we get this Lindy Lewis case settled."

"Now?"

"Right now! This one's big?" Ed's voice vibrated
over the line.

"Ed, I'm going to be pretty busy for awhile," Reed
stalled. "Can't it wait?"

"Nah, I need you on this one!"

"What's going on?"

"Ten million big ones on a dame. Carmen Ciem.
Fell out a window. Young husband. Looks fishy."

"Where?" Reed asked.

"Lake Calhoun. There's a sizable bonus in it for you
if you can crack this one!"

"Okay, give me a few days." Reed slammed down
the phone. Christ, what the hell would he do now? Ed
and the insurance company wouldn't be happy after he
told them Lindy had slipped right through his fingers.
He grabbed his leather jacket and left the motel. They
should have been on the road to the Brainerd airport by
now!

Goddamn, when would he learn? His face was
frozen in a grimace as he swore and crossed the street
to the cafe. He'd catch a ride from one of the guys,
check on the house and pick up his car.

The Woodsmen cafe had stood on the same corner
since Reed had been a kid and had come with his folks
to spend his summers swimming and fishing at their
cabin. Of course, the owners like his parents were gone

now and the new generation had refurbished. But the tradition continued of serving good food at reasonable prices to the tourists and the small population that resided in the community. The building was made of logs, weathered now to a glossy silver gray and nestled in amongst the block long business district. A hardware store, bakery, a sewer pumping and well drilling company, and of course a Legion club; a popular bar and liquor store occupied the main street. A real estate office and a church stood on the same side of the street as the motel Reed was staying in. He pushed the door open and walked into the cafe, to the aroma of cinnamon rolls, bacon and eggs. Today his stomach was a mess of nerves.

"Morning Flo," he greeted the waitress and swung a leg over a stool at the counter.

"Good to see you Reed," she thrilled. "Just awful about your house. Coffee?"

He realized he hadn't eaten since yesterday morning and before he did anything he needed food. "The works Flo, please," he said then.

"Morning," Jerome, who sat on the next stool said as he raised blood-shot eyes and nursed his coffee with shaking hands.

"How you doing?" Reed asked.

"Oh, I've been better," Jerome said while scooping runny eggs on his fork after Flo brought him his order.

Jerome had been a fixture around town too since Reed had been a kid. No one knew how old he was, but people figured he must be somewhere in his nineties. He'd spend hours in the cafe drinking coffee and then limp down the street to be the first customer in the Legion club. A brimmed feed cap firmly covered his bald head, and a walrus mustache adorned his face. He always left a trail of Old Spice shaving lotion in his wake and his usual dress was a faded bib overall, a plaid flannel shirt with a tie knotted at his throat. He would say, "now he could wear all those ties he'd gotten from the kids over the years."

"Tough about your place Reed," he mumbled between bites.

"It'll be months before it's livable, they say." Reed was tired, but forced himself not to think about Lindy's disappearance, or the next job coming up. Stan, the cook came out of the kitchen carrying a coffee cup and joined the row of men who lined the counter. His white apron splattered with spills.

"You back for awhile now Reed?" He fumbled in his shirt pocket for a cigarette, lit up and took a deep drag then exhaled a stream of smoke upwards.

"Doesn't look like it." Reed gulped his coffee. "Company's got a new case waiting for me, they say. I'm not done with the last one!"

The locals nodded their heads in unison at Reed's apparent frustration. After wolfing down his breakfast he asked, "Can I hitch a ride from one of you over to my place to pick up my car?"

The roads were covered with snow, the sky gray as Reed rode in Joe Johnson's pick-up. He pulled the collar up on his leather jacket and blew on his hands. Even before the vehicle had stopped, he was staring at the spectacle going on in his yard. His heart plummeted as he saw a large crane lift what was left of the roof of his house and drop it on the ground, exposing his living room and kitchen. Most of it smashed and covered in ice. Although, through a broken window he could see the oak dining room table and chair set that had belonged to his folks and that he'd painstakingly refinished stood untouched, the centerpiece of sunflowers intact.

His neighbors, Joe and Abby were there on the sidelines. "Hell of a thing," Joe muttered, shaking his head and pulling his cap down further. "Reed, we cleared out the barn and I got my boys here so we'll help load your things. Be safe at our place until you can move back in."

"You sure Joe?" Reed asked then and said, "Thanks, I'll move my car out of the way." He walked over and using an extra key to open the door, got in and sat down with a sigh. Just then his eyes fell on a brown paper bag lying on the floor, the top folded down neatly.

What the hell, he mumbled and reached down and opened it. Goddamn, it was full of money!

- 3-

Lindy and Solly huddled together in the early dawn as plumes of fire shot high into the sky and clouds of black smoke engulfed the house. Then Lindy gasped "my car," and ran dragging the blanket and clutching the box, thankful she had an extra key for the ignition safely hidden under the seat. She backed the BMW away from the house, swerving back and forth across the cobble-stone driveway in her haste to get to the safety of the street. Sirens began to pierce the air and as she joined Solly again and they stood staring at the scene, they were soon surrounded by fire-trucks, police cars and then a ambulance.

"Is everybody out," a man called?

"Yes," Lindy exclaimed tearfully.

"Okay, move back. Looks like it's a goner!"

Lindy and Solly ran through the dew covered grass, stumbled over the hoses the firemen had tossed out in the middle of the yard and climbed back into her car.

"What am I going to do now?" Lindy wailed as she watched her second home go up in smoke. Her hair stuck up in tangled blonde tufts and her face was streaked with soot.

"We'll think of something," Solly said and added, "I got my suitcases out so we've got some clothes to wear." She had been in Savannah for just a few days.

In a vulnerable moment Lindy had called her and she'd said, "Solly, I bought the cutest house and it has an extra bedroom. Come on down!"

"I'm on my way!" Solly had replied excitedly.

***

Lindy had seen a sign posted on the lawn by a house one day as she had been sight-seeing around the older part of Savannah. "For Sale by Owner," it read. On impulse she'd stopped and went to the door. A little elderly woman had answered her knock.

"I saw your sign, and if it's convenient for you I'd like to see your house," Lindy had said.

"Oh my yes, come in." The lady held the door wide for Lindy to enter, and then closed it with a bang. "Hurry, mosquitoes you know!"

Lindy held out her hand and said, "My name is Lola Lang."

"And you can call me Madame Fitsgerald," the sprightly woman said as they shook hands.

The house was a small two-storied Tudor style, painted yellow with white trim and stood daintily at the rear of a grass covered lot. As Lindy stepped into the vestibule a floral scent tinged with cinnamon surrounded her, tickled her nose.

"I have to ask you to take your shoes off. You see I wear house slippers, to keep everything fresh you know." Madame reached up and tightened the knot of gray hair that seemed to tilt on her head when she moved. She opened a closet door. "Here are some slippers for you." She handed Lindy a pair of multicolored crocheted booties to put on.

Lindy's glance swept over the living room as they talked and she immediately fell in love with the Victorian decor. "It's lovely," she murmured.

"Well, yes it is. Now I've decided I'm going to join my boyfriend at a rest-home," she smiled and went on, "And I'm leaving everything. Everything goes; furniture and dishes too."

"Can I see?" Lindy asked and then followed Madame Fitsgerald around the house as her top knot bobbed and her steel framed round glasses perched precariously on the tip of her nose.

The living room held a flowered couch and two velvet chairs, small tables adorned with lace doilies, and lamps with fringed shades. Crystal figurines stood here and there. The walls were rose colored and the trim cream. The kitchen was small and spick and span. Cupboards and appliances were cream colored with pink walls and accentuated with lace curtains.

"Now let me show you the upstairs," Madame said with a hand on the railing. "I can't go up and down much anymore but at the Pines where I'll be living, everything is on the first floor. I'll be right next door to Huey, my boyfriend you know."

"I see," Lindy replied taken with her charm.

"I have two bedrooms up here, each with its own bathroom and as you can see, a balcony for each one," Madame Fitsgerald exclaimed proudly.

Lindy's eyes widened in pleasure at the four poster beds covered with crocheted bedspreads, gleaming wood floors, and especially the French doors that opened out to the balconies that were surrounded by the tops of trees. Leafy ferns stood on spindly legged tables in the sun filled rooms and gave off a mossy scent, and mixed with the heavy potpourri from downstairs. Maybe just a little bit much, Lindy thought as she rubbed her nose, almost ready to sneeze.

"I've lived here over fifty years," Madame Fitsgerald said. "Raised a son here, but he's gone too." She sighed as a sad look came over her face, then brightened and continued, "Now me and Huey are going to have some fun before they lock us in for good over there at the home!" Her eyes twinkled.

"What are you going to do?" Lindy asked curiously.

"Oh my, we're going to see the country. He's Indian, you know. So we're going way up north to the plains to visit his family. And while I'm there I'm going to stop in Minnesota and look up a niece. And maybe we'll try our hand in those casinos." Her cheeks were rosy as she talked. Lindy smiled at the little lady, liking her sprightly manner.

"The closets are small. Miss Lang, you know long ago when the house was built people didn't need much space." She opened the door for Lindy to glance into its depth.

"That's not a problem," Lindy said, "I don't have much anyway."

"Oh my, I hear the kettle whistling, we can have our tea now." They walked down the stairs slowly as Madame Fitsgerald gripped the railing, then stood for a minute to rest her legs when they got down to the bottom. "Come sit down while I get things ready."

Lindy sat down in the living room and let her eyes roam around the peaceful setting. Minutes later, Madame Fitsgerald placed a tray with a tea pot and matching china cups and saucers on the coffee table and sat down, then busied herself pouring tea. Lindy sat, totally in love with the ambiance of the house, charmed by the quiet neighborhood. She had so longed for a home of her own again; a place to feel safe in.

Did she dare ask the price? Should she spend more of her dwindling money? She sipped her tea and crooked her fingers delicately around the cup handle just as Madame Fitsgerald did.

"Tell me Miss Lang, do you like my house?"

Startled out of her thoughts, Lindy exclaimed, "Oh yes!"

Madame Fitsgerald beamed and nodded her head. "I can see you're just the person I want to have my things. I want you to have it."

"But—, what is the price?" Lindy dared to ask finally.

Perched on her chair, Madame Fitsgerald adjusted her top knot, pushed her glasses back up on the bridge of her small nose and said, "One dollar!"

"One dollar?" Lindy echoed.

"One dollar," Madame Fitsgerald repeated. "I told myself this morning, I would give this house to the one person that I found who I thought would love it and take care of everything." She smiled at Lindy, sipped her tea and then exclaimed "I've decided to give my house to you!" A satisfied look spread over her rosy face now.

"For one dollar?" Lindy asked again dubiously.

"That will make the sale official. Oh my, aren't you interested?"

"Yes," Lindy exhaled a breath. "But, I can't—." Taken aback at Madame Fitsgeralds outlandish offer, she sat back on the couch and shook her head in disbelief.

Madame Fitsgerald waved her hands in the air. "Miss Lang, I don't have any family and there's no one else. I'm going to get rid of everything I have while I know what I'm doing and have some fun!" She smiled, "The place can be yours, but there's one thing you've got to promise me."

Lindy's hand shook as she held the fragile tea cup. "What?" she managed to ask still astonished.

The little lady looked at her expectantly; her top-knot listed dangerously to the left as she leaned over and whispered, "You've got to promise to take good care of my friends who visit from time to time."

"Why, they will be welcome anytime," Lindy solemnly promised not realizing Madame Fitsgerald meant her ghostly buddies who came and went freely in the house.

Madame Fitsgerald beamed. "I'll call Van Dyke, he's an attorney you know and he lives next door. Oh my, you see I packed my suitcases bright and early this morning too so I'm ready to go.

By the end of the afternoon, Lindy had paid the dollar and stood in her new home as Madame Fitsgerald picked up her bags, blew her a kiss and ran to catch a waiting taxi. And now just a few days later, her perfect world had crashed to the ground!

- 4-

What the hell—? Reed muttered as he reached in the paper bag and took out a handful of money, then dumped the contents out on the car seat and stared. He blew out a jagged breath and counted. An even fifty thousand dollars! The same amount he had paid out the day before in court to cover Lindy's fine! It could only mean one thing, she had lied! Instead of the money being in South Carolina like she'd said, she had had it with her all along. He sat back in the car seat, deeply anguished.

Goddamn, what kind of game was she playing?

"Hey Reed," Joe called out and waved from the side of the house where he and Abby stood. Forcing his attention back to the present, Reed put the bag in the glove compartment and walked back to where his neighbors waited.

Joe continued, "We can go in now and get your things out. Reed, you know we can bring Boomer over here to keep watch, he won't let anyone near the place without taking off a leg."

"Thanks Joe, that sounds like a good idea," Reed agreed.

The day flew by as Abby, Joe and their boys helped him pack up what was still usable and move his belongings over to their barn. He took one last look at his home as it stood covered in blue tarps. The lawn was already full of holes, and the trampled grass; a soggy mess. Even the trees looked bedraggled.

He slept fitfully that night as Lindy's perfume from the pillow she'd slept on the night before haunted him. Finally in frustration, he got up and flung it outside. He awoke early and after getting ready to check out of the motel looked at her suitcases.

What the hell was he supposed to do with them? He finally loaded them in the trunk of his Corvette, checked out of the motel and headed to Minneapolis. His attitude pissed, but the three hour drive flew by as he pushed his speed to the limit amidst a plume of cussing about that damn woman!

Hadn't their love-making meant anything? Apparently nothing, he mumbled. Then swore again for thinking something could be rekindled after so many years.

The low slung car hugged the road and his CD player hummed country as he finally turned into the underground parking at the First Federated Insurance Company in Minneapolis. A huge enterprise known world-wide that insured anything you wanted to cover; Homes, cars, businesses, people and their parts. It had been in business for decades. If he had wanted, he could have been employed full time, but he liked to think he was semi-retired.

Fat chance, he muttered as he took the elevator up to the top floor.

"Reed Conners," Mona, an old friend and sometimes lover, exclaimed when he walked in, then jumped up from her receptionist's desk and wrapped him in her arms. "Where have you been?" she asked smiling up at him.

Reed returned her greeting by running his hands down her back and onto her fanny. She stepped back out of his reach and slapped at his hands. "You never change."

Reed grinned and raised them in defense. "You do that to me!"

Mona smiled demurely. As a woman in her middle fifties, she was the picture of a modem woman. Slim and fit and beautifully groomed with short black hair curled stylishly around her heart shaped face and an unlined creamy complexion with perfectly applied make-up.

"You're not so bad yourself," she replied as she looked him up and down. Reed had unzipped his leather jacket and stood unabashed at her scrutiny of him in his black designer jeans and Armani sweater. Then she said seriously, "Reed, I'm so sorry about your house."

Reed shook his head. "Yeah, I was gone at the time when the storm came through."

"I remember, we got just the edge of it here. You did get the check for damages didn't you?" Mona walked back to her desk and sat down, adjusted the skirt of her rose colored suit.

"Yeah, and the guys are working on the place now," Reed answered. He nodded towards the closed oak doors. "What kind of mood is Ed in today?"

"Well—, okay unless his wife calls again. She's been a bitch lately ever since her last face-lift failed." Mona choked on a giggle.

Reed grinned. "Better check in. How about dinner?"

"Wonderful. At Gina's?"

"I'll meet you there at five," Reed said and walked into Ed Anderson's office, CEO of First Federated Insurance. Holding the phone to his ear, Ed waved Reed over to a chair, as he bellowed to someone, "Just get it done!" And then into the intercom to Mona said, "Hold my calls!"

The two men had been acquaintances for years and then later became good friends when Reed started working for the company as an investigator. Ed had spent many weekends out on Birch Lake with Reed fishing for walleye.

Turning his full attention to Reed, he reached over and shook his hand. "Thanks for getting here so soon," he said in his usual brisk tone after an exchange of greetings."Okay, let's get down to business." He pushed a mountain of papers out of the way on his desk and looked at Reed expectantly, then sat back in his chair. "Okay, let's wrap up the Lewis case first!"

"Ed, there's a problem!" Reed said as he took off his jacket.

"What," Ed asked curiously?

"I need some more time. So far I've got fifty thousand of the million here." He opened his briefcase and put the money on Ed's desk.

"What happened? I thought the case was closed." Ed's face flushed beet red as he rolled his chair back and stood up.

Reed ran a hand over his face. "Goddamn, I thought so too!"

"Didn't she have the rest of the money with her," Ed asked?

"Just the fifty thousand dollars!"

"What about the rest?" Ed sat back down.

"She said it was in a safe deposit box in South Carolina. We were going there to pick it up!"

"Well- what happened?"

"She took off right under my nose," Reed finally admitted.

Ed was silent and drummed his fingers on the desk and then turned away and stared out a window.

Reed's face was set in hard lines. "Ed, I need two more weeks. I will find her and get the rest of the money back to the company!"

Ed swung around and faced him. "Reed, I'm taking you off the case. You're too close; I've decided to assign Baker."

Reed stood up, put his hands on the edge of the desk and leaned in. "Christ, Ed I've got a lot invested in this one!" Should he tell Ed the whole story?

"A week?" he asked. Not willing after all to admit to Ed she had played him for a fool.

"Nope, can't do it!" Ed said then. "Sorry, standard procedure. Reed, you're one of my top investigators and I need you on this new case!"

But Reed's face was a mix of frustration and distress as he slid Lindy's file over to Ed. Goddamn, he couldn't give up now, he'd lost her and although he was comfortably well off, he had lost his own fifty thousand dollars as well!

"Okay buddy no hard feelings," Ed said shaking his head, and then handed the new file over to Reed.

"This is big and time is running out! Like I said, ten million on this dame. Carmen Ciem married a guy fourteen years younger, seven years ago. She was sixty two now. Lived in a mansion over on Lake Calhoun.

Went over a third floor balcony and splattered on a brick courtyard. No pre-nupts."

Reed opened the bulging folder.

"The case is at a standstill." Ed exhaled, "Reed, there's a hefty bonus in this one if you can save my company the ten big ones!"

Reed stood up. "Okay, I've got to locate a place to stay." He put the file in his briefcase and wondered if he could regain enough to cover his losses!

But goddamn, how the hell would he have time to run down Lindy and investigate this new case too?

He checked into a motel close to the Calhoun area called the Settle Inn, unpacked and hung up his clothes and took off again in his Corvette. Within minutes he was in the neighborhood of old money; with well-tended homes, stone columns, bricked driveways and marble fountains. He drove on until he found Carmen Ciem's address and exhaled a breath as he saw the lavish house with the breathtaking view of the lake. As he neared, an eight foot fence of concrete guarded the pink stucco fortress. He stopped and got out, walked up a hill where he could get a better look at the place. Here he could see the back and side of the house. Three floors looked down to a patio and a large swimming pool, covered now for the season. Pots of green shrubs placed around it gave the place the look of a setting out of a magazine. As he walked back to his car, he could see the front entrance. Two huge stone lions sitting

back on their haunches guarded the rose colored double
doors.

   Now why the hell would Carmen Ciem kill herself?
He got in the Corvette. Something about this stinks, he
mumbled.

-5-

Lindy and Solly watched in horror as the fire leapt with hot lashing tongues demolishing the walls, and the roof of her house. Sparks and debris flew up in the air, and then fell to the ground. Firemen frantically dragged ladders and hoses, radios blared with instructions, water flowed everywhere. The dense smoke was heavy with odors, while the air hummed with obscure noises. All of it taking only a few hours to leave a pile of charred boards, and blackened pieces of odd shapes lying in amongst sodden ashes.

Lindy put her head down on the steering wheel of the BMW as sobs shook her body, and tore at her heart. Her second home was gone. Her beautiful little house she'd only spent a few nights in. How could this have happened just when she'd found this safe haven?

A fireman stepped up to the car window and adjusted his hat. Wiped his forehead.

Lindy wiped her eyes with a soot covered hand, smearing her face. Solly sat quietly beside her in the car.

"You better find a place to stay and then call your insurance company. It's out now, but we'll be around to keep an eye on it."

Lindy looked at him blankly. It was now after eight o'clock in the morning. In just a few hours Lindy's life had changed again. Homeless, with just a pair of pajamas to her name. She straightened up, took a deep breath.

"Solly, let's find a motel, take a shower, and get some rest."

Solly wiped her face on her shirt sleeve and picked a piece of mascara off her eyelid. "Cripes, I hope I haven't brought you bad luck by coming here."

"Why on earth would you say that?" Lindy started the BMW and drove slowly down the street.

"I'm kind of scared to think about it again, but my asshole husband said that's my karma." Solly chewed on her lower lip and looked out the window, then turned her gaze towards Lindy again. "I'm serious; he used to tell me all kinds of spooky things. Like I was responsible for his failing business. If his car broke down. If he gained weight. One time he told me I had given him VD. I had never been with anyone else."

"God Solly, he blamed you for his failures?"

"Oh sure. I finally got it when he said he needed to be around someone younger and full of life. Not an old woman like me."

"And I suppose you took all his BS seriously!"

"Of course I did. It's been two years now since our divorce and I finally realized I'm okay, and not the drudge he made me believe I was. Sorry, I didn't mean to bring this up now, but, he had me convinced for a long time that I was the cause of bad luck to anyone around me."

"What a jerk! For Pete's sake, Solly don't give it another thought."

"I just wanted you to know."

"Solly, forget it." As they turned onto the freeway, Lindy took one last wistful look back at her burned out house, and swallowed the lump in her throat. They drove aimlessly in silence, each lost in their own thoughts. Finally, signs advertising short term rentals along the highway caught Lindy's attention. Something new for the traveler; Furnished apartments, called the Shamrock Inn. A laundry, a restaurant and it promised quiet hominess. Lindy turned off the highway and parked.

"Solly, you look better than I do, could you go in and register. Tell them we had a fire."

"Sure. Thank goodness, I had enough brains to take my suitcases out of the house; we're about the same size so you can use whatever I've got."

"Thanks. Here's some money. Tell them I'll make arrangements after I've cleaned up." Within fifteen minutes Solly was back waving a room key, and motioning to Lindy where to park.

"Really nice people," she said as she reached in for her cases, after Lindy had parked the car. Lindy carried the shoe box under her arm, the only possession she had left. As they walked side by side through the parking lot, Solly looked at the box Lindy had clasped under her arm, and curiosity got the best of her. She had to ask "Lola, for Gods sake, what's in that damn box?"

Tired and stressed, Lindy started to giggle helplessly. "It's full of money," she gasped. Solly's eyes grew large. Her full lips opened as she stared.

"Cripes," she whispered and joined in Lindy's laughter. What a pair they made as they stumbled through the parking area. Solly's kimono in red silk streaked with soot. Her feet, stuck in rubber thongs clapped as she walked. Lindy's blue and white striped pajamas, gray with soot. One sleeve ripped open. Her feet were bare, but her red toe-nails were perfectly manicured.

"Full of money?" Solly asked incredulously.

Lindy sobered. "No--, just pictures and some papers." They reached their apartment and unlocked the door. After checking out their new home, Lindy collapsed on the couch and put her head back on the cushion. "Oh Lord Solly, I'm sorry I got you into this."

"Well, I needed some excitement in my life." Solly smiled, "Although, this wasn't what I'd planned." She sat down in an easy chair and put her feet under her. "I hope I've made my last bed though. I figure I can take it easy for about two months. What about you?"

"I don't know yet." Lindy groaned and went on, "Do you mind if I use the shower first?" What the hell would she do now? Her plans of settling down had been smashed again. She stood in the shower and let the water run from hot to cool, as her mind fumbled for a strand of normalcy.

"Are you all right in there Lindy?" Solly's voice echoed through the door. Lindy came out of her fog.

"Sorry, I'll be out in a minute." She stepped out, reached for a towel. Oh Lord, she was tired. She stood in front of the mirror as she dried herself off. Black circles edged her eyes, and even though she straightened up with determination, her small frame sagged. She took a shaking breath. She needed to just stay in bed; be warm and safe, relax and feel her body melt into the mattress. She opened the bathroom door.

"Solly, I'm going to bed. Are you okay?"

"Sure, I'll be fine." Lindy went into one of the bedrooms, closed the door, and hid the shoebox under the bed. She flipped the covers down and crawled in. With a sigh, she took a deep breath, covered her head and closed her eyes. Peace at last! She slept through the afternoon and awoke with a start to a knock on the door. She sat up.

"What?" she answered puzzled at her surroundings.

"Lola, cripes, I was getting worried about you." Solly stepped into the room.

"What time is it?"

"It's almost evening. I made some coffee and got some rolls from the restaurant next door."

"Lord, I'm starved," Lindy mumbled and got out of bed and wrapped a bath towel around her naked body. The December air, damp and cool seeped inside the rooms and Solly had turned the lamps on against the gray day. A television set flashed brightly colored pictures of a parade. As Lindy sat on the couch and sipped her coffee she exclaimed, "My God, it's almost Christmas, isn't it? That's one of the holiday parades!"

Solly sat cross-legged on the floor and her face had a forlorn look. "You know, I kind of miss cooking and baking. The last few years I invited some neighbors over."

Lindy's hair hung straight and un-combed as she watched the television and thought about those past dinners she'd cooked. No, she would not look back! She reached for a cigarette.

"Let's go out and have a big dinner, that's if I can wear something of yours."

"Sure, and I think a cocktail would be nice too, don't you? To celebrate our escape from the kitchen."

Solly stood up and winked. Her European accent heavy.

"Hmm-, a brandy Manhattan. Yes!" A flush brought color to Lindy's pale features, a slight sparkle back to her eyes. She dressed in one of Solly's long skirts and a matching sweater. Her shoes were a little too big for her, but they solved that problem by stuffing the toes with toilet paper. They agreed she'd wear this again the following day to shop in, when the stores opened after the holiday.

The BMW roared to life as they spun out of the parking lot and into the freeway traffic. In the short time Lindy had been in Savannah, she had discovered a renovated warehouse district on the waterfront. An area of a dozen blocks of outdoor cafes, coffee houses, antique shops, boutiques, and gift shops. The architecture, done in old world French. Entertainment went on continuously, with music for dancers, dreamers and lovers. The sun came out as they stopped at Aunt Chiladas. An elegant outdoor restaurant, with tables covered in soft yellow linen and adorned with crystal wine glasses. A chef with a tall white hat presided over a grill that gave off tantalizing aromas of steaks, roasting sweet potatoes and baking bread. Lindy had already made an impression as that blonde with the long cigarette holder as she'd sat for hours, drinking minted iced tea and soaking up the warm sun over the past weeks. Their stomachs growled as they were escorted to a table under a huge umbrella and the spreading branches of a magnolia tree. Fragrant flowers scented the air and mixed with the mouth-watering food cooking nearby. A strolling band of musicians serenaded everyone with haunting sounds of a clarinet, an accordion and guitars. As Lindy and Solly relaxed and enjoyed their cocktail, Lindy blinked her eyes at Solly's question.

"Lola, I know it's none of my business, but shouldn't you call your insurance company and report the fire? Your house was insured wasn't it?"

-6-

Reed Conners drove away from the posh neighborhood where Carmen Ciem had lived, his mind already at work. He needed to study the files, but first he had to meet Mona for dinner. It was close to five o'clock and about twenty minutes to Gina's restaurant. The skies had turned dingy gray with sleet and the late afternoon traffic had come to a complete stand-still as commuters hurried to start the weekend. Reed turned the heat up in the Corvette, punched in the CD player and eyed the line-up of traffic, bumper to bumper.

Goddamn, he grumbled as he drummed his fingers on the steering wheel. He should have been sitting at home with his feet up on an ottoman in front of the fireplace, reading one of his mysteries. Instead, here he was homeless, starting a new case, still trying to find Lindy Lewis and out fifty thousand dollars. Finally the traffic began to move and the cars inched along.

Gina's restaurant, a Minneapolis landmark known for its steaks, was centered in the heart of downtown. A lifesize bronze statue of a nude woman stood next to the burgundy canopy that stretched over the doors and matched the window coverings through which a soft rosy glow escaped. As Reed drove up, a uniformed valet stepped out and held the car door open. A doorman ushered him in. He stood for a moment and savored the tantalizing aromas, then walked up to the elegantly dressed woman standing in the foyer. A Mae West look about her.

"Hello Gina, how are you beautiful?"

"Well, it's about time you came back to my town darling." Gina clasped him to her ample breasts. They stood back, looked each other over and hugged again.

"I see business is good as ever."

"Yes, thank God. That's why I get up every day."

"You should quit and take it easy, Gina."

"Are you crazy? I'm thinking of remodeling!" She walked to her hostess desk and opened her reservation book.

"Will you be having dinner alone?" Her blue gown fit her perfectly. Diamonds sparkled on her fingers and ears.

"Mona is going to join me."

"I see. Reed, why don't you quit running around and pop the question? You couldn't find a nicer girl!"

Reed grinned as he said, "Gina, stop trying to marry me off."

"Okay, okay." Gina laughed good naturedly. "I'll keep a nice table for you kids."

Reed found a stool at the bar and ordered a Crown Royal and savored the cool whiskey as it slid down his throat.

Mona walked in and took a stool next to his, leaned over and kissed him on the cheek. Her rose colored suit jacket hung casually over her shoulders showing a lacy black, low-cut blouse. She carried a mink coat. She'd swept her hair back off her face, and the lines around her eyes only accentuated their blue depths. She turned towards Reed, crossed her legs, smiled and pointed to his glass.

"I'll have one of those, too." Reed and Mona had been friends ever since he had started working for the First Federated Insurance Company. Their easy friendship had stayed at a playful level. They admired each other but were not willing, or able to move their relationship out of the safe area and experiment with emotions.

"I'm starved for one of Gina's steaks, Mona, let's go to our table." After they were seated and ordered their dinner Reed asked, "What do you know about Carmen Ciem?" Mona swallowed a sip of her drink and gazed out the window for a second.

"You know years ago I used to see her at a health club. She'd come in for a jazzercise class. I didn't know her, just knew who she was. I heard she was a model around town back in the seventies."

Reed buttered a roll and popped the golden warm bread in his mouth and asked, "Was she married?"

"I heard she was divorced. Had kids."

"What else?" Reed lit a cigarette and sat back.

"It's so long ago, Reed. I heard she had small parts on television, and she worked as a waitress in restaurants around town." Mona shook her head, "I just can't believe she would kill herself!"

"Well that's what I've got to work on." Their conversation changed to easy chatter as their dinner arrived in which they ate with relish. After coffee and cordials, Mona stood up.

"It's been wonderful as always, Reed. I've got an early day coming up tomorrow so I've got to run, but I'll cook dinner soon and call you."

Reed laid some bills on the table, and after saying good night to Gina, guided Mona out to her car and safely on her way. But, as they had stood under the canopy waiting for their cars, Reed glanced over as he'd heard a car start up on the street, and for a moment his eyes connected with those of someone in a black sedan.

Was it just a coincidence? Or had this person been interested in what he was doing? Back at his motel, he spread Carmen Ciem's file out on the coffee table and began to read.

Carmen Ciem owned Georgiana's. A fortune five hundred business and her financial worth was figured at approximately two hundred million. She had started selling products door to door for the struggling business, managed to get a loan and bought out the company. She had been born in the middle forties and as an only child lived on a farm with her parents. She'd married at a young age and had two children. Reed picked up a picture that was clipped to the file. She had been a real beauty! Shoulder length blonde hair flipped back off her forehead and accentuated high cheekbones. Thick lashes edged smiling brown eyes. Full lips opened to perfect dazzling teeth.

She'd married Tony Roman seven years ago. Reed studied his photograph and the profile that had been done on him by the Police department. He was a good-looking Italian; forty-nine years old, six feet tall, and one hundred and eighty pounds. Graying black hair, blue eyes, and a mustache that failed to cover the man's weak lips. He'd quit his blue-collar job to pursue a career in acting and had had several bit parts in movies. At the time Carmen Ciem had died, he'd been in Hollywood for an appointment with his agent, Bobby Olson.

Reed lit a cigarette and jotted down the name. Next in the file, Hilda and Otto Sorenson. A Swedish couple who had worked for the previous owners and came with the house twenty some year's ago; Hilda was the housekeeper and cook, and Otto, the gardener and chauffeur. Hilda had found Carmen's body and called 911. Carmen Ciem had two children; a son, who was an accomplished musician and Director of an Art College and a daughter who had majored in business finance and was a CEO of a company. Both were accomplished professionals and vehemently protested their Mother's suicide.

"Impossible," they insisted, "Her husband killed her!"

-7-

"O f course there is insurance on the house."
Lindy replied to Solly's question. She had
thought of nothing else since her house had
disintegrated into a pile of ashes. Madame Fitsgerald's
neighbor, Attorney Van Dyke, had taken care of the
transfer of title and the other necessary papers,
including insurance forms. That was only after he had
painstaking explained to Madame Fitsgerald the course
of action she was intent on pursuing.

"I have no family and I can do anything I want with
my things," she had exclaimed. So the insurance was
in order but there was one big problem, all the papers
were written out to Lola Lang! Lindy took another sip
of her Manhattan.

"Have you thought of rebuilding?" Solly asked concerned, "it's such a beautiful area."

Lindy tried to smile at her new friend, but for a minute wondered if she had made a mistake in inviting her to come to Savannah, then brushed the thought away.

"I've got to think about that," she answered.

Their waiter brought menus and laid them down on the table. "Can I bring you ladies another cocktail?" He stood ready for their order.

"Yes," Lindy and Solly said in unison, then laughed. He hurried away and within minutes was back. As they lifted their glasses and took long drinks, Lindy's eyes were drawn to a man across the room. Just as her glance connected with his, the stranger raised a newspaper to cover his face. A prickle of apprehension shot through her body.

Was he watching her? And if so, who the hell was he?

It was early afternoon at Aunt Chilada's and the restaurant buzzed with business. The working crowd had come and gone and was being replaced with people out for a leisurely dinner. Strolling musicians were nearing the girl's table with smiles on their faces. The accordion player's fingers flew over the keyboard as he played 'Lady of Spain' and stopped at Lindy's side. Solly was enthralled with the guitar player as he looked deeply into her eyes. Lindy hummed along with the music as the trio entertained the customers. Her mind wandered. It had been so long since she'd even thought of those old love songs. Songs she'd learned from her Mother as she was growing up on the little farm hundreds of miles away. One of the few bright spots of her childhood had been when her folks had bought her a guitar. She remembered running her fingers over the beautiful, shiny, smooth finish and covering it with an old piece of material to keep it dust-free.

Her eyes had a faraway look as she remembered her mother's patience as she had written out cords for the guitar, words to songs for her. She remembered the excitement of having time away from the never ending work and being able to practice. She'd learned "church songs," and began to sing in public, especially in Luther League. She remembered imagining herself being up on a stage and going far-off to Hollywood and becoming famous like Loretta Lyn. She hummed along with the trio. This time they were playing a love song that she remembered singing years ago. The words came instantly to mind.

Her voice rose and fell with the clarinet, the accordion and the guitar as the boys in the trio stood at her table. Then the music turned her thoughts to Reed Conners and their college days and their love so intense, so fresh. She wondered how things would have been now, if they'd stayed together. If they would have married, would they have been happy together with kids and approaching middle age?

She lifted the Manhattan to her lips. With a sigh, she realized how just one decision had changed the course of her life.

She took another sip of her drink as her mind wandered miles away and her lips absently formed the words to another familiar song. If only her husband hadn't gotten sick. Pain flashed over her face as she remembered. That love had been gentle and caring and the years had flown by as they rebuilt that old house. Damn, she had thought he would be around forever to take care of her, but he'd died and that was when all this craziness had begun! Her thoughts raced over the last year as her face shadowed a mixture of emotions.

Coming out of her reverie she suddenly realized the accordion player was talking to her. "May we join you ladies?" he asked flashing perfect white teeth.

Lindy forced a smile.

"My name is Taylor, this is Tyler and this is Toby. We're the Georgia Tea's!" The three men bowed at the waist as they stood by their table.

"Okay," Lindy managed to say. Solly was all aglow. They pulled up chairs and motioned to a waiter.

"We'd like a bottle of your best champagne. We need to celebrate this little lady's break into show business!" Lindy fluffed her hair at their boisterous praise.

"I'm serious, you're good Lola. Have you thought about going professional?" Lindy laughed and went along with their joking. "I played around with the idea years ago."

"Lola, this town is short on entertainers. It wouldn't be hard to put together a group." He reached for the bottle of wine the waiter had placed on the table and filled their glasses. "Here's to fun and fame for you, Lola," he toasted. The ping of the glasses musical as they all raised them in a toast. Lindy smiled again and fluttered her eyelashes at the handsome men in fun. A flush spread over Solly's face after exchanging a kiss with Tyler.

Later, as Lindy had fallen into bed just a little bit tipsy after several bottles of wine had passed over their table, that stranger's face appeared again just as she was drifting off.

The next morning Solly was up as usual and had coffee and croissants laid out when she came into the kitchen.

"Are you ready to go shopping today?" Solly asked as she passed Lindy a cup.

"Absolutely! Just as soon as I have some caffeine." Lindy pushed her hair out of her eyes.

"Where should we go?" Solly asked.

Lindy tucked her feet under her. "There's a mall near here where I've seen some nice stores."

"Lola, you should make a list." Solly said and fussed with her robe.

"Lord, I need everything. I guess I'll start with underwear and make-up. But first I'm going to take a shower."

She went into her room and closed the door then reached under the bed for the shoebox. By now the edges of the cardboard container had become somewhat frayed, and the Reebok emblem on the cover had dulled. As she began to count the bills her breath caught when she found there wasn't as much left as she had thought. She'd have to be very careful now. No more of those Armani dresses and Prada shoes. This time she would have to be satisfied with clothes off the racks. She slid the shoebox under the bed after taking out several bundles of the cash.

They shopped for lingerie and make-up, then found a department store and soon their arms were laden with Lindy's purchases. "But I shopped wisely," Lindy said as they each ordered a salad and iced tea at a snack bar later. On their way to the car, Lindy noticed a small boutique nestled on an avenue. "Let's just take a small peek," she said but the minute they stepped into the store, all her good resolutions went down the drain. Pulling out another bundle of money she'd taken along just in case, she asked the saleswoman to wrap up the dress and shoes that just happened to fit her perfectly. Well, she needed just one original ensemble to feel good!   When they got back to their apartment, Solly reminded her again that she should call the insurance company.

Lindy agreed and went into her bedroom and thanked God, all the papers had been safely in her car when the fire had broken out. Now she carefully paged through the file, Van Dyke, Madam Fitsgerald's attorney and neighbor had given her, and found the name of the company. She perched on her bed and her hand trembled as she dialed the number to the Triple Insurance Company. A woman answered her call.

Lindy's voice caught in her throat at the possibility of what she could be getting herself into. But she forced herself to go on, "I'm calling to report a fire, my name is Lola Lang and my house burned."

"Sorry to hear that, Miss Lang. I'll connect you with someone who can help you."

And within seconds a man came on the line. He cleared his throat, "I'm John Houston. Are you insured with us?" His brisk manner unnerved Lindy further.

"Yes--." Lindy managed to say. "I bought a house that formerly belonged to Madam Fitsgerald." She gave him the address, and then sat in dread as his computer hummed. After a few minutes he came back on the line.

"Okay, first I'll need to see the policy. Then I'll need to check the Fire Marshal and the Police reports." A moment passed and he went on, "I can see you sometime in the next few days."

She hesitated, "Let me ask, Mr. Houston, what other papers will I need to bring?" There, she'd asked, she may as well hear the bad news.

"Well, Miss Lang, besides the insurance policy, the deed for your house and of course, your driver's license with your picture and your social security card."

Lord, just as she had expected. She was sunk. She couldn't open up that can of worms by showing her identification that read Lindy Lewis. And, she had nothing official that read Lola Lang.

What the hell would she do? What could she do? After counting the diminishing pile of money, she just had to figure out some way to collect the insurance on the house. After all it was her money now!

"And later, if the reports check out I'll need a list of all the contents in the house you lost. You might start thinking about that now," he continued.

"Thank you," she replied and hung up the phone, by now a nervous wreck. But as she stood in the shower a day later, she suddenly remembered something. And it could work! She dressed in a new red dress.

"Solly," she said telling a little fib, "I need to go down to the insurance company, will you be okay?"

"Sure," Solly replied, "I'm going to watch television and take a nap."

Lindy got in her BMW but instead of heading downtown to the business district, she turned off the busy highway into the warehouse area. Minutes later, she walked into The Raven; a small dark bar wedged in between a shoe repair shop and a laundry.

"Hi handsome," she said and slipped up on a bar stool.

The bartender turned from the television he'd been watching. "Lola, you're looking fabulous!" He reached for a bottle of brandy and poured her a shot.

"You're positively too much." Lindy smiled and raised the liquor glass, but only let the fiery liquid touch her lips. She needed to stay sharp. Just after coming to Savannah, she had met this man in and around the bar scene and even kissed him in a moment of lust the last time they'd run into each other. He was a local player.

"I haven't seen you at Aunt Chilada's lately." He swiped a hand through his expensive haircut.

Lindy reached over the bar and ran a finger over his lips. "You haven't forgotten about me already have you?"

He looked her up and down and said, "Who could compare?"

She took a small sip of the liquor, just enough to give her courage. Then said, "Last week you said you could get me anything I needed in this town. Is that true?" She smiled seductively and leaned closer showing him some cleavage.

He grinned. "Sure, everything's for sale. Why, what do you need?"

Without batting an eye, Lindy said, "I need a driver's license and a social security number."

He studied her for a minute and her heart began to thud in her chest. "No problem," he said then, "but it'll cost. Cash!"

"I've got cash," she managed to say and this time took a sizeable sip of the liquor. Her throat burned.

"I'll need to make a call. Wait here." The bartender turned and disappeared through a door.

Was he calling the Police? She gulped down more of the brandy. Should she leave now? Get away while she still had time? Swallowing hard over her racing nerves she forced herself to sit tight. Then she remembered all that expensive jewelry and his clothes and guessed he had to have something shady going on the side, as he sure couldn't afford his lifestyle working in this dump!

"Okay gorgeous," he said a few minutes later and put a scrap of paper on the bar. "This is what it'll cost you. Can you handle it?"

Lindy's eyes grew large at the amount, but what choice did she have? "Yes," she answered.

The bartender busily wiped the bar as he exclaimed, "Sweet! Bring back the cash and a picture of yourself."

Lindy slid off her stool, anxious to get out of there.

He winked and asked, "Anything else for you beautiful?"

Lindy leaned over and kissed him. Touched tongues. "See you in an hour," she said and hurried out to her car, not sure if this had been a good idea or not.

When she got back to the apartment to pick up the money, she collapsed on the couch and to Solly, said, "I've got to go back downtown to the insurance company with some more papers. Then later I've got to start a list of everything that burned up in the house. Everything!" She brushed at her hair with a shaking hand. "Right now I can't remember a thing!"

Solly turned off the soap opera she had been watching. "Lola, I can help," she said, "I need something to keep busy with."

Lindy shook her head in dismay at the humongous project. "Lord, I don't even know where to start. Everything came with the house: Dishes, linens and all that old furniture."

"Lola listen, I know there were a lot of antiques. I have to apologize, one day when you were out, I snooped." Solly picked at her lower lip and looked uncertain. "Sorry, I didn't mean to be nosy. I was just curious to see all your beautiful things," she added.

"Well," Lindy hesitated not sure of what she wanted to say. She was just a little bit upset at Solly's inquisitiveness.

"Lola, cripes, I can help you. When I was going through my bad time, to take my mind off things, I used to go to estate auctions, haunt the museums and I learned a lot about antiques."

"Really?" Lindy exclaimed now with interest.

"Yes, you know I'm sure that was an original painting you had in the foyer! And then that big collection of depression glassware, and you had a set of early Royal Dalton in the china cupboard. That Beidermen chest in your bedroom was the real thing! Lola, do you know what that could have been worth?" Looking doubtful for a moment she paused, then went on, "Those dining room chairs? I'm not so sure about!" Solly stopped for air, her face flushed. "You must have special insurance on all that stuff!"

Lindy smiled, this was better than she expected. "Solly," she said forgetting her previous testy feelings, "Would you be a dear, and start that blasted list for me please?"

-8-

Reed paced around his room in the motel with the Carmen Ciem file in his hand. Ten million was the amount his company would have to pay out unless he could prove her death was a homicide. First thing tomorrow he would track down Tony Roman and the Sorensons.

He had been going nonstop since leaving Birch Lake early that morning and now was totally wiped out. He dropped his clothes over an armchair and got into bed, but soon found it didn't have down-filled pillows and quilts like he had at home. Irritated, he tossed and turned for hours. It had been only a few days since Lindy had come back and begged for his help and safety from that asshole Mario. He jerked at the covers on the bed, aggravated by their rough texture. Goddamn, he'd gotten the fraud charges against her dropped and was supposed to escort her to SC to get the million back for his company. And, he'd even paid her fine of fifty thousand dollars with his own money after listening to her promises. Now it seemed like a dream. A nightmare!

What the hell was up with that woman anyway! He was still grumbling the next morning as he showered and dressed.

The December weather; clear and cold, biting even, woke him fast as he left his room and got into his car. Thank God, he didn't have to go through downtown again. Damn crazy people to put up with fighting traffic twice a day. This time he drove right up to the gate at Carmen Ciem's house, pressed a button and waited.

"Who's there?" A woman's voice, heavy with a Scandinavian accent asked.

"Reed Conners. I'm from the First Federated Insurance Company." The gate opened smoothly. Reed shifted gears and a soft growl invaded the quiet neighborhood as his Corvette moved over the curved brick driveway. He parked in front of the portico where the two stone lions guarded the rose colored door. A cold wind swept up off Lake Calhoun and ruffled his sandy hair as he rang the doorbell and patiently waited. Finally the door opened but a gray-haired woman firmly blocked his entrance.

"I need some identification," she said in a brisk manner fitting her appearance. Her hair was lacquered to a sheen and held securely in a tight French roll. She wore a black uniform and apron. Reed opened his billfold and took out his company picture. He stepped back so she could get a good look.

"Sorry to intrude. You're Mrs. Sorenson?" Reed asked after she had studied the card and returned it with a scowl. He looked around her into the foyer. One quick glance told him the lady who had lived there had exquisite taste.

"Yes, young man, I'm Mrs. Sorenson. Now what do you want, I'm very busy!" She stood with her hands on her hips, an impatient look on her face.

"Well, I'll try to make it brief. You found Mrs. Ciem?"

"Yes." Her piercing blue eyes told him nothing. Reed took out a notebook, a pen. Most people began to feel uncomfortable when they saw you were about to put their words on paper, but Mrs. Sorenson didn't flinch.

"Could I come in and sit down for a minute?" Reed asked.

Mrs. Sorenson turned to walk away and he followed her through a sitting room filled with pastel covered couches and easy chairs, by a book- filled library and finally into the kitchen. Here the house had a cozy feeling, with blue and white checked curtains at the windows that overlooked the lake, and a matching

cloth over a round table in a corner. The house was
silent except for a robust polka coming from a small
radio that sat on the kitchen counter.

"Otto's music." Mrs. Sorenson said and turned it
down. She busied herself setting out coffee-filled
mugs. Put a plate of doughnuts on the table and sat
down. After adding cream and sugar to her cup and
stirring, she blew on the mixture and sipped loudly.

"May I call you Hilda?" Reed asked. At her nod he
went on, "You found Mrs. Ciem?" He watched her and
although she was being accommodating her manner
seemed just a bit on the nervous side.

"Yes," she said now. "Otto was busy trimming
some trees down by the water. I had Mrs. Ciem's
breakfast ready at the usual time, but she didn't come
down. She always liked to eat here in the kitchen and
we'd go over things for the day."

"Was it unusual for her not to be up?" Reed
watched Hilda's face.

"Yes," Hilda replied. "Mrs. Ciem was always up
early." She picked up a doughnut.

"Did you go up to her bedroom, or call to her?"
Reed leaned back in his chair.

"Well yes, I went up to see if she wanted her
breakfast in her sitting room. She didn't answer when I
knocked on her door."

"She wasn't there?" Reed asked and took a
swallow of his coffee.

"No-- I thought she must have gone out. Most of the time she had Otto drive her though."

"Then what did you do?"

"I came back down here and started my usual cleaning. On Thursdays, I vacuum." Hilda put her cup down on the saucer and tried to cover the rattle of china with a cough.

"Go on." Reed said.

"It wasn't till close to noon when I rolled the vacuum into the sun-room, and there, right outside the window was Mrs. Ciem."

"Where?"

"Outside, just laying there on the patio floor." Hilda blew out a breath. "It was awful, just awful!"

"I can imagine. Where had she fallen from," Reed asked?

Hilda sniffed, "The third floor, the Police said she must have tried to open a window in the sitting room up there and lost her balance."

"Where was Otto all this time?"

"Well, he came in for morning coffee and went right out again. Those trees, you know."

"I understand you and Otto were caretakers for the previous owners and Mrs. Ciem hired you both to stay on." Reed watched Hilda closely.

"That's right," Hilda replied and tucked a strand of hair back into the tightened coiled roll on the back of her head. "We have an apartment over the garages."

"Is Mr. Roman around this morning?" Reed asked.

Hilda's face hardened for just a second. "He's here somewhere, he was down for breakfast."

"What's he doing?" Reed asked curiously.

"Well, I can't say. We don't see a lot of him." Hilda stirred her coffee.

"Where is he now?"

"Probably in the garage, he likes to tinker around with the cars. Her cars," Hilda added with annoyance creeping into her voice again.

"How many are there?" Reed had taken notice of the numerous garage doors on the building attached to the side of the property.

"Four," Hilda answered.

"What does Mr. Roman drive?"

"He usually drives the Prowler. It's a purple color. Mrs.Ciem bought it for him a few years ago."

Reed drank the last of his coffee. The guy had been lucky, marrying into money.

"What are the other cars?"

Hilda sat back in her chair and straightened her apron. "Well there's the Mercedes, the town car and a Mustang. Mrs. Ciem liked to drive that herself sometimes."

"Did her kids come over often?"

"They used to. Not so often lately."

"They didn't get along with Mr. Roman?"

Hilda hesitated, "I couldn't say, Mr. Conners."

"I understand," Reed said. He pushed his coffee cup aside. "I'd like to talk to your husband."

"He keeps pretty busy, but I'll call him." Hilda went to the back door and called out. In a few minutes Otto came in and looked expectantly at Reed. A short man, in his sixties clad in bib overalls. He took off his billed cap and ran a hand over his white forehead, flattening his hair as Hilda whispered to him. He walked over to the table.

"About time someone checks into this. The Police were sloppy," he mumbled. Reed stood up and extended his hand. "Name's Reed Conners. Why do you say that?"

Otto shook hands, they sat down and he reached for a doughnut. "Well, things haven't been so good around here for a long time."

"Now Otto." Hilda's voice had an edge as she handed him a mug of coffee.

"Well, I'm right, ain't I?" He flashed her an irritated look and took a loud slurping drink of his coffee. Put the cup down with a bang.

"Where were you the day Mrs. Ciem died?" Reed studied Otto's face with interest.

"I was down by the water trimming trees all morning. Didn't see or hear anything. Course, I had the trimmer going most of the time."

"Had you noticed anyone new around the neighborhood lately?"

"Nah. It's pretty quiet around here."

"How do you get along with Mr. Roman?"

Otto hesitated, chewed his doughnut. "Well---, he's different, can't quite put my finger on it. I try to stay out of his way."

"Do you think he's involved in his wife's death?" Reed asked then.

Otto sat up straighter in his chair as Hilda's intake of breath echoed in the room. "Well we'll see," Reed said and stood up not expecting an answer. "Thanks for the coffee and the delicious doughnuts, Hilda," he said nonchalantly. As he turned to go he didn't miss the look of relief on her face, a relaxation of her shoulders. He sensed there was more, much more to their story. And he knew they had to be very nervous now that their livelihood seemed uncertain after so many years of easy living amongst such luxuries. He'd be back!

-9-

Lindy rushed into her bedroom and closed the door. Well, now maybe Solly's snooping might pay off. She couldn't think about it anymore right now, she had to get back to The Raven bar with the cash for her new identification. She sat down on the floor, pulled the shoebox out from under the bed and began to count out bills. Lord, this would make a big dent in her money!

Her thoughts ran unleashed. What if the insurance on the house was delinquent? But hadn't Van Dyke, the attorney, said it was paid up for the year. Her stomach flipped. Just how much investigating did insurance companies do before paying out? But, they'd paid out in a couple of months after her other fire, and only later the company had decided something wasn't right and called in a special investigator; none other than Reed Conners! For a moment, her heart ached as she remembered her brief liaison with him just a few weeks ago. Remembered his efforts that cleared her of the fraud charge. She shook her head to chase away the feelings. No time, she whispered to herself, she'd think about that later.

She'd been so nervous when she'd talked to the adjuster at Triple Insurance and he'd confirmed the house was insured for five hundred thousand dollars! With a rider on the contents! Well, this was not the time to turn tail and run. She jammed the bills in her purse and ran out of the apartment, butterflies churning out of control in her stomach and within thirty minutes she was back at The Raven. The bartender was leaning on the bar, eyes turned to the television.

"I'm back," Lindy said and settled on a stool, out of breath. He turned to her and in a low voice asked, "Got the money?"

Determined not to be daunted, she sucked in her breath. "Hey, slow down, how soon do I get my papers?"

The bartender's eyes swept the room. "I'd say around noon tomorrow." He reached out a hand. "Got the picture?"

"I stopped at an instant photo place." Lindy handed him a picture of herself. Blonde hair and brown eyes.

"That'll do." He looked around the room again and put his hand out for the money. "Not so fast," Lindy said, "I'll pay half now and the rest when I get what I need." She'd seen that on television one time.

The bartender paused, "Sorry, no dice. That's not the way it works. I need the money up front!"

Lindy hesitated, then realizing she didn't have a choice reached in her purse for the money and passed it to him quickly.

"Okay, sweetheart." He winked at her, stuffed the bills in his pocket and turned to wait on some men at the other end of the bar. Lindy slid off the bar stool as a loud whistle pierced the air.

"Come on over baby, I'll show you a good time," someone said amid more whistles and cat calls. Chills went up her back as she sidestepped a biker, a bandanna tied over his hair.

Oh Lord, was she totally crazy handing a stranger thousands of dollars? Someone she'd met just a couple of times?

As she hurried out, she eyed the run-down neighborhood. Old men sat in plastic chairs in front of a sagging building that looked like a grocery store. Relieved that her car was still there and in one piece, she got in the BMW and locked the door. She sped back to the safety of her apartment where Solly sat with a tablet and pen, busily writing.

"How's it going?" Lindy asked as she dropped her purse on the coffee table and sat down with a groan.

"Well, I think I've got the things in the kitchen done." Solly sat back and reached for a cigarette.

"You mean everything?"

"Cripes, everything I can think of. Listen to this." Solly began to name the appliances, pots and pans, linens, and antique dishes and pictures. Lindy looked at Solly, remembered the insurance rider on the antiques, but did Solly really know as much as she said she did?

"I've put down a price of replacement on everything so far. I may be off, but we've got to put that down and when we're finished we'll have an amount to work with."

"Thanks Solly, I'm no good at this, I hope you don't mind doing it." Actually, she was relieved. Something like this would have driven her nuts.

"I need something to do; besides, I have a good memory and a good eye."

Lindy relaxed, put her feet up on the coffee table and blew some stray hair out of her eyes as Solly went into the living room to start another list. She couldn't help thinking; I'm lucky to have Solly here to do this. But what's in it for her?

The next morning, after their coffee and croissants, Lindy said "I've got another errand to do today, Solly. I shouldn't be more than an hour."

"Do you want me to go along for company or keep working on the list?"

"Solly, you'd be so bored. Could you please keep working on those lists?" Lindy breathed a sigh.

"Cripes, I don't have anything else to do." Solly sat on the couch in her usual at home attire; a tube top and bikini underpants. Her blonde hair was a mess, a cigarette in one hand and a cup of coffee in the other. The television was turned on to a morning show where a weather forecaster was predicting blizzards for the northern plains.

"I'm so glad to be out of that God forsaken country. Do you miss that frozen tundra you're from Lola," Solly asked? For a minute the thought tugged at Lindy's heart, knowing she wouldn't be able to go back to Minnesota, for sometime anyway. She pushed it aside though and put a smile on her face.

"This is so much better Solly. Don't you just love the sunshine and the flowers everywhere?" She got up and opened the door and breathed in the fresh morning air.

"It's gorgeous! But, don't you miss your family?"

"Hmm-- sometimes." Lindy sipped her coffee.

"I would love to have someone in this country besides my son. Oh well--," Solly sighed and picked at her lower lip, her eyes shaded and far-off.

"Solly, you'll have more friends, and then they'll become your family."

"I suppose. Don't you get lonesome, though?"

"Some--," Lindy replied and smiled, "then I just go shopping." She got up and stretched. "Right now, I've got to get ready to go back downtown again." She changed clothes and fled the apartment, but her foot trembled on the accelerator as she drove. She parked in the now familiar trashy neighborhood and hurried into The Raven bar. Today the place was full, a mix of working men in plaid shirts and dusty caps, some in expensive clothes wearing a lot of jewelry. Music blared and the smoke and whiskey fumes were heavy. Heads turned towards her as she hesitated in the doorway. Whistles filled the air.

"Hi ya baby, c'mon over," echoed at a pause in a song from the jukebox. A dark skinned man wearing his long hair in a pigtail made kissing sounds. Lindy walked in feeling the hungry looks greedily devour her body as she stood at the bar and looked around anxiously for the bartender. Then her heart lurched. A stranger stood in his place.

Oh Lord, she was going to faint! Had she just given her precious money to a slick operator and he'd disappeared with it?

-10-

Reed left Hilda and Otto Sorenson, the housekeeper and caretaker, sitting in the kitchen and let himself out the tall double doors. Hilda's footsteps echoed on the marble floors in the foyer as she hurried behind him to apparently make sure he left. He stood for a minute and looked around. Earth-toned cobblestone bricks sparkled on the driveway in the morning sunshine and lead to a large garage. He walked over to an open doorway and called out, "Hello is anyone here?" There was only silence. "Anyone here?" he repeated.

"Yeah." A deep voice answered.

Reed walked in and stood for a minute and waited for his eyes to adjust to the shadows. "You Tony Roman?" he asked. Now he had a good look at the man with the voice. He stuck out his hand.

"Who wants to know?" Tony Roman turned from leaning over an open hood of a car, but ignored Reed's outstretched hand and put his hands in his back pockets and stood with feet apart in a defensive manner.

Reed sized him up quickly. Late forties, six feet, two hundred and ten pounds. Italian with a Brooklyn accent. His black hair had traces of silver; his body was muscled and tanned.

Reed looked around at the shiny cars and whistled. "Fine looking wheels!"

"Yeah," Tony Roman said.

A man of many words. Reed pulled out one of his cards. "Reed Conners, I'm from the First Federated Insurance Company."

"So, what do you want from me?" Tony Roman stood firmly planted in the same spot.

'Just some things I need clarified."

"Like what?"

"Where were you when your wife died?" Reed asked.

"Like I told the Police, I was in Hollywood. I'm an actor." His teeth were beautifully capped.

"You've got witnesses?"

"Sure. Bob Olson, my agent."

"I'll need an address and a telephone number for him." Reed reached in his pocket for his notes and began writing, then asked, "How long were you and Mrs. Ciem married?"

"Seven years." Tony's face cracked for a second. Almost looked real until Reed remembered he was an actor. "Look, you can get all this from the Police. I'm tired of all this crap!" Tony Roman turned and walked away.

Back in his motel room, Reed studied his notes and the file. And shortly after he called it a day and went to bed, he fell into a dream. A grin crossed his face as he and Lindy were in his boat out on his lake. They were laughing together. A deep sigh of contentment settled in his chest as he reached to lift a strand of her hair that had fallen over her face. Then abruptly he was awakened to the phone ringing next to his ear, only to find it was a wrong number. As he sat on the edge of the bed, his mind still numb with sleep, the dilemma he was in came rushing back!

Where the hell was she? How could he concentrate on this new case and still have time to look for her? This is the last goddamn time I'll ever let a woman get that close. When I get my place fixed up again I'll be damned if I'll ever leave the north!

Even though it was the middle of the night, Reed showered, dressed and stomped around the room mumbling as he grabbed his jacket and slammed out of the motel. He got in his Corvette and drove fast, until

he came to a bar. Three Crown Royals later, he
returned to his room. Now he was drunk and pissed!

The next day, still in a bad mood he went back to
Carmen Ciem's house unannounced as before.

"Again? I thought we answered all your questions,"
Hilda said after he rang the bell at the gate. Actually,
he didn't have anything further at the moment until
some papers arrived. Just wanted to catch the
occupants unaware. See their reaction.

"How are you?" He asked as he stepped into the
now familiar foyer after Hilda had grudgingly opened
the door. Today, her uniform was gone and she was
dressed in a chic black suit. The jewelry looked real
and her perfume smelled expensive.

"I'm just on my way out." She blocked Reed's
entrance into the room further.

"That's okay; actually I wanted to see Mr. Roman."

"He's not here; he's on his way back to Hollywood.
Otto took him to the airport." Hilda looked at her
watch impatiently.

"For how long?" Reed asked.

"He didn't tell us." She shook her head and
shrugged her shoulders.

"Okay, sorry to intrude, Hilda. Have a nice day."

He went out the rose colored double door, and then
stepped back in the room. Christ, now he was
beginning to feel like the bumbling Colombo character
portrayed on television; preoccupied and forgetful. He
cleared his throat.

"Hilda, didn't Mrs. Ciem have any relatives?" Reed stood in the open doorway.

"Her two kids, you know."

"No one else?"

For just a minute Hilda stood silent, her eyes widened, "I've never heard of anyone. Now, I really must go!" She closed the door in Reed's face.

-11-

As Lindy perched on the stool at The Raven bar, her eyes adjusted to the darkness, her nose to the grease, sweat and liquor fumes. Cat-calls and suggestive jeers echoed in her ears. She held her purse securely in her lap and adjusted her shirt with her other hand. Thank God, she'd worn one of Solly's long skirts and a loose blouse and not one of her new shorter outfits.

"What'll you have?" The new bartender asked as he winked and wiped down the bar with a gray rag.

"Where's the other bartender?" Lindy asked nervously and leaned away from the man on the next stool who was grinning at her.

This bartender leaned over the bar and stroked her hand. "Won't I do?" Lindy jerked her hand back.

"Hey, you get all the good-looking ones," the man on the next stool mumbled drunkenly.

"Nah, this one is for me!"

Lindy swung around and looked into the face of a huge man leering from the other side. Gray hair hung out of a wool cap. A full beard, stained brown around large lips, leaned only inches from her face. He continued, "I bet the pretty lady wants a fancy glass of wine. I'll buy."

The bartender left and returned with a water glass filled to the rim. The fumes of the dark wine rose up to Lindy's nose, pungent and raw. Her stomach lurched. She turned to slide off her stool and sucked in her breath. Three men stood just behind her, hemmed her in. One put his booted foot on the rung of her stool. His breath foul with whiskey.

"Excuse me," Lindy said in a faltering voice. The men leered at her and moved in closer.

"Dance with me," one of them said as he swayed from side to side mouthing the words to Willy Nelson's, 'Born to Loose.' His large hands stroked his crotch. His faded red and black jacket was edged with dirt and grease. She tried to slip around the men and get away. They moved in closer.

"You can't leave, you're mine," the man in the plaid jacket said and put his arm over her shoulder, pulled her towards him. Lindy sat frozen, helpless. The music roared in her ears, smoke burned her eyes. A hand reached out and pushed her skirt up, grabbed her bare thigh. She slapped at it. The steely grip didn't budge.

"She's mine!" echoed in her ear. Lindy sat pinned in, pinned down in the middle of the cluster of men. A hand stroked her hair. She jerked her head away, tried to get up. The men stood firm in place, their sweat and foul breath engulfed her.

Suddenly, a man yelled, "get away from her, assholes, I saw her first!" Out of the corner of her eye, Lindy saw the flash of a knife, as a man pushed his way towards her. The crowd parted, but not before blood shot out of the arm of the man in the plaid jacket who held her thigh. With a groan he crumpled to the floor. The man with the braid in his long hair held the knife. The men stepped back, retreated. Lindy leaned into the bar, tried to make herself smaller. Her face sickly white, her eyes desperate. Suddenly, a shot echoed in the room, then silence except for the blare of the music. The men stood frozen, mouths agape.

"I'll blast the first one that moves," a voice shouted. Suddenly Lindy was pulled off the stool, pushed through the crowd into a back room. She stumbled blindly. Her blouse was torn, the belt on her skirt untied, but, she had held tightly to her purse. Lindy's legs gave out and she fell into a chair as the door slammed.

"Christ, you sure know how to start a riot!" A familiar voice belonging to her friend, the bartender, surprised her dogged thoughts.

"Well, where the hell were you?" Lindy exploded after she regained her composure.

"You could have gotten yourself killed!" The man kicked some boxes out the way and walked over to a battered desk and sat down on the edge.

Now she was pissed. She glared at him. "Have you got the papers or did you just steal my money!" She blew out a breath.

He took an envelope out of his shirt pocket. "Here, good as gold."

"They better be good," she fumed and quickly looked over the Georgia driver's license, and the social security card. They both read Lola Lang. They looked real, but then how did she know anyway.

"Now get me out of this hell-hole," she declared and he led her to a back entrance. Sirens screamed in the distance as Lindy sped away from The Raven bar, thankful, her car was still there and in one piece. Back at the apartment, she joined Solly in the living room.

"How are you coming with the list?" She asked and sank down on the couch. Her legs were still weak.

"I'm through, Lola, but you need to check it over to make sure I've reported everything you lost. I may have overlooked some things."

Lindy sighed. She'd gotten quite used to loosing everything by now. First in her house fire up north, and then when she'd left all her beautiful clothes at Reed Conner's place. A blade of guilt cut through her heart at that thought.

"Lola, are you okay? You look a little pale." Solly handed her a cup of tea and sat down cross-legged on the floor. Now that Lindy was home safely, she was more shaken than ever, but answered evasively, "I must be coming down with something."

Lindy studied the list of contents that Solly had worked on for the insurance company, pages listing each article and estimated value that had burned in the fire. It looked good, but she really didn't know. When she came to the personals, she was totally surprised. Eleven pairs of underwear. Four pairs of nylons. Gucci black pumps and matching purse. Solly had even included the small box that Lindy had hidden in the back of her closet. Not anything of value, just a glass door-knob from her first house, the mansion up north.

A frown crossed Lindy's face as she skimmed the lists further. Just how thorough had Solly been when she'd admitted to snooping through her things. And if she'd found even these things, she'd certainly found the money tucked under the bed. Her real identification in her billfold. A trickle of apprehension spread down through Lindy's body. Keeping her eyes averted, her mind flew ahead.

Who was she? Some kind of spy? Or just a nosy old lady like she'd said. Lindy had been burned too many times lately. She remembered Dade Lampart in

Dallas, and Mario in Hilton Head. The phone rang, jangling her nerves. She jumped up and answered.

"Miss Lang, Triple Insurance. I'd like you to come in tomorrow morning. Also if you've got your inventory list ready, I'd like to see that!"

"What time," Lindy asked and swallowed hard.

"Nine o'clock." The man's voice was brisk and business like.

"I'll be there." Lindy put the phone down nervously. Thank God, she had things ready just in time.

The next morning, Lindy dressed in one of her new dresses. A bright red A-line with spaghetti straps. A jacket covered the low cut top. She stood in front of the floor-length mirror. Was it too short? Her heels too high? Or, maybe that was good! Oh Lord, she was tired of worrying.

Downtown, at the insurance company she was ushered into an office. She sat nervously twisting a tissue. I've got nothing to hide, she reassured herself defensively. After what seemed like an hour, the door opened and a gray-haired man came in. He reached out a hand and introduced himself. "I'm John Houston, Miss Lang." Lindy sat up straighter. Everything about him was gray. Hair, suit, shoes, socks, even his complexion had a somber look. He sat down and opened a file.

"Miss Lang, I'll need to see your identification and your insurance papers." She busied herself taking her billfold out of her purse and laying the cards out on the table. Placing the envelope containing the policy next to them, she took small quiet breaths as he studied her picture on the driver's license, and compared signatures. She stifled a nervous gasp when he stood and said, "I'll need to copy these."

After he left the room Lindy smoothed her dress and fluffed her hair. She pushed down a little voice that scrambled to be heard that said, run! He was back minutes later and asked, "Have you got your inventory list?" Not so much as a half smile had escaped his thin face. Maybe, he owned the company. Lindy handed him the papers and asked, "Mr. Houston, I lost everything I owned in the fire, so just how much money can I plan on getting?"

Mr. Houston fussed with his mustache, brushed it one way and back again. "Well, if everything checks out, the house was insured for five hundred thousand dollars. Also Madam Fitzgerald had special coverage on all her antiques so we will call in specialists for comparable estimates."

Lindy stifled a smile just in time, and then managed a tear to roll down her cheek. She fumbled in her purse for a tissue and turned her soulful eyes towards him. "I loved that house!" she managed to say at last.

On the way back to the apartment, she tried to relax, thankful this part was over. If this comes through, she promised herself, she would settle down and get serious about life! Invest the money and get a job! But what about Solly? Should she confront her and demand to know her agenda or should she just wait and watch?

-12-

Reed Conners stood on the portico of Carmen Ciem's house and felt the breeze of the slamming door on his face as Hilda impatiently hurried him away. Today, she certainly didn't look like the housekeeper in her expensive suit and make-up. He heard the wrought iron gate close behind him, and the lock click into place as he left the property. He drove slowly through the neighborhood nestled in around the Lake Calhoun area, the biggest and busiest lake in Minneapolis, where brick houses stood securely behind fences and mature trees swayed in the morning breezes. Smoke from wood-burning fireplaces tickled Reed's nose as he lowered the car window in the Corvette to get a better look around. The holidays were approaching and workmen were busy at a corner house putting up Christmas lights and garland on a wrap-around verandah.

Who were these people that lived behind closed doors and locked gates? What did they do and what were their thoughts? It looked pretty cold and lonely to Reed who was used to the cozy friendly atmosphere of his small northern community. He drove for a few minutes and then circled back to Carmen Ciem's house and parked down the street, out of sight. Maybe he'd just watch for awhile. Let his mind run through the facts. Later, he had an appointment with Joe Baker, the guy at his insurance company who had taken over Lindy's case.

Reed sat in the Corvette with the window open and inhaled the brisk morning air off the snow covered Lake Calhoun. He pulled the collar of his brown leather jacket up, lit a cigarette and let his thoughts ramble.

His company, First Federated Insurance, would not pay out ten million dollars until they were certain without a doubt, that foul play was not involved.

The facts, as reported by the Police department, stated Carmen Ciem had died from a fall from an upstairs balcony. Who would benefit from her death? Her husband, Tony Roman, a small time Hollywood actor? Her son and daughter? Not likely since both had successful careers and not a single blemish on their histories. Hilda and Otto Sorenson; Carmen Ciem's live-in housekeeper and all around handy man and chauffeur?

Were they responsible for Carmen Ciem's death, and now had done away with her husband, since they'd said he'd left town?

Reed put out the cigarette, turned on some music, Miles Davis this time. Just so he wouldn't look too suspicious parked in this affluent neighborhood he took out a map and pretended to study it. He had just lit up another cigarette when a car drove past.

Goddamn he muttered, what the hell was going on? Hilda sat at the wheel of a red Mustang. Carmen Ciem's car. Dark glasses covered her eyes. He waited until she turned a corner and then started the Corvette. Just as he turned onto a main street the Mustang merged with traffic headed for the freeway. He accelerated and caught up, leaving only a few cars in between. Now this was interesting. He followed her through a tunnel and onto the freeway. His speedometer read seventy five miles an hour, then eighty. For an old gal, she sure knew how to handle a car. He had to admit, he got tense in some of the traffic tangles that seemed to be an everyday thing here in Minneapolis. She slowed as she approached the bluffs overlooking the Saint Croix River near Stillwater.

As a kid, Reed had visited the area with his parents and had been fascinated with the scenery. It was just as splendid now, as it had been then. Trees grew out of the rocks, which reached dozens of feet high over one side of the highway. On the other side the water sparkled below in a river stream as it flowed gently over small rapids.

He followed Hilda into the town and down the one street, bordered on both sides by antique shops and restaurants. She took an abrupt left turn and went uphill into the residential area. Being careful not to be observed, Reed waited through a yellow light before following her. Keeping well behind, he saw her turn into a driveway and go up to a house. Saw her take out a key and go inside. Window shades snapped down in the front windows.

What the hell was she up to? The neighborhood was old and some of the houses needed help. Overgrown lilac bushes edged the back yards.

Reed parked across the street and down a few houses, stretched his legs, pushed the seat back in the Corvette and settled into wait. As he sat, the early afternoon sun clouded over and a wind off the water from the river below the hill sent up a bone-chilling whine. Dead leaves swirled on the snow banks around his car. After two hours, he was just about to give up and start back for his appointment in Minneapolis, when a sleek burgundy town car slid into the driveway. Reed sat up, instantly alert. He held the map up in front of his face, and watched out of the corner of his eyes as a woman climbed out and hurried up to the house, her face almost covered by huge dark glasses. The door opened quickly and she disappeared inside.

Now who the hell is this woman? Reed muttered
and checked the time. Forty minutes until his
appointment with Baker, and Joe would be pissed if he
was late.

He knew he had to get a car phone, but it would be
a goddamn nuisance as far as he was concerned. A guy
couldn't even enjoy the pure silence of his car anymore.
He took down the license number of the town car along
with the address of the house.

The countryside flew by as Reed drove back to
Minneapolis and to the offices of the First Federated
Insurance Company. Mona smiled at him with her
usual classy greeting.

"Have you got plans for tonight?" Reed asked as he
sat on the edge of her desk and looked her up and
down. Goddamn he was lonely, needed some warm
affection. She smiled, stood up and planted a kiss on
his lips. Her perfume enveloped him. He inhaled the
fragrance from her skin, her hair. "Damn you smell
good," he murmured in her ear.

"Should I meet you at Gina's?" Mona stepped back
out of his reach, and raised an eyebrow teasingly. "Or
should we do take-out at my house?"

"Let's have a cocktail and decide. Okay?"

"Sounds fine." Mona sat back down at her desk,
tucked a strand of hair behind her ear. Reed nodded
towards Joe Baker's door.

"Is he in?"

"He's in and waiting for you. I'll meet you when I close up shop." Reed glanced back at her as he stepped out of the reception area. Mona's black hair curled around her face, spiked effectively on top. Today, she wore a beige cashmere dress. Low cut in front. Her full sensuous lips were painted a brilliant red. As Reed had tasted her kiss, he was momentarily reminded of the picture of those lips that hung over the Red Dog bar in Dallas where he and Manny had waited for John Thomas, Lindy Lewis's assailant. Lindy Lewis again. Goddamn! That woman always invaded his thoughts when things looked promising with someone else.

Reed adjusted his jeans against the tension in his groin and pushed the door open to Baker's office. He had gotten to know Joe when he'd joined the company and they had spent many hours drinking coffee going over old and new business. Joe was a family man, with a wife and six kids. His blond hair was thinning and his middle was starting to bulge. His good humor was catchy, which gave him an edge. Right off, people trusted him.

"How's it going Joe?" Reed walked in and greeted him.

"Hey Conners, good to see you, have a seat."

Reed pulled out a chair.

"Thanks for coming in," Joe said and went on," I've spent the last two days reading the file on this Lewis dame. How the hell did she get away?"

"I let my guard down," Reed admitted. Be damned if he would tell anyone they'd slept together!

"Well, here's what I got so far. Zilch. Nada!" Baker put his feet up on the desk and leaned back. Reed turned his chair around, leaned his chin on the top. Baker loosened his tie and opened his shirt collar. "How long since she split?"

"Over three weeks." Reed exhaled, shook his head.

"I take it she's still traveling in that BMW?"

"As far as I know. Of course by now she could have gotten rid of it." Reed got up and paced, ran a hand over his face.

"We've got the warrant out. Hell, we'll catch up with her soon." Baker said confidently then went on, "No one stays lost forever. Is that photo of her a recent one?"

Reed took out a cigarette, lit up and took his time inhaling.

"Jeez man, do you have to?" Baker waved a file in the air.

"You sound like Murphy! Who knows about her, the last time I saw Lindy Lewis, her hair was blonde and she wore brown eye contacts."

"I'm thinking she's in Chicago. Lost herself in the crowd."

"No--, I don't think so." Reed sat back down, crossed an ankle over his knee. "She hates cold weather. I think she's back in the south."

"How much do you think she's got left of that million?"

"Christ, not much I'll bet, she's got expensive tastes."   Reed remembered the suitcases of expensive clothes she'd left behind at his motel.

"Well sometime soon, she's going to run out of money and will have to get a job. It's not hard to track someone once they use their social security card. We'll have her then!" Baker tossed the file down on his desk with finality.

Reed walked out of the office with mixed feelings but, he had to admit, also relief that she was still safe out there somewhere.

-13-

Five hundred thousand dollars on the house! And more from the insurance on the antiques, Lindy whispered as she drove away following the meeting with John Houston at the Triple Insurance Company. She had just brought him the insurance papers, and her new driver's license and social security card.

But lord, had he suspected they were fake? When he'd stepped out of the room to make copies had he really called the authorities? He hadn't seemed too friendly when he'd said it would take weeks to process.

Lindy squared her shoulders. What would she do while she waited! She needed to relax. Get away from her worries and then thought with a stab of guilt, Solly too! She turned the BMW around and headed across town to Zelda's. At this time of the day, the parking lot was beginning to fill with the lunch crowd. She found a space at the end of the lot and parked.

The temperature was already in the high eighties with the humidity rapidly keeping up. Lindy ruffled her hair and took off the jacket that matched her dress. She sucked in her stomach and pushed her chest out. Maybe she'd get those implants after she got her money. She caught a glimpse of herself in a window when she opened the door to the restaurant and smiled.

Zelda's was an upbeat, trendy restaurant next to the water in the old recently restored part of Savannah, Georgia. The brick building was overgrown with an ivy vine that attached itself as it spread to anything that got in its way. It never turned brown and never died and even an ax couldn't control it. And which, northerners paid big money for and tried in vain to grow. She adjusted her smart new Armani sunglasses and stepped into the busy place. The aroma of garlic and fresh baked bread tantalized her growling stomach. Chatter was loud and animated.

'This is just what I needed," she murmured as she sipped a tall frosted Margarita and lit a cigarette. She relaxed and felt the tension flow out of her body. In the middle of her second drink, she began to think seriously about the evitable changes she'd have to make soon. No more drifting. She had to have a plan. When this money came through she had to figure out a way to not squander it. It might mean that she'd have to find a job again. A shudder shot through her at that thought. And maybe she should move. The southeast was wonderful, but a niggling feeling seemed to urge her to get out fast. Not back to the north certainly. Well, there's the east and the west. She'd take her money and go somewhere. There, she'd made a plan!

Lindy slammed the door when she got back to the apartment just to let Solly know she was back. She and her new love, Toby, from the band called the Three T's were seated on the couch intently watching an afternoon movie. They both turned to Lindy as she sank into a chair, shed her shoes and put her feet up on the coffee table. Solly's eyes were clouded with love and desire as she nestled in the arms of the musician. They were in love, Solly had confided earlier.

"I was beginning to worry Lola, you were gone so long." Solly sat up and brushed at her hair.

"Oh sorry," Lindy said, "I got tied up downtown."

"I hope the list I made for you for the insurance company was okay." Solly picked at her bottom lip, looked doubtful.

"As far as I know it was fine." Lindy sighed. "Of course, how would they know what I had in the house anyway, and, they have pictures of the antiques?"

"Cripes, maybe I was way off on pricing. You know, on linens and dishes. And I just guessed on all those knick-knacks."

"Ahh, don't worry about it, Solly. You did a better job than I could have. Besides I'm sure they have guidelines they go by."

"What are you going to do after you get the insurance?" Solly asked and looked at Lindy expectantly.

"I really don't know. I've got to see how things go." She didn't really want to divulge anything yet.

"How about you, Solly? Have you made any plans?" Lindy asked hoping she had thought about the future. "Do you want to stay here in Savannah?"

Solly looked up at her new love. "Hmm-1 think so. I love this town and the weather. I asked about a job here in this hotel complex and I can work here if I want to." She snuggled in closer to the man's embrace.

"I'm glad, Solly," Lindy said and sighed, inwardly relieved. But she worried again, for sure Solly had found her real identity when she had admitted to snooping through her things, and also the box of money hidden in her bedroom? Why hadn't she said anything? What was her agenda anyway?

God, she was restless and tired of all this uncertainty. And even though she'd just gotten home, she got up and slid into her sandals again and said, "Why don't we go out for awhile?"

"Cripes, what a good idea." Solly exclaimed and took her friends hand and pulled him to his feet. "The band starts tonight over at a place called the Wing Joint, we were over there earlier."

"Is that the place on the beach by the lighthouse?" Lindy opened her purse, took out a compact and checked her face.

"You should see it Lola. The outside deck goes out over the water. Let's go there and we can watch the sunset."

"I'll drive my car and follow you two over there." Actually there was a reason Lindy wanted to drive alone.

As she drove through town, the late afternoon sun glistened off the green vegetation, catching the brilliant colors of pansies and geraniums planted on the street corners of Savannah. Heads of kale grew as a decorative plant, its large green or burgundy cabbage-like leaves delicately edged in white. Before coming to the South, she had only seen this plant's leaves used as a garnish in restaurants. Bamboo bushes were common, also the Tamarack evergreen. Huge stately water oaks laced with Spanish moss still fascinated her. Nearing the ocean, hills and valleys of marsh land glistened with oyster beds which fed off the tides that washed over the shores. Cattails and sea oats grew here and there along the edges.

Lindy inhaled the wonderful smell of the salt water; felt the air begin to cool as she neared a familiar area. She held her breath as she turned a street corner not sure of what she would see. And there it was. There stood the blackened remains of her beautiful house.

Parts of a wall still stood here and there amongst the heaps of ashes.

She stopped the car and stared at the horrible sight. Then tears flooded her eyes and her shoulders sagged in sadness.

Life would have been so pleasant living there, so safe. She sat huddled in sorrow and time lost its cadence when suddenly a cloud seemed to form above the ashes. Her breath caught as she stared at it, fascinated as it turned into shadowy silhouettes, resembling human shapes. The already cool air turned icy cold and then suddenly the shapes turned into what seemed to be a whirling dervish. It stood still for a moment and then came towards the car. Lindy sat stunned, and then it suddenly disappeared.

"What the hell was that?" she whispered, shaken to the bone as she drove away. Could it have been those friends of Madame Fitzgerald's protesting lose of their home?

She joined Solly and her boyfriend out on the deck at the Wing Joint. When he left to get ready for the evenings entertainment, they sat mesmerized along with the other customers and watched the awesome scene unfolding before them.

The setting sun was a huge orange globe slightly hidden behind a lacy cloud. The glow not only illuminated the water in brilliance but, edged it in pinks, mauves and purple. The oyster beds in the marsh shone like black pearls. Now the sea oats and cattails edged the picture in a matte-like finish. Each second the scene changed. Conversation dwindled as everyone watched the fascinating splendor. The whole panoramic show took only a matter of minutes before the sun sank into the ocean. The people sat in hushed silence in the purple afterglow.

"Have you ever seen anything like that?" Solly finally managed to ask.

Lindy shook her head. "Wow, it's something, isn't it?"

"I'm never leaving this place. I want to see this everyday, Lola." Solly's eyes grew large. "Even in Norway, we never had anything like this."

"That's what they say on the brochures, 'You'll never want to leave after seeing our sunsets.'"

"Lola," Solly asked curiously, "Isn't it weird to see Christmas decorations and hear the holiday songs when there's no snow?"

Lindy nodded, sipped her drink and blew smoke in the air, remembering the holidays in the north with her family and friends. The music started then with the Three T's coming on stage dressed in Santa Claus outfits. Their hair and false white beards clashed dramatically with their dark complexions as they sang Jingle Bells with a Jamaican beat. Lindy tapped her toe and hummed along with the familiar song. Suddenly her heart jumped in her chest. Her breath caught in her throat. She set her glass down carefully and looked again. Same sandy hair and broad shoulders. As the man at the bar with his back to them, lifted a glass of beer his actions seemed so familiar.

Oh my God, could it be Reed? Had he found her here in Savannah? Chills crept up her back as she thought of what he would make her do.

Was there a back way out of the place? Could she slip out without him seeing her?

Well, now she wouldn't have to worry about a future, the law would have that planned for her. And, she was so close to getting her money from the insurance.

Her eyes bore into the man's back and suddenly, as if on cue, he turned and looked right at her. Lindy stared aghast, right into the eyes of a stranger. From the front, his features were altogether different. Dark eyes, a long nose, lips almost covered with a mustache. She quickly averted her eyes, and with a trembling hand took another drink of her Margarita. The alcohol caught in her throat as she gulped, but her shoulders sagged with relief.

"I've got to leave," she whispered to Solly who had looked at her in surprise. She grabbed her purse and stood up on shaking legs and hurried out of the Wing Joint.

Oh lord, she thought panic-stricken, first I see apparitions in the ashes of my burned out house and now I thought I saw Reed.

This is not good!

-14-

Reed left Joe Baker's office at First Federated Insurance and got into his Corvette. Goddamn, how would he really feel when Joe brought Lindy in? Like Joe had said, sooner or later, she would be found! The whole thing was out of his hands, unless he could wind up Carmen Ciem's case, fast. He drove the few blocks to Gina's restaurant, located in the heart of downtown Minneapolis. As he approached the door and gave his car keys to the valet, the familiar landmark brought back memories of his law school days, when he and his buddy Tanner Burk would bring a special date. Their money was short and the times were few. One time, he and Lindy had been there for her birthday. Now, Tanner was dead and Lindy was a fugitive!

"Reed Conners, it's good to see you again so soon." Gina pressed him to her ample breast. "You're just as handsome as ever." Her bracelets jangled.

"How are you Gina?" Reed stood back and smiled at his friend.

"I'm great. Business is great. What more can I ask!" Her platinum hair was swept up in curls that framed her forehead. Her gown was a flaming red. Diamonds sparkled in her ears. "Will you be in town for a while this time?"

"Not sure, I've got a case that might drag on." He nodded towards the bar. "Is Mona here yet?"

"She sure is." Gina shook her head. "Reed, I wish you two would take my advise and not waste anymore time!"

"Well." Reed mumbled at a loss.

"I mean it, Reed. You don't want to be alone when you get to be my age."

Reed winked at her. "Gina, you can't kid me, you've got the best of both worlds and you know it."

"Shush, come along now." She laughed and ushered him to the bar where Mona sat perched on a stool, a martini in one hand.

"Hi, beautiful," Reed said and leaned over and planted a kiss on her lips.

Mona put her glass down and smiled. "Good to see you too. How did it go this afternoon with Joe?"

"Nothing new so far!" He motioned to the bartender and ordered a Crown Royal on ice.

"Is it true you've known this Lindy Lewis since college," Mona asked curiously?

Reed cleared his throat and gave her a sharp look. "Mona, it was a long time ago."

"Well," Mona persisted, "why is she so hard to find? Why can't you get the case settled?" Mona sipped her drink, studied his face.

Reed motioned the bartender over. Goddamn, he hated to be pressed. Stalling for time, he said, "We'll have another," then took out his cigarettes and snapped his lighter.

"What's this woman like?" Mona asked.

Reed leaned back on his bar stool and crossed an ankle over his knee. "What do you mean?"

"Well, just a woman's curiosity. What does she look like, that picture in the file didn't tell me much!"

He shrugged his shoulders, took a big swallow of the second drink the bartender had just placed on the bar.

"Hmm-, I don't know."

"Well?" Mona waited.

"I guess she's good looking. Why?" he asked.

Mona smiled demurely. "I'm just curious what this woman has that has got the company's two super sleuths by the short hairs."

"Yeah?" Reed mumbled, slightly irritated. "Hey, I'm starved, lets not waste time talking about her." He nodded at the bartender. "Tell Gina we're ready for our table.

"We'll have the prime rib," Reed told the waiter a few minutes later as they were seated in the elegant dining room. As they sipped after dinner cordials Reed reached under the table and ran a hand over Mona's thigh and felt the heat.

"Should I follow you home?" he asked. Some TLC was just what he needed after being trampled on by Lindy.

"I'd like that" Mona smiled seductively. She reached for her mink coat, and gathered her purse.

One thing about Mona, she knew how to enjoy life. She was independent and beautiful and had come from a family of money. Her home was in a downtown high rise overlooking the Mississippi River and the city. A doorman opened the door for them; an elevator operator took them up to the nineteenth floor. As soon as she locked the door, Reed took her in his arms and his hungry lips found hers. She dropped the mink and began unbuttoning his shirt and tugging at his belt when he picked her up and carried her to the bedroom. He laid her on the king-sized bed and as his lips began a downward journey, her purring murmurs of ecstasy filled the night.

Hours later Reed untangled himself from her warm embrace and sat up on the edge of her bed.

"Do you have to go?" Mona whispered and stood up, unabashed by her nakedness. She put her hands on her hips then and went on, "Reed Conners, you come to town, buy me dinner a few times, get me in bed and then I don't hear from you again for months!" Her face was clear of make-up, her hair messed.

"Come here," he said and pulled her down to his lap, ran a finger over a breast and kissed a nipple. "But you're never out of my thoughts!"

"Oh sure," she laughed. She busied herself tying the belt of her robe. He gathered his clothes scattered on the floor and went in the bathroom and turned on the shower.

"Well, when will I see you again?" Mona asked as he stood at the door ready to leave a short time later.

"I'll call you. I promise," he said, his thoughts already miles away!

-15-

Lindy ran out of the Wing Joint restaurant on shaking legs. Lord, if that man had been Reed Conners, what would she have done? Well, it wasn't him and she couldn't worry about it now, she just needed a little more time.

If only the insurance company would get on the ball and give her the damn money! The days passed slowly for her, and each time the phone rang her heart jumped in her throat. Solly was gone a lot with her boyfriend, so the apartment was lonely and quiet. Her nerves were taut. She tried exercising, but got a backache, bought herself some yarn and attempted to start an afghan, but threw the bundle of twisted wool in the trash. Finally, out of desperation she went out to shop, window shop that is, being that was the one thing that could occupy her totally. She passed the days and also picked out a new car. Instead of a red BMW convertible as she had thought she'd get this time a silver Lexus called her name.

Another week went by and when she came back to the apartment after wandering through the shops again, the flashing light on the telephone summoned her attention. She picked up the receiver and listened. She had a message. Her heart thumped.

"Miss Lang, John Houston from Triple Insurance. I'd like to see you tomorrow morning at 9:00 in my office."

Lindy put the phone down and blew out a nervous breath. The time had come! She'd either get the money or they'd arrest her. She tried to sleep that night, but at three AM tossed the blankets aside, got up and made a pot of coffee and sat on the couch huddled in a robe. A cloud of cigarette smoke circled around her head. Her stomach was tied in knots. Finally, after hours of staring at the television, it was time for her to get ready and see the man that held her future in his hands.

A somber receptionist ushered her into the same office as before, and minutes later John Houston entered carrying a thick file. He cleared his throat as he sat down behind his desk. His greeting was short with not a trace of a smile on his face. Lindy's voice faltered as she squeaked out a hello. She'd worn a two-piece red suit. Just to add some severity to her outfit she'd slipped a scarf around her neck to cover the low cut neckline. She smoothed her skirt down and wondered, too late, if it was too short to wear to collect her money. She clutched her purse in her lap.

"You owned the house how long?" John Houston's piercing eyes shot a quick peek at her legs.

"Well," Lindy stammered. "Just a few weeks."

"Hmm- unbelievable!" The man paged through the file. Not saying anything more as he studied the pages.

Lindy swallowed over a lump of nerves in her throat. Outside, the skies were leaden and soon a spatter of rain began to drum against the window panes. The small office became humid and the man's powerful after-shave suddenly brought on a wave of nausea.

Oh Lord, Lindy thought desperately, he knows! He must know I bought my ID. And, he probably knows about my fire up north! But she forced her breathing to slow, her face to relax.

"Yes, well." John Houston straightened in his chair, ran a hand over his gray mustache. He shuffled some papers, and then went on, "Your attorney was thorough in the transfer of title." He read some more notes and looked her squarely in her eyes. "The fire Marshall and the special Investigator have determined and concur the fire was caused by a defective air-conditioner."

Lindy held her breath, her eyes riveted on his lips as he went on, "Your house was insured for five hundred thousand dollars. Are you planning to rebuild?" He asked looking at her expectantly.

Rebuild, was he crazy? "I'm not sure," she managed to say.

"We can turn this around and mortgage a new property for you. I advise you to invest right away, but that's your choice. Now, about the antiques, that amount comes to several hundred thousand dollars. Madam Fitsgerald left you some pretty unique pieces!"

Good lord, she had had no idea those paintings were authentic. And then those funny looking tables and knick-knacks? This was more than she had dared to hope!

The intercom buzzed, and after a hushed conversation, John Houston stood up and said, "Excuse me for a moment, Miss Lang. I have to attend to a slight problem out front. There are some magazines on the table as it might be a few minutes."

Lindy tried to smile, but her mouth was so dry her lips stuck to her teeth. He closed the door and left.

Had he gotten a last minute call from some official? Maybe they had a hidden mirror in the room where they watched for guilty signs! She'd read that somewhere. Oh Lord, her mind was in a whirlwind. Just in case someone was watching she nonchalantly yawned and reached for something to read. She paged through the New Yorker, a month old Money, and finally found a People magazine that was current. Even the antics of the Hollywood natives could not interest her today. But, she pretended to read, just in case.

What was wrong with her? Why was she feeling guilty, she wasn't responsible for the damn fire that burned the house!

After what seemed like hours, John Houston came back in the room carrying a file and took his seat behind his desk. He shuffled some more papers, sucked a tooth. Perspiration trickled down between Lindy's breasts, dampened her armpits as he finally said, "Miss Lang, I suggest you go straight to your bank and put this safely away." Then he handed her the check. Lindy's hand shook as she reached for it. Then she steadied herself and smiled at the little man and poised her legs seductively.

"Thank you, Mr. Houston," she said and left his office forcing herself to walk slowly and not run like hell. When she finally reached the safety of her car, her nerves got the best of her and she put her head down on the steering wheel. Tears of relief flooded her eyes and rolled down her face, but a few minutes later, she regrouped and smiled.

Yes, she'd stop at a bank, then collect her things at the apartment, leave a note for Solly and be on her way. To where? She didn't know, but she'd know when she got there!

-16-

Reed left Mona's bed sated, but perturbed about her questions and her sudden change in attitude. She'd never been so clingy, so inquisitive. That had been the one good thing about their relationship that seemed to work for both of them. He got back to his room at the motel and picked up the phone to make a call.

"Bernard? Reed Conners. Yeah, I'm back in town again. Buddy, I've got some things I need you to check out. Otto and Hilda Sorenson at this address. Tony Roman, same place. This house in Stillwater, Minnesota." He paged through his notes. "Oh yeah, this license number on a car. Thanks, I'll check back."

He threw his clothes on the bed and hit the sack and spent the next days watching Carmen Ciem's house. Saw Hilda go over to the big house every morning. Saw Otto clear snow off the porches and driveway. At night, the caretaker couple would turn off the lights in the mansion and go back to their apartment above the garage.

He wondered what the hell they did now that their boss was dead and her husband was away. He studied the file again and again. The medical examiner declared Carmen Ciem had died sometime around dawn. Hilda had found her employer laying three stories below the upstairs balcony on the tiled courtyard many hours later. On a Monday, over two months ago. During that time he had been in Dallas chasing down John Thomas, escaped prisoner and killer of his friend, Tanner. The same man who had infiltrated his company, First Federated Insurance.

It was late in the month of January and Minnesota was deep in a bone chilling winter. Goddamn, this was the time of the year he should have been tucked down in his log home at Birch Lake, a fire roaring in the fieldstone fireplace, reading from his collection of mysteries.

He dressed hurriedly as today he was going to meet with his friend Bernard, the whiz on the computer. That man could find out everything about anybody. Reed's knock echoed in the barren halls of a downtown rooming house.

"Conners, you're looking good," Bernard greeted him.

"Yeah, what did you find?" Reed unzipped his jacket.

"Not too much yet, but here it is." The metal creaked as the crippled man straightened up in his wheelchair. "Hilda and Otto Sorenson are clean. No arrests, not even a parking ticket. They came here in the early eighties, got jobs with the former owners on that property. Have been at that address ever since." Reed already knew this.

"They have any money?" he asked.

"Some. I found four hundred thousand."

"Where'd they come from Bernard?"

"Not a clue. But get this; they withdrew a hundred grand right about the time that old dame sailed over the railing." Bernard's chair creaked as he shifted his weight.

"No shit!" Reed lit a cigarette. "What about that address in Stillwater?"

The wheel chair creaked again as the man shuffled papers. "The house is owned by a group of investors, taken care of by a management company. The rent comes in promptly each month by money order. A cover up, you can be sure."

Reed exhaled a frustrated breath. "Anything on the car?"

"Yep, rented by a broad. Ann Ramsey."

"Who the hell is that?"

"Don't know. Came in to rent and paid cash. Want me to go further?"

"Christ, yes!" Reed jotted down names and dates. "What'd you find on Tony Roman?"

"Ha, now that was easy. Romanopulis is his family name. Grew up in Chicago in a poor Italian neighborhood. Never did have a real job until he copped this peach driving the Ciem dame around in her collection of swanky cars. Had some arrests for small time."

"When did he come to Minneapolis and land this job?"

"He started paying taxes just a little over eight years ago."

"Anything else?" Reed asked as he took out his billfold and slid a hundred dollar bill on the table.

"Didn't take him long to get in her bed." Bernard shook his head. "I'll call if anything else pops up."

Back at his motel, Reed ordered a sandwich and coffee from room service and sat at the desk. If the caretakers had some money, why were they still working? Why weren't they retired and living in Florida or Arizona like most people their age?

And especially, why had they taken a hundred thousand dollars out of their savings? Was it to pay someone to murder their boss?

And, what about Tony Roman? He definitely had gotten lucky. The one time Reed had seen him, he'd been in the garage. His six-foot frame matched Reeds, but of course being a Hollywood actor, he was tanned, slim and in shape.

Well, what the hell else did the asshole have to do, but make himself pretty? Reed snorted in the silent room. The big question though was, what did a smart business woman like Carmen Ciem, featured in articles time and again about her successful cosmetic company, see in this nobody? Granted, he could be called good looking, with his curly black hair and blue eyes, but why wouldn't she just have an affair with him and not get into the complications of marriage?

The afternoon flew by and as evening approached, Reed drove back to the Calhoun lake area, parked on a dark street and watched the house again. This time the lights didn't go out at seven o'clock as usual, when the caretakers would lock up and go to their place over the garage. The kitchen lights stayed on. Then a bedroom light upstairs came on. Carmen and Tony's bedroom? Another snapped on, on third floor. What the hell were they doing? It was time he paid another visit.

He rang the bell from the now familiar front portico and glanced over at the stone lions sitting on their haunches guarding the entrance. He punched the bell again. After minutes the door was jerked open and Hilda stood there, out of breath. Her face was devoid of make-up, her hair messed.

"You again?" Her voice didn't hide her resentment.

He loved to catch people unaware. "Sorry to bother you," he said innocently,

"May I come in?"

Hilda bristled. "You could have called. I'm very busy."

"This won't take long." Reed pushed the door wider and put a foot over the threshold. Hilda's eyes widened in alarm.

"What is it you want?" She didn't invite him in for coffee and doughnuts like she had before, but stood with hands on her hips. An irritated look on her face.

"I'll keep it short, Hilda. I know you and Otto have been here for over twenty years working on this property."

"I told you that." Hilda looked him square in the eyes.

"Well," Reed dragged it out, a sly look on his face. "Where did you and Otto come from? Are you natives of Minnesota? I figured I'd give you a chance to bring me up to date. Save us time." Hilda's face turned red. Her eyes blazed.

"We're investigating everyone!" Reed added and watched her reaction.

"You're saying I'm a suspect? You think I had something to do with Mrs. Ciem's fall?"

"Until we get the facts, we're looking at everyone." Her face went from red to a ghastly white. "Now I'll ask again, where are you folks from?"

Hilda huffed. "We came here from Illinois, answered an ad for a couple to be caretakers."

"That was before Mrs. Ciem bought the property?"

"I told you that."

"Then?" Reed stared at her.

"Well, we stayed," she answered defiantly.

"Where'd you get four hundred thousand dollars?"

Hilda paled again, stepped back. Then fire lit her eyes. Her head jerked towards Reed.

Reed lowered his voice. "I said, where did you get that kind of money?"

"That's none of your business. What right?" Hilda drew herself up and folded her arms over her chest.

"All the rights in the world, Hilda. What did you do with the hundred grand you withdrew from your bank account?"

A small nerve twitched under her left eye as she hissed, "Get out. Get out of this house!" She pulled the door open and held onto the knob.

Reed stepped out, then turned back to her. "I'll be in touch." The door slammed. A lock snapped. "Stirred her up a little," he muttered as he walked down the drive to his car. He felt eyes follow his every move. Was it Hilda's guilty stare or was it those damn lions ready to pounce?

He drove off and headed for Stillwater. He punched in the stereo; Stevie Ray Vaughn this time, lit a cigarette and as usual got stuck in a traffic jam going out of Minneapolis. This time it took almost an hour and a half to get there. Tonight, the bleak looking house stood silent. A crest of snow covered the porch. Reed waded through the drift and knocked on the door.

Nothing. He knocked again and stepped back as a growl came from inside. Low and angry. He knocked again. Now a clacking echo like an animals claws on a bare floor. Then, a heavy thump against the door. Christ, a dog. And a big one!

The shades were drawn as before. He went next door, but again no one was home. Across the street and several houses down, he got lucky.

"That place?" a gnarly old man said, "They come and go."

"Who lives there now?" Reed asked patiently.

The man hoisted his overalls. "Lately, some old lady."

"Do you know her name?"

"Nope, no business of mine." The man turned and closed the door in Reed's face, but not before Reed slipped his card into the doorframe. "Give me a call if you see anything, will you?" he added.

He drove back to Minneapolis. Tomorrow, next on his agenda was Sloan and Associates. Mrs. Ciem's lawyers.

"Thanks for coming Mr. Conners," the attorney said shaking hands. "We've got trouble!"

-17-

Lindy tucked the check into her purse, and then took it out again, looked at the big numbers in unbelief. She'd just gotten almost another million dollars!

Lord, where could she hide it? She remembered the heartbreak when that thief had stolen her car with all her money in it, in Dallas. She peered out the window of the BMW. Someone could be lurking in this parking ramp; this was where crimes were notoriously committed so she tucked the check safely in her bra. She started the car, came down the circular exit and entered the street, then peered anxiously back over her shoulder, just to make sure Mr. Houston wasn't following her and wanting his money back.

The insurance had finally come through without a hitch and she was very rich again. Richer than before and life was great! Rushing back to the apartment she grabbed her clothes, dropped her make-up in a shopping bag, and then sat down to write a note to Solly.

Deciding not to confront her after all, Lindy wrote, "Solly whoever you are, thanks for all your help. I've decided to go north for awhile. I'll let you know where I am. Here's some money, have fun!" She counted out five thousand dollars from her cash in the shoebox and put the money with the note in an envelope and propped it on the coffee table. Someday maybe they'd get together again. There, she was ready.

With her arms laden with clothes and plastic bags, she closed the door. Sadly, she left the sunny city of Savannah, Georgia and headed out to the first highway she came to and turned into the traffic. As she drove along signs advertising Hilton Head, South Carolina began to appear.

Could she go back there? No, better to stay away from that place. Shivers brought goose bumps when she remembered how close she'd come to getting herself killed after seeing Mario shoot that man out on the ocean. In that luxurious floating palace he'd said was his. From now on she vowed she'd be very careful about getting involved with anybody.

She drove for hours and finally was forced to stop to rest in Myrtle Beach, South Carolina. The signs advertised sunny beaches, fabulous foliage, a carnival atmosphere, and freedom from boredom of every day life. She found a motel and lugged her clothes, bags and of course the shoebox, lighter now, but the knowledge that she had a lot more money tucked safely in her bra lightened that scare.

The motel was nestled next to a hill, with the ocean not far away. One room with a bath. Not big, but furnished in white wicker furniture with turquoise carpeting. Pictures of tropical flowers adorned the walls, sea shells sat on the coffee table. Paperback books were stacked in a bookcase, along with a television. It was eleven o'clock at night and she was bone-tired from the stressful day she'd had in Savannah that morning. She undressed, dropped her clothes on a chair and got into bed. She slept for several hours and for some reason awoke. As she snapped on the bed-side lamp, her tired eyes flew open as something scuttled across the carpet and disappeared under the couch. She sat frozen for a minute them jumped out of bed, then quickly back in and tucked her feet under a blanket.

What the hell was that! A mouse? It was huge and it had horns. What kind of beast was in her room? She perched wide-eyed in the bed, whatever it was, was still under the couch!

Should she call the office and tell them she'd seen something dart across the floor. Would they think she was nuts? Well, she couldn't go to sleep now; not with some creature on the loose. She sat huddled on the bed. Then she began to feel ridiculous. Why was she afraid of some small creature, hadn't she been born and raised on a farm? Although, the time she'd peeked up in the attic of her house in the north and found it crawling with carpenter ants, that had really scared her! Well, she was braver now. She gathered her courage, jumped out of bed and ran over to the couch, lifted one end and let it fall with a bang, then watched wide-eyed as a big brown thing scuttled across the room and disappeared under her bed. That was it! She slid into her jeans and shirt, ran out the door and over to the motel office.

"There's something in my room, this big!" She held her hands out six inches to make a point. "What the hell kind of place is this?"

"What?" a surprised night clerk looked up from a book he'd been reading.

"For God's sake!" Lindy huffed. She followed him back to her room and stepped gingerly inside. "Over there!" She directed the man with his flashlight and broom to the side of her bed. He leaned down and shined the light, swished the broom and suddenly the thing ran for the open door and the outside. Lindy jumped up on the couch.

The man stood up and laughed heartily "No problem. It's just a palmetto bug, sometimes called a cockroach. They sneak in sometimes, but they don't hurt you."

"Don't hurt you, good God, you could die of fright though!"

"Well, it's gone now Miss, get some sleep." The guy left shaking his head. Lindy was wide awake. She sat in bed in her clothes and looked around the room warily. Should she leave and get back on the road? But her body ached from fatigue, and her eyes burned. Maybe she could fall sleep for a few hours.

Finally drifting off, she was immediately caught in a nightmare. She was driving faster and faster on a highway trying to get away from a noisy trucker that was too close, then he hit her bumper with a loud bang and began shouting at her. The wind whistled. Then a hair-splitting crash echoed in her dream and she sat straight up in bed. For the second time that same night she was awake. She sat dazed as her room lit up, as the walls seemed to waver as a clap of thunder roared. Suddenly, she realized that the nightmare she'd had was really the screaming wind and rage coming from a huge storm. Instead of a truck driver yelling at her, it was someone banging on her door, shouting, "Tornado, get down!"

The wind howled fiercely, the curtains began to swish in and out against the flimsy windows. Another flash of lightning lit up the room and then a crash of thunder. She dashed into the bathroom and got into the bathtub. At least, it was better then crawling under the bed. Then, she remembered the shoe-box and the check and crept back into the bedroom and clutched the box and the check to her chest as she got back in the tub. If anything happened now just after she'd gotten the money, life just wasn't fair. She covered her head with her hands and cowered while the wind seemed to blow right through the room. A loud roar started and grew more intense as if it were a train headed right for the motel. She closed her eyes and felt the cold porcelain of the tub chill her body and she prayed.

Oh God, this was it. Lindy lost track of time as she repeated all the little prayers she could remember from childhood. Her tears mixed with the words. Outside the storm raged. She could hear glass breaking, ear-splitting thunder. Then suddenly it stopped and there was only silence. Just a gentle rain tapped on the roof. She crawled out of the tub and on trembling legs walked out of the bathroom. Glass from the window lay on the floor smashed into a million pieces, the shade and curtains hung haphazardly. She gaped in horror through the open window and saw across the parking lot where the next building had stood, was now a pile of broken lumber. Trees were uprooted and lay like scattered toothpicks. Wires twisted everywhere. When she looked out to where she'd parked her BMW. It was gone!

She sucked in her breath. How could a car disappear? She opened the door and stepped outside into icy air. There, off to the side lay another pile of destruction, this time twisted metal. Cars interwoven like pretzels. She ran for the phone, but of course that was dead. Terrified, she wrapped a blanket around her shoulders and sat Indian style on her bed, looking like a frightened little kid instead of an over forty year old woman.

It was deathly quiet. She jumped up and peered outside again. Was she the only one left alive in Myrtle Beach? The rain had stopped and the clouds had begun to move out. A sliver of sun peeked over the horizon as daybreak began, as if nothing had happened. She wanted to run for help, for some human contact, but she didn't dare step outside amongst the wires and glass. Then she heard sirens, a welcome noise that grew louder and louder. A police car screeched to a stop, then a fire truck. Men scattered. Lindy waved her arms frantically.

"Here, over here," she screamed.

"Are you okay?" someone yelled.

"Yes," she answered in a shaking voice.

"Stay inside, we'll get you out soon."

Lindy watched as the place became frantic with action. An ambulance arrived followed by two more. Her heart hammered in her throat as she saw people carried out of the wreckage next door, placed on stretchers and hurried away. Hours went by, her stomach ached from hunger, from fear. She held the shoebox to her chest. Here she was in the middle of this devastation, lucky to be alive, with tons of money but, stranded!

Finally a city bus lumbered in and a voice boomed on a horn, urging everyone to gather their belongings and board for a ride to another motel down the road. The driver stepped out and offered his arm to the dozen people that stood nervously clutching their belongings, darting frightened looks across the parking lot at the piles of lumber and unrecognizable twisted objects. Lindy sat with her clothes and paper bags in the first seat.

"Where are we going?" she asked forlornly.

"Just down a way to the Saratoga. It's owned by the same people."

Lindy's room here was identical to the one she'd left; white wicker furniture, turquoise carpeting. She dropped her things and turned on the television to the scene she'd just left.

"Tornadoes are rare at this time of the year especially, usually we're plagued with hurricanes earlier in the season," the newswoman said. "The death toll remains uncertain. At this point we just don't know for sure. As we turn our cameras to the opposite side of this motel complex, a building stands untouched. It was more than likely protected since it backs up to a hill in back. That pile of twisted metal you see over there is cars!"

Lindy's heart skipped a beat. The phone rang just then saying there was food ready for the newcomers. It was a Tuesday, the middle of January and her plans had gone to hell. Now, she had to face the fact that had been niggling in the back of her mind; if she turned in a claim to her insurance company for her demolished car, it would mean instant disaster. She would be traced! Lindy Lewis, right here in Myrtle Beach, South Carolina. Sick at heart, she realized she'd have to give up the money it was insured for. She didn't dare take the chance. Later that morning, she showered and dressed and called a taxi.

"Take me to the nearest bank," she told the driver.

"No problem," the banker said a few minutes later as he studied the piece of precious paper, "but we need forty-eight hours for it to clear." Lindy's heart sank.

"But--," she stammered.

"Come back in two days, Miss Lang." On the way back to her motel, she stopped at a car dealership and found the same silver Lexus she'd looked at before in Savannah. Not one to waste time she cornered a salesman.

"I'll take this one, and would you have it serviced and ready for me on Thursday. I'll be back!"

The next two days seemed to be the longest of her life. On Thursday, Lindy was back at the bank.

"Everything is in order, Miss Lang, may I advise you on what kind of investments would be wise at this time," the banker said as he sat behind his massive desk.

Lindy had thought it out and answered matter-of-factly, "Actually I want five thousand in cash, a check for thirty thousand dollars made out for a car I'm buying, and another check for the remainder."

Aghast at her independence, the banker whispered, "but it isn't safe, Miss Lang."

"I'm investing it in my families' bank." A little lie, but it was her decision. No one was going to touch her money!

"Miss Lang," the man persisted patiently, "we have many good investments available here!"

Undaunted, a few minutes later, she walked into the car showroom and bought her Lexus. Within an hour, Lindy was on the road.

-18-

Reed sat in a soft leather armchair after shaking hands with Mr. Sloan, Mrs. Ciem's attorney. The office was luxuriously furnished in maroon colored leather furniture. One large wall was filled with books. A Picasso adorned another. The twelfth floor overlooked the downtown Minneapolis skyline. Sloan leaned forward as he sat at his mahogany desk and folded his arms over his broad chest. The afternoon sun caught the shine of manicured fingernails. His tailored suit and silk shirt and tie were magnificently matched blues.

"How's the investigation going Mr. Conners?"

Out of habit, Reed sized up the man. Middle forties, sun bleached brown hair, expensive cut. Fine wrinkles around brown eyes. Thin face, trimmed mustache. Capped teeth that flashed brilliantly against a tan. Six feet, one hundred and eighty pounds, trim and in shape.

Not one to give out information until he was good and ready, Reed replied, "Very interesting so far. What's up?"

Sloan opened a file. "Here's what is going on; Carmen Ciem made out a will ten years ago leaving the bulk of her estate to a college in her hometown of Blue Rock Falls, in Wisconsin. Right now, the President of that school and his lawyers are in town breathing down my neck! So, do you have any idea when you can wrap this up?"

Reed shifted in his chair. "I'm working on an angle, but, it would help if you would fill me in on the entire contents of her will!"

Sloan turned a page in the file. "It's confidential until it is read. But in this case I feel I can divulge the contents to you. Five million goes to each of her kids, and one million to an aunt. Her longtime house-keeper and caretaker get the house. The rest of her estate goes to her hometown college."

Reed sat back, put an ankle over a knee. "So, Roman's out of luck?"

"Yes, according to this, Mr. Conners. She never did change anything after marrying that man. I called you because I'm willing to bet right this minute Tony

Roman is out in Hollywood looking up one of those slick lawyers!"

"You could be right, I'll be in touch," Reed said and left the attorneys office. He needed a big steak.

Gina's was quiet this time of the day, even Gina was gone, which left the restaurant lacking in color. Her stand-in led Reed to a corner booth. As he waited for his steak and after a smooth Crown Royal began to relax the knots in his stomach, his mind wandered. It had been in this exact spot he and Tanner Burke had sat so many years ago. The occasion was bittersweet. Tanner was graduating from law school a year ahead of him, as he'd taken a year off to settle affairs when his parents had died in a car accident. They had been roommates all through those years, their minds fresh and alert. They were in their early twenties and the world lay open and unexplored. They had both worked as cooks and waiters to pay for their tuition, books and rent. Goddamn, he missed his buddy! Just a short time ago, Tanner had been alive, so in love with his secretary Sierra Ames. Then, so broken when she'd died and so insistent that she'd been murdered. Now they were both gone!

He remembered Tanner had grown up in north Minneapolis. He had said it had been a flourishing community of ethnic families in modest homes. He had been an only child and sometimes rebellious. Reed remembered him saying his father wanted him to come into the family business with him, a sausage making factory. Tanner had said, 'I've seen enough of dead animals, I'm going to be a lawyer and make millions'. His father had refused to pay for his schooling and saw him as a traitor to a respectable family tradition.

Tanner had been a skinny kid, fresh out of high school when he and Reed had sat next to each other in their first classes in college. He was of Italian descent; black curly hair, brown eyes that the girls loved, he soon learned. His wardrobe consisted of faded jeans and plaid flannel shirts. If an occasion called for dress, he'd slip on a threadbare corduroy sport coat. That same coat was around all through college and law school. As the years slipped by, they studied late into the night after closing the restaurant, then got up at the crack of dawn for classes. After Tanner graduated, Reed was restless and lonely without his buddy. It was during this time Lindy Lewis had come into the restaurant and applied for a job as a waitress. Not long afterwards, they settled into living together.

Damn--, Reed muttered that her name had come up again in his thoughts. He raised his whiskey glass and drank deeply, tried to focus his thoughts on the familiarity of Gina's restaurant and away from the painful memories, but it didn't work. After Reed had graduated from law school, he had gone back to his home town and hung out his shingle. The first years were slow, but he had the advantage of inheriting some money from his parents, and a beautiful ranch just out of a town called High Landing. Over the years, he and

Tanner would get together and go on fishing trips, sometimes to an island in Canada, so remote that the only access was by air. The years went by and gradually they had found less and less time to get together. The last few times had been after Sierra Ames had died, and he and Tanner had studied the files looking for a clue to her death.

Later, Reed had sold the ranch and moved to his cabin on Birch Lake. He'd taken a part-time investigative job with the First Federated Insurance Company, and to his dismay, that was when he'd become involved with Lindy Lewis again.

Goddamn, he swiped a hand through his hair, he missed Tanner. Even though a few years would spin by sometimes without a phone conversation, their friendship was always there. When Tanner had gotten shot, Reed guessed he was on his way up to go over the files again.

Why the hell hadn't he called Tanner and told him he had closed up shop and moved to the lake? Well hell, it didn't do any good to keep blaming himself, it wouldn't bring his friend back.

Reed ran a hand over his face, swallowed hard over a catch in his throat. Determined, he picked up his notes and began to study Carmen Ciem's case again and went over what he had learned so far about her death. But it wasn't enough, he needed answers!

Just then the waiter brought a steaming platter with the mushroom loaded steak and set it down in front of him, then added a baked potato and hard rolls. By now, his thoughts had totally bummed him out but maybe the food would fill the holes. But as he wolfed down the delicious cuisine it, didn't help.

So had Tony Roman sent his wife over that balcony railing after finding out he was not included in her will? Or had the caretakers finally gotten tired of waiting on her!

-19-

The music flowed from the radio in Lindy's new Lexus, smooth and vibrant, as she drove through the countryside nearing the Virginia state line. Cattle and horse farms covered vast miles of grazing lands, now lying with a drift of snow here and there. White board fences sparkled in the early evening sunshine and large signs above gates advertised breeding and riding stables. The houses were built out of red brick trimmed in white, with long low white barns scattered around the yards. She began to relax as she gazed at the new landscapes, feeling safer now that she was far away from Savannah. She took one hand off the steering wheel and patted her hair, took a quick look at herself in the rear-view mirror. Now that she had the money as soon as she came to a place she liked, she'd take time to shop and fix herself up. Her hair was still blonde, but needed a touch-up. Her brown contacts? Well, maybe she'd keep them. But, she was a little nervous about traveling alone, especially after the things that had happened to her, but she patted her left breast, reassured that the plastic covered envelope was still safely tucked inside her bra. The shoebox, in the tire well, in the trunk. Still, she noticed the curious looks she got from strangers on the country roads. Men in ranch trucks, with western hats and dogs perched on the front seats next to them. Well, she had an idea. She stopped in a town called Lynchburg, found a toy store and within a few minutes was back on the road. A big black stuffed Labrador sat up on his hind legs next to her on the front seat of her Lexus.

Okay Pal, you're my protector! She giggled as she drove off. She traveled through the eastern states, staying close to the coast and only stopping long enough to eat, sleep, and shower. As she approached the New England area, evergreen and fir trees stood majestically along the highway. The houses were plain two story structures, unadorned, weathered, some painted white. Lindy remembered they were called salt box homes and turned to her traveling companion. By this time she had grown used to talking to her stuffed dog on the lonely roads.

"Pretty straight laced, don't you think?"

The traffic zoomed around her as she neared the downtown area of Boston. To her dismay, the city didn't have skyscrapers, shiny shopping malls or paved streets that she'd expected, instead the store fronts were old and the streets were cobblestone. She'd read somewhere that the important people lived in Beacon Hill; an exclusive area close to theaters, shops and restaurants.

"What do you think big boy, should we take a look," she asked her traveling companion?

The weather had taken a turn and was warm and sunny, and outdoor cafes were doing a flourishing business. Lindy parked the Lexus, set her stuffed companion down on the floor of the car, and walked along studying the people on the sidewalks, listening to their eastern accents. She found a place that really excited her. Armani, it said on a sign and next door in a cordoned off area was a café called Inga's. She was seated under an umbrella with a perfect view of the store windows and the shoppers strolling by, enjoying a respite from the usual dreary weather. Long skirts, perfectly coifed hair, and carefully applied makeup seemed to be the look of the natives. She ordered a vegetable pizza and a glass of iced tea. As the large doors opened and closed on the Armani store, scents of delicious fragrances filled the air. And how she loved expensive perfumes!

She spent the rest of the day shopping in the store, and hours later, walked out clutching the elegant black and white bags. Her cheeks were rosy after all the compliments the trained staff had heaped on her as she chose several outfits. Her cash was slightly lower after her exhilarating shopping spree and a drop-in at a beauty shop for a touch-up and a quick mani-pedi, but she needed it and of course, deserved it.

This time she wouldn't have to leave all her belongings behind as she'd had to do when she'd been at Reed's house in Minnesota. As she walked back to the Lexus, she gawked at signs advertising apartments for rent in the Beacon Hill area. Lordy, four thousand dollars a month for a one bedroom, and five thousand dollars and up for a two bedroom!

After a night of rest and dressed in a new outfit, she drove off again. A brochure she'd seen in the hotel intrigued her, Newport, Rhode Island, approximately four hours away. The only thing she had previously known about the place was that the Newport jazz festival was an annual event at this exclusive resort town located on the shores of the Atlantic ocean. And, of course the playground and summer homes of old well-known millionaire families; such as the Asters, Dupont's, and the Rockefellers.

Even though it was too early for the tourist season, the quiet town was beautiful, with seasoned trees and low buildings weathered by the ocean air. Signs advertised tours of mansions built along the roaring waters. Lindy parked the Lexus.

"You can take a nap now," she said as she laid the stuffed dog down out of sight and covered him with a blanket. She took a quick look around to see if anyone was near enough to see her, then smiled and wondered why she hadn't thought of getting a pet before. Especially one like this, one that had a button that you could press to make it bark and growl.

She adjusted her designer sunglasses, put on a black floppy hat that matched her outfit and walked into a restaurant, a place called Ye Old English Pub. To her delight, she created a flurry of interest from the bar as heads turned to her as she stood waiting to be seated. She did sneak a curious peek at the seemingly solo males and had to admit it felt enticing to be noticed after being alone on the roads for days with only a dog to talk to, a stuffed one yet!

She bought a local newspaper and studied it as she ate her dinner and made her plans. The next day she went to a bank and rented a safe deposit box to stow her cash, but even after charming the banker, she found she had to wait for the huge check to clear.

"It's customary," the man said apologetically, taking in her appearance.

Lindy hated waiting, but she smiled sweetly after realizing her flirting wasn't going to get her anywhere, "I'm relocating here, so I'll be back after I've found a place to live. I'll be looking for some investments then."

She'd seen an interesting advertisement in the paper. It had read; in return for hosting tours, the experienced female could live rent-free in a cottage by the ocean.

Bright and early the following day, Lindy applied for the job. She had dressed with care in a black and white checked cashmere suit, with a hem-line that just touched her knees, black snake-skin high heels and a large purse. Her newly touched-up blonde hair; shining and chic.

"May I have your name please?" A young man with a heavy Eastern accent asked as she entered the private employment agency.

After practicing late into the night, she replied easily now, "Lili Lane," matching his articulation.

"Well, Miss Lane," he replied after looking her over from head to toe, "if you can transcend yourself into another era, you just might be what we're looking for!"

And Lindy thought, this just might be what she had been looking for too!

-20-

Reed finished his steak, then gathered his files and left Gina's restaurant. Snowflakes mixed with rain fell lazily from the dark sky. A north wind tore at his clothes as he waited for a valet to bring his car.

"Nice to see you again, Reed," the doorman said as he waited with him under the green canopy.

"Same here." Reed shrugged into his jacket against the cold. "Tough time of the year for you guys to work outside." He nodded towards the valet who had just spun up in his Corvette.

"Nah, Miz Gina got us a shack to get warm in." The doorman nodded towards a utility building off to the side of the parking lot. A light shone through a window of the small structure that overlooked the front entrance and the drive-up to the restaurant. The valet joined them and they stood together companionably.

Reed had known the two men for years; homeless brothers whom Gina used to feed. He heard, long ago that they'd made the mistake of trying to steal from her. The story went that she'd personally beat the hell out of them, then promised that if they straightened up, she'd hire them. Apparently things had worked out. They were devoted to her, acting as chauffeurs, handymen, and of course their duties at the door of the restaurant. They stood side by side in their down-filled jackets and caps with ear flaps turned down, and slapped their hands together against the cold.

"Did you fellows know Carmen Ciem and her husband, Tony Roman?" Reed asked as he started to step off the curb. The brothers looked at each other, then nodded. "They'd come in sometimes," the smaller of the men replied as he pulled off his cap and scratched his gray hair.

"What did you think of them?" Reed turned to him.

"Man, she was a looker you know. He'd get pissed when men would eye-ball her."

The other chimed in, "To bad about her."

Reed stepped back on to the sidewalk. "Has he been in since she died?"

"Few times," one said, and the other nodded.

"Was he alone?"

The smaller man, apparently the talker of the two, shook his head. "One time I saw him sitting with a woman at the bar." He looked over to his brother and they nodded again.

Reed put his briefcase down on the ground, stuck his hands into his jacket pockets. "You know who she was?"

"Nah--, but ask Leon the bartender, he knows everybody." The brothers nodded their heads in unison.

"Thanks guys, I'll be back shortly." Reed picked up his briefcase, went back into Gina's and took a stool at the long polished oak bar. Colored Tiffany lights sent a soft glow over the room. Hundreds of bottles of liquor were lined up on the shelves and glasses gleamed on racks. Dean Martin's voice crooned, and delicious aromas escaped from the kitchen. A couple sat at one end of the bar, intent on looking into each others eyes.

"Evening again, Leon, damn freezing out there!" Reed unzipped his jacket.

"Hey, Conners, Crown Royal?" The bartender leaned up against the bar, cigarette in hand as he watched a television set. Reed laid his briefcase on the bar and nodded as Leon took a bottle of the best off a top shelf and poured a generous shot in a snifter.

"It's on me. I hear you're in town again for awhile." Leon was another of Gina's faithful employees, having worked for her for years, not only as her bartender, but as the bouncer if someone got too rambunctious. And if Gina approved of someone, you knew they were good people.

"Thanks buddy." Reed took a big swallow of the whiskey, savored the warmth. "Great stuff. Yeah, guess I'll be here for a while."

"How are things going? I hear you're working on that big case involving that Ciem chick."

"Right, what do you know about her old man Tony Roman?"

Leon raised his eyebrows.

"You know him?" Reed asked and lit a cigarette, sat back on the barstool, and exhaled.

Leon laughed as he wiped the bar "The guy likes to be known. Comes in here and walks around introducing himself."

"Did they come in a lot?"

"Quite a bit. Yeah, he thought he was pretty suave."

"Was he?"

"Nah--, most people thought he was a phony." Leon reached for a liquor bottle and filled a coffee cup.

"How so?" Reed asked.

Leon took a long drink. Exhaled loudly. "He was a big spender and would buy drinks for everyone." He shook his head and laughed again. "Then he'd toss me a credit card that had her name on it."

"How'd she react to that?"

"She'd just smile. Later on though--."

"What?" Reed asked again.

"At first, I could see she was definitely swayed by his attentions, but later, I'd guess she was glad he was in Hollywood and out of her hair."

"Have you seen him since she died?"

"Oh yeah, he's been in. Tries to appear grief-stricken, but I heard him hitting on a chick. Didn't sound too sad to me!" Leon turned to wait on a group of boisterous patrons that had burst in the door. Reed stared at the bottles across the bar. His face grim. What was Roman's real story?

"Why so glum handsome? Come and join us." Reed turned as a soft voice whispered in his ear. He exhaled at the surprise. A blonde with a drink in hand smiled brazenly at him. She leaned in and ran a hand over his jaw line. Put a finger on his lips. "I want to feel those on me!"

"Right now?" Reed asked warily.

"Why not, the night is still young." The woman teetered on her high heels. He looked her over. Not a day over twenty-one. He put an arm out and steadied her.

"Sweetheart, I think it's about done for you."

"Ah--, you're no fun." She pouted and went back to her group, leaning off-center as she picked her way around the bar stools. Leon came back and shook his head.

"Thank God, they've got a driver." He smiled. "They're all drinking iced tea now, and they can't tell the difference."

"Oh man, to be that young and carefree." Reed swiped a hand over his forehead as a headache began to take hold. He glanced over at the people as they roared with laughter over something someone had said.

"Leon, do you know the woman Roman was hitting on in here?"

"Yeah man, the same one that just hit on you." Leon jerked his head towards the blonde a few stools over.

"Her? What's her name?"

"Legs, that's all I know." Leon laughed. "Did you catch those pins?"

"No--, wasn't interested at the time." Reed turned towards her and met her come-on look with a grin. He got up and strolled over.

"Legs, huh?" The blonde giggled. He leaned over and raised her chin, kissed her lips. "That's for now," he said "I've got to take off, but why don't you meet me here tomorrow, say around four?"

"You mean it?" She smiled crookedly.

"Absolutely. Remember now, tomorrow!" Reed went back and put some bills on the bar, winked at Leon. Outside again, the north wind still howled, but the valet had the Corvette at the curb, running and warmed up. Reed handed him a twenty and roared off.

- 21-

Lindy slipped into a puffed sleeved pink dress and pinned the coronet of flowers into her hair. She wiggled her fingers into sheer lace gloves, and took up the fan that completed her outfit and swished it over her face. She'd practiced her speech and learned how to drop her "r's" like the easterners. Today was the first day of her new job.

When she'd first arrived in Newport, Rhode Island a week ago she'd seen an advertisement in the local paper seeking a tour guide and caretaker. With a plan in mind Lindy had applied for the job and was now settled into the small house on the property with a fabulous view of the Atlantic Ocean. She had been absolutely taken in by the beauty of the mansion, not that she planned to work for long, but for now the disguise would keep her safe and busy while she pondered her future options. Her money was tucked away, and she planned to take her time and be very careful how she spent it this time. She'd taken the position and settled in.

She would play the role of Lili Ashton, daughter of the infamous Anne Ashton. Her eyes roamed around her new living space and out to the crashing waves of the ocean far below the cliff the cottage was built on. Then she gazed out the window on the opposite side where vast lawns framed the spacious home of the millionaire railroad family who had lived there decades ago, before it was donated to the historical society. She'd learned that the three-storied house contained thirty thousand square feet of living space but was considered small by comparison to some homes along the oceanfront. Glassed-in porches and open-railed decks jutted out from all sides. Sharp-edged gables protruded high above the red tiled roof. Thick hedges separated the early sprouting lawn where not a weed dared to show its rangy head. Huge stone urns stood in the four archways on a marbled courtyard loaded with wintering kale and pansies.

Lindy exhaled in bliss at her good fortune. She was far way from Savannah, Georgia and the worry that the insurance she'd collected could be recalled. Away from Hilton Head, South Carolina and any repercussions from the murder Mario D'Agustino had committed, that she had witnessed. Far away even from Reed Conners. For a minute her heart fluttered at the memory of their lovemaking. Then turned to dread at how thoroughly disgusted he must be at her now. She swished the fan across her face again and straightened up. Well, she didn't have time for misgivings now. She had a new life far away from anyone from her past and she had met Sid.

She lit a cigarette and put it in a long, jeweled holder like the one Lili Ashton was known to use, and gazed at her reflection in a mirror. Well, she did look the part of the brazen daughter she was to portray. She had done a little research on the family prior to the interview, and had decided she'd change her first name to Lili, just in case she got the job. And it had worked.

Lili's mother, Anne Ashton inherited her vast holdings from her Father who had emigrated from England, and started a railroad that made him outrageously rich; and as his only child, Anne had became a very wealthy lady. Her hand in marriage was sought world-wide, but she didn't want anything to do with these so-called aristocrats who were only interested in her because of her money. Instead she married a weak-willed man named Charles Ashton. Lindy had studied numerous portraits of the couple which clearly depicted the husband's role, as it showed Charles sitting on a prissy chair and Anne standing majestically at his side, one hand on hip. Another of Anne Ashton sitting in a throne-like chair in the morning room. Not a line creased her creamy complexion. Sleek black hair held high on top her head with jeweled combs matching dark eyes that sparked a no nonsense look.

Lindy practiced her lines using her new eastern accent as she stepped outside. The cozy little house she had moved into was an authentic Oriental pagoda painted red with a black roof, with curved edged corners uplifted to the skies. Anne Ashton had had it built after one of her trips to the Eastern countries and used it for herself when she needed religious solace. No one else was ever allowed inside her hideaway. Later, after she'd taken ill, she'd lived there believing the fresh ocean air would regenerate her.

Glancing at her watch, Lindy realized it was nearing one o'clock and time for her to start work. She adjusted her dress to show cleavage, fastened the flowers tighter in her hair. Sun warmed her back but a cold ocean breeze fluttered her long skirt as she hurried over to the Ashton mansion. Sid met her at the door. He took her in his arms and kissed her passionately. He was clad in a perfectly cut black suit. A gleaming white shirt set off his tanned skin.

"Lili Lane, you look fabulous! You should see the crowd of people waiting in the vestibule. Looks like around fifty."

Oh God, she thought suddenly, what was she doing here anyway? Why wasn't she on a beach drinking Margarita's somewhere! She swallowed over a lump of nerves as Sid ran a finger down inside the front of her dress.

"After the tour is over I've got something planned for you." Lindy smiled at him momentarily pleased, then opened the door to a room filled with a sea of faces.

"Good afternoon," she said and waved the fan over her flushed cheeks and stepped into her role. "I'm Lili, Anne Ashton's daughter." She smiled demurely at the crowd of curious tourists. "I'd like you to meet my family," she said and pointed to the many framed portraits. "My Grandparents, and my Mother and Father. As you can see, picture taking was serious business in those days." The crowd studied the brown toned portraits of the Ashton family and smiled at the sober faces.

"Now if you will follow me, we'll go to my Mother's parlor first." The tourists tromped along with Lindy as she went on, "Here she'd visit with her guests and serve tea." This room was filled with brocaded sofas and chairs, ornate tables and lamps. A huge French door opened onto a view of the grounds and the ocean. A throne-like chair, done in a dark blue brocade, delicate carved oak arms and legs sat among the lavish furnishings.

"This, of course, was my Mother's chair." Lindy had gotten over her stage fright and quickly hid her face behind the fan as a giggle threatened to slip out. She pictured bossy Anne Ashton sitting in the ridiculous chair holding court. She sobered and went on.

"My mother imported all her furnishings from England, her father's homeland, believing no one in this country had the finesse and skill to dress her home." The tourists admired the tapestry materials, silk shaded lamps and art work. Next, they toured bedrooms and dressing rooms, and several of the guest rooms, which numbered in the twenties. Lindy showed the tourists through the various rooms used only for entertaining, as the people gawked at the luxurious settings.

"If you'll follow me again we'll go to the kitchen and then to the rooms in the other wing of the house." Here highly waxed wood floors creaked as the crowd of people dutifully followed Lindy into the no frills wing. She took a breath as she began to feel faint, if only she'd taken time to eat properly earlier, instead of that cold pizza and coke she had left over from the night before.

She led the group of curious tourist into the huge dark cavern that was the kitchen. Blackened stoves stood along one side of the room, and cupboards filled with dishes lined another. A coffee grinder, ice cream maker, griddles and waffle makers used on the wood burning stoves were displayed on the worktables.

"As you can imagine, my Mother never set foot in this room!" Leading the group further down a hallway, Lindy pointed out," Here are the rooms for the staff.

Mother employed no less than fifteen people, some of them just to take up positions she felt looked appropriate to her role as a rich society matron." Stepping into the corridor, she opened a small cube-like room, plainly decorated. A stuffed teddy bear sat on a narrow cot next to an old fashioned school desk.

"This was my room. I lived here until I was sixteen years old. My nanny and tutor lived next door. I ate my meals in the kitchen."

"You mean you didn't live on the other side with your parents?" A wizened little lady in blue pedal pushers asked.

"Oh no, rich people didn't have time to be fussing with children, they were too busy! They had parties to give and social functions to attend."

"When did you see your parents?' Another tourist asked.

"Every evening I could visit for an hour as they relaxed with a cocktail before they left for the night or had guests in. Of course, I couldn't touch them since they were dressed in their fine clothes."

"Didn't you eat your meals with them?"

"On Sundays, I'd get to have breakfast with them.

"The last room I'd like to show you is the ballroom," Lindy said as they went back to the front wing of the mansion. She swung huge double doors open to the gleeful surprise of the tourists. After the dinginess of the back wing they'd just left, this room took their breath away.

Victorian styled sconces lit the room and two huge crystal chandeliers highlighted a ceiling painted in beautiful shades of pastel colors depicting blue skies, clouds and cherubs frolicking in a summer garden. A tall, marble fireplace next to French doors took up another wall.

"Once a month Mother would give a ball and her guests were invited to step outside for a breath of cool air between dances." She threw open the doors to a marbled courtyard.

"At midnight, a supper would be served." Lindy opened another set of doors and led the way. "This room could hold up to one hundred people." She pointed to the length of the highly polished table, with two seemingly endless rows of brocade covered chairs. The table was set as if ready for a party. Crystal sparkled, sterling silver gleamed, tall candlesticks and flower arrangements nestled among paper thin china.

The tourists stood awed at the sight, looking out of place, clad in their shorts and comfortable walking shoes.

Lindy took a deep breath. Lord, she was tired. Her underarms were damp, the pins in the flowered head-piece stabbed her scalp. She sneaked a quick look at her watch. The trek through the house was to be an hour long and to her relief she saw it was going on two o'clock.

As she stood at the door thanking the group for coming, she hoped the tourists would take the hint and leave quickly. The same little lady in blue pedal pushers who had tagged closely at her heels, totally caught up in the moment, said, "I don't like your Mother Lili." Her visor had slid down past her eyebrows and Lindy hid behind her fan and stifled another giggle.

"Well, Lili, how'd it go?" Sid asked as he locked the door after the last tourist had finally left.

"Fine--," Lindy murmured then added, "But, you know, I saw something really strange as we passed one of those rooms upstairs!"

-22-

Reed flung his jacket down on a chair in his motel room, dropped his briefcase on the desk. A flashing red light on the telephone caught his attention.

"Got a message for me?" he asked the desk clerk as he lay down on the bed after punching the pillows into a comfortable mound.

"One," a woman answered, "Here's the number." He recognized it as the company that insured Lindy Lewis's car. He'd been in contact with them, but had been informed she'd paid her premium up for a year, her address then had been in Minneapolis.

"Too late to call tonight," he mumbled looking at his watch. He turned on the television to the late news just as a blond reporter opened the show standing among ruins caused by a storm in the south.

"It's been several weeks now and as you can see in the background, clean-up is still being done. Millions of dollars of damage has been reported."   Reeds attention suddenly focused on the screen as the camera showed homes blown apart, businesses flattened and then came to rest on a twisted mass of cars swept into a pile of wreckage. And there at the top of the pile a shiny black BMW perched. The front intact, but the back of it flattened.

He sat up on the bed and groaned. Could that wreck be Lindy's car?   Nah, couldn't be, too much of a coincidence! Right now, he needed a night's rest to get away from the mess going around in his head. Within a few minutes after his head hit the pillow, he was sound asleep.

He awoke as the alarm on his Rolex watch buzzed in his ear. After showering and getting dressed in his usual attire of pressed jeans and a sweater, he walked over to a diner for coffee and the morning paper. He sat at a table by a window in downtown Minneapolis and watched the hustle of people on the street hurrying by, clutching their coats and scarves as they trudged to their appointed places in the work force. As he drank his first cup of rich, black coffee and felt the caffeine kick in, adrenalin flowed through his body. Energy and confidence took shape, but then restlessness. Goddamn, he'd wrap the Ciem case up fast, straighten out Lindy's chaos and go back to his place and relax. Take it easy for a few months until fishing opened in the spring. To hell with trying to figure out why people did what they did. He was tired of all the BS!

But first today he needed to swing back to Stillwater and take a look around that house that he'd seen Hilda Sorenson and that other woman enter. From what the neighbor had said, an old woman lived there. But what was the connection? He needed to ask the Sorenson's some more questions. Never mind that Hilda had literally thrown him out of the Ciem house. Later he had a date with Legs. Tony Roman's acquaintance.

He shuffled the paper to the sports page. Football was done for the year, basketball bored him. Too soon for baseball. He checked his watch, flipped his cellphone on and dialed the number to Lindy's insurance company, punched in the extension.

"Bob Burns," the agent answered

"Hey Flash, Reed Conners. I got your message last night."

"Yeah. How you doing?"

"So, so. What's up?"

"Something curious. I got a call from a Police department in Georgia. Storms down there."

"I saw that on the tube last night." Reed took a sip of his coffee.

"Well, a car registered to Lindy Lewis turned up, smashed to hell."

"Yeah?" Reed's heart took a leap.

"Here's the strange part. It's been almost a week and we haven't had a claim. Not a word!" Reed drummed his fingers on the table top.

"When did you get the call?"

"Yesterday, from Savannah. The wreck has stood around for days, so they put a tracer on it."

"Okay, thanks Flash, I'll stay in touch."

"Hey pal, you got a cell phone yet?"

"Didn't have a choice. Here's the number." Reed jumped up from his table, paid his bill and started off to Stillwater.

The icy wind blew gusts of freezing snow across the highway. The sky looked dingy and forbidding as usual. Reed groaned as he drove, trying to concentrate on the Ciem case, while the present whereabouts of Lindy invaded his thoughts.

So where was she now? She couldn't have been hurt or someone would have known. And knowing how she liked to fly around the country, what was she doing for transportation? He dialed the number of his company, First Federated Insurance and brought them up to speed on the report he'd gotten. As he held on to the phone with one hand the wind caught the car and swerved it almost into the opposite lane. He threw the phone on the car seat, jerked the wheel just in time to miss an oncoming truck.

Goddamn phones, he mumbled.

He retraced his tracks to the white frame house in Stillwater and circled around the block. The sagging porch and sidewalk had been shoveled he saw. Parking down the street by a warehouse he sat back to wait and watch. Smoke poured out of the chimney, but the shades were drawn as before. He slipped in a Santana CD. And after only a few minutes he was in luck as suddenly the front door burst open and to his surprise a big brown German shepherd bounded out. The dog lifted a leg by a drooping maple tree and then began to run around wildly in the front yard. Reed watched as a woman stepped out of the shadowed doorway, leaning heavily on a cane. A scarf tied around her head hid most of her face. She stood huddled against the north wind in short sleeves as she looked helplessly after the running dog.

Reed got out of the Corvette and walked towards the house. The dog picked up his scent and ran full force toward him. The hair on the back of Reed's neck stood up as the animal neared then it slowed down to a walk and bared his teeth and growled.

"Good boy," Reed said and held out a hand, palm up, aware that he could loose not only a finger but a whole arm. The dog growled again and moved closer. He sniffed at Reeds hand.

"Good boy," Reed said again warily as the low growl turned into a whine. He stroked the dog for a minute then said, "Let's go home." He took hold of the dog's collar and gently led him towards the house. The woman had gone back into the building, but held the door open a few inches and peeked out.

"Hello," Reed called out to her, "seems he wants to play." The dog burst back inside the house pushing the woman out of the way. She caught the side of the door to keep from falling, clutched her chest and shivered. As the scarf slid off her head, her hair hung gray and wispy, drooping from a top knot on her head. Her clothes were wrinkled and spotted with food stains. Reed sized up the room inside behind her and saw it needed drastic help.

"I just moved in down the street, so I'm your new neighbor," he said and smiled. "Can I help you with anything?" The woman darted frightened looks at him, then out the door and up and down the street. "You've got quite a dog." Reed went on and watched as the big animal circled the room, sniffed the corners of the couch and began to tear up a pillow.

"I--." She opened the door wider and motioned Reed towards it then gave a shriek as the dog dashed to her side and stood between her and Reed. Backed her further against the wall.

"Are you okay?" Reed asked.

The old woman seemed dazed. "Go, go!" she whispered and put her hands up in dismissing manner. The dog growled at her movement. "They'll be here soon."

Reed watched her. "Are you going out?"

She pushed little wire-rimmed glasses up over her nose and suddenly smiled. "I've just sold my house and I'm going to live with my friend at a nice home." She patted the loosened top-knot of her fly away hair and then suddenly self-consciously picked at food spills on her clothes.

"Well, that sounds nice for you." Reed returned her smile.

"We're going to a casino too," she added.

"Really, you gamble?"

"No--, yes, I think so." Her hand stopped in mid-air. "I've been ready to go." A puzzled look spread over her lined face.

"Well, can I do anything for you while you wait?" Reed wanted to get into the house and look around, but he couldn't show too much curiosity and scare her. She turned and began to walk away, apparently forgetting him still being there. The dog leapt into action and herded her into another room.

What the hell was going on? But Reed had no choice but to close the door and leave. He walked back to his car and waited to see if anyone was really coming to pick her up, but no one showed up after an hour. On the way back to Minneapolis, he dialed the Sheriff's department in Stillwater.

"There's an elderly woman living alone who needs help," he reported.

"Where, and do you have a name?" a woman asked.

"No, but she's terribly confused. Seems to be either drugged or senile. Has this big dog that looks dangerous."

"Okay, I'll let Sheriff Finney know and to check on her." She asked for the address.

Reed headed back to Minneapolis to the Ciem house. It was early afternoon and he noticed the shades were drawn on the Sorenson apartment over the garage. When he rang the doorbell at the main house the chimes echoed in the silence. As he stood patiently waiting on the porch he noticed a corner of a paper sticking out of the mailbox. He looked around for any curious onlookers then reached in and pulled it out. It was addressed to the paperboy and read, "please don't leave the paper as we'll be gone until Saturday." It was signed Hilda Sorenson, housekeeper.

Great! Reed leaned over to shield his actions from the street as he slipped it back in the box. Today was Friday. This was just the chance he had been waiting for!

-23-

Lindy collapsed in Sid's arms, still puzzled about that mysterious room in the mansion. He ran his hand down her back, pressed her hips to his and held her in a firm grip. His hardness probed her belly.

"I need you Lili," he whispered in her ear. Lindy's pulse raced. Her breath was heavy. Even though she was bone-tired after the tour of the Ashton mansion, he could do that to her.

"Why don't you come over to my place? I've got a bottle of wine." Her eyes held a teasing look as she stepped back.

Sid pulled her close again and ran his tongue down her neck, opened the neckline of her dress and found a nipple. Lindy's knees sagged and she clung to him for support. It had been so long since anyone had cared for her, filled that vacant space in her heart. Not since Reed! No looking back she reminded herself. Reed was over for good! She opened her eyes wide, for a second bewildered at seeing this stranger at her breast.

"Lili, come with me." Sid took her hand.

To hell with Reed Conners, she scolded silently and stumbled along. Her pulses racing again. "Where are we going?" she gasped.

"You'll see." He put an arm around her waist and led her down a hallway to the end of a wing into the Ashton's sleeping quarters.

"We can't--! This is Anne Ashton's bed," Lindy murmured.

"Sure, we can Lili." Sid guided her over to the four poster bed, pulled her down to his lap. He unbuttoned her dress and slipped it off her shoulders. Unhooked her bra and slipped the wisp of lace off. A minute later, Lindy daintily stepped out of her panties and stood before him, not a wee bit embarrassed at her nakedness. This man excited her, made her feel again.

Time flew by then as she closed her eyes and opened herself to this man that had come into her life. Although she'd only met him a few weeks ago, he guessed exactly what she needed. As they lay in each others arms later, Lindy gazed around the room of the long deceased Ashton's. She could picture the domineering Anne Ashton dictating to her husband when and where she wanted sex. If she wanted it at all.

She pictured Anne straddling the hips of her timid husband, banishing a whip and riding him. Lindy giggled helplessly. She sat up and wiped her eyes.

"Lili, what's so funny?" Sid asked suddenly alarmed at her outburst. He patted his mussed hair into place and ran a finger over his mustache. Lindy sobered.

"I'm just thinking about the Ashton's." But suddenly she needed to get away, out of these dead peoples' bedroom. The room smelled musty, old. She climbed out of the bed, gathered her clothes and hurriedly dressed.

"Sid, I'm not so sure I want to be a caretaker of this place too. It kind of gives me the creeps!"

"Lili it's simple. All you need to do is check the front and back alarms, just come in and go to the east wing and you can do it from there, before midnight each night is good." He slid out of bed and started getting dressed.

"Has there ever been a break-in?" Lindy asked, still not convinced.

"No, not since I took over." They walked out of the mansion. "Okay, my sweet, I've got to run, I'll see you tomorrow." He waved as he got into his Mercedes.

Lindy went back to her cottage, threw her clothes on the bed and opened the windows to the ocean breeze. She slipped into a robe and put her feet under her as she sat on the couch and relaxed, relieved to have the first day of her job over. It really wasn't so bad, and maybe she'd do it for a month or so. In the meantime, she'd have time to decide where she wanted to live. This was going to be her town.

She lazed the day away watching television and napping. Then later remembered it was time to check on the mansion. She found her jeans, a shirt and slipped her feet into a pair of sandals. As she hurried over the path, a sliver of moonlight lit the path. A fog horn sounded far out over the water as she climbed the steps that led to the back door. She clasped her arms over her chest against the chilly air.

She put the key in the lock, found the light switch and turned off the alarm. She hurried through the dingy halls to the wing that she was familiar with, moving fast by that door again. The one she'd asked Sid about and that he had avoided answering.

The next week went by quickly as Lindy led her daily tours through the mansion. One day, after a tryst with Sid in Anne Ashton's receiving room, as they were getting back in their clothes, Lindy said, "I'd like it if we went out to dinner together." She paused as she buttoned her dress and looked at him.

"Lili, my sweet, I'm sorry I have a commitment tonight."

"Well, you're not married are you?"

"God no!" Sid knotted his tie, buttoned the French cuffs of his shirt.

Undaunted Lindy persisted. "Well then, what is it?"

Sid tucked his shirt in his trousers, picked up his jacket. "Lili my love, I promise when I get through working on this deal I'm involved with, we'll do the town." He leaned over and kissed her and hurried out the door. In the few weeks Lindy had known Sid, not once, had he invited her out for a sandwich or a drink.

She fluffed her hair, picked up the coronet of flowers from the floor and hurried through the mansion. As she passed that same door that led into the mysterious room, a light seemed to emanate from under the closed door. Lindy stopped for minute. It couldn't be the sun. It had been hidden all day under voluminous clouds. She walked briskly back to her small house.

The weekend loomed ahead and Lindy was restless. She'd spent time looking for real estate but still hadn't found something she'd liked. The prices were outrageous, but then what could you expect, this was a part of the world that offered people sun, sand and fun. Her sex life was okay, but her social life hadn't happened.

She dressed in one of her new outfits; an Avocado coarse linen, long skirt and top, and a matching long coat imported from India. This had cost a bundle when she'd bought it at Armani's in Boston, but it certainly had an elegant look. She slipped her bare feet in a pair of Prada high heeled sandals. At the last minute she grabbed a tan straw hat and adjusted it at a jaunty angle, and added her designer sunglasses. She did look good!

She drove around Newport acquainting herself with the delightful shops and restaurants, felt the intriguing ambience, then found Shirlee's, the place she'd heard about. A piano bar and restaurant located next to the water with a deck that extended over the glistening bay. The day was unusually mild and Lindy settled under a gaily striped umbrella and ordered her favorite drink. As she sipped her Manhattan she sat back and lit a cigarette and put it in the long holder she'd snitched which was part of the outfit she wore for the mansion tours. She was sure she made a glamorous picture in her hat and dark glasses. How she loved it!

Later, as the sun slipped over the horizon Lindy took off her hat and glasses, just as the owner and entertainer came out and sat down at a grand piano. Earlier, Lindy had read the clippings used on the menu cover depicting the entertainer's life. How she'd come to Newport, Rhode Island, fifteen years ago and met and married a native. Then read she was from her own home town in Minnesota!

Shirlee was a tall brunette with smiling blue eyes, well built and beautiful. She sat in the spotlight at the piano nestled inside a u-shaped bar, as her adored followers clustered around the outer edges on stools. Her voice was low and sexy as she accompanied herself beautifully on the baby grand and Lindy hummed along to the familiar songs. At the end of the night, after Shirlee thanked the patrons for coming, she walked directly over to Lindy's table.

"I see you're alone."   The entertainer smiled. "Thanks for coming."

"Lovely place, I've enjoyed the evening."   Lindy stood up and gathered her things.

"Would you care to join me for a cup of coffee? I need to stick around and lock up after the clean-up crew is done."

"Sure, I'd love to," Lindy agreed. By now, after enjoying numerous cocktails she had completely forgotten her commitment to check the mansion before midnight.

"Some brandy should warm us up too."   Shirlee reached across the bar and laced their coffee cups with the amber liquor. They settled on stools at the bar.

"I loved all your songs," Lindy said.

"I noticed you seemed to know all of them." Shirlee took a breath and sat back on the bar stool. "I've found that most people like the golden oldies." After a moment she looked at Lindy questioningly. "Haven't we met?"

"I don't think so. My name is Lili Lane." Lindy lit a cigarette and blew out a cloud of smoke.

"Hmm--, you look familiar."

Lindy laughed. "I've been told I have a familiar face."

"No seriously, where are you from?"

"Florida," Lindy answered. By now she had become so used to hiding her real identity it just flew out of her mouth.

Shirlee leaned in closer. "I could swear you have the same northern accent as I have. I'm from Minnesota."

"Well, I am Scandinavian." Anxious to leave this particular subject, Lindy said, "I read all the news clippings about your career, have you ever regretted your decision to stay here?"

"Not at all. I fell in love with the place and shortly after, met my husband." Lindy adjusted her long skirt over her legs. "I've been looking for a house; I'm planning to stay here."

"Great. Are you single?" Shirlee asked.

"Yes. I have been for a few years now."

"Well, this is a paradise. You won't be lacking for escorts." The late night customers had left and waiters gathered glasses. A cleaning crew piled chairs on top of tables. A vacuum cleaner hummed.

"It looks like you've got a gold mine here!"

"I've been lucky. Of course, we're just getting into our tourist season. Tell me, what have you been doing since you got here?"

Lindy laughed, "I've been working as a tour guide. It's just temporary."

Shirlee poured another hefty splash of brandy in their cups. "Really? That sounds interesting. Where at?"

"It's one of those big places along the ocean. I do an hour leading people around and then keep an eye on the building at night. The Ashton house," Lindy added.

Shirlee sucked in her breath, clunked her coffee cup down on the bar and exclaimed with alarm, "Oh my God, not there!"

-24-

Reed replaced the note that Hilda Sorenson had left for the paperboy back in the mailbox. He left Carmen Ciem's house, took off in his Corvette and spent part of the day working on a plan. At four o'clock he was back at Gina's, refreshed after a shower and ready for a tall cool drink. And, ready to talk to the blonde Tony Roman had been seen pursuing. But, would she remember to show up after last night's alcoholic haze she'd been in?

"Afternoon Leon," Reed said as he slid onto a bar stool. "Crown Royal." He reached into his coat jacket for a cigarette.

"Hey, what's new?" Leon reached for the bottle and poured a hefty amount over ice.

"Not much."   Reed looked around the bar. "Has Legs been around?" He took a swallow of the liquor.

"Nope, haven't seen anything of that bunch. Did you connect?"

"She's supposed to show up about now."

"Doing some research are you?" Leon smiled and collected glasses from the bar. "Always   looking   for answers." Reed raised an eyebrow, an innocent look on his face. Just then, the girl walked in. She hesitated and looked around, then saw Reed at the bar. He turned just as she was about to tap him on the shoulder.

"I wasn't sure you'd show up," he said somewhat surprised.

"Really!" She smiled, showing braces on her teeth.

He stood up while she got settled on the next stool. "What would you like to drink?   Should I call you Legs?"

"Why not, but my name is Marty."   She was wearing a leopard print coat, with matching high heeled strapped shoes. Her silver hair was cut in a boyish style, strands hung down over large blue eyes. There was a saucy look about her as she winked at the bartender.

"I'd love one of those drinks with an umbrella. Rum something."

"Right."   Leon smiled. She unbuttoned her coat, crossed her legs, and smoothed a short black leather skirt down over her thighs. The effect was not lost on Reed. However, he reminded himself, she was too young and he didn't need another complication in his life.

She sighed and blew out a breath that raised her bangs. "My lord, I'm tired."

"Hard day?" Reed took a drag on his cigarette.

"Just got through work. I've got to say, I made all those old ladies look good though."

"How so?" Reed looked at her curiously. She laughed merrily and sampled the tall pink drink Leon put down on the bar for her. "I'm a hair stylist," she said and twirled the little umbrella from it with her perfectly manicured finger-tips. She reminded Reed of someone he'd seen on one of those sitcoms on television; cute and witty.

"Do you come here often?"

"Why, are you interested?" She gave him a seductive look.

He leaned towards her and grinned. "Are you hungry? Would you join me for dinner?"

"Would I!" She answered happily as Reed picked up their glasses and guided her into the dining room which was quiet at this early cocktail hour. They were seated in a secluded corner.

"I love this place," she gushed as she ran her fingers over the linen tablecloth, the crystal glasses.

"Gina does have class. Order whatever you'd like," Reed said as they studied the menus in silence.

"I'll have the lobster," she said.

After they'd finished dinner and sat back to relax with foamy mint drinks, Reed cleared his throat.

"Marty, I hear you're seeing that movie star, Tony Roman." Marty's eyes lit up with a dreamy look. "Would he be my competition?" Reed took her hand, stroked her fingers.

She smiled demurely and fluttered her eyelashes. "Maybe."

"Well, what's he got that I haven't?" Reed asked jokingly.

She stuck her tongue out and licked some cream off her upper lip. He felt her relax. She smiled again at him. "He said when he gets famous he wants me to move to Hollywood too. And, he's rich!"

"Well damn, how long have you been seeing this guy?"

"For a few years. He bought me this." She held her arm out to proudly show of a gold braided chain bracelet on her wrist.

"That's beautiful. Where does he live," Reed asked innocently.

"Oh wow, he's got this huge mansion. No kidding!"

After Reed paid the bill and walked her out to her car, he hadn't found out anything new except that Tony Roman had apparently played around before his wife died too. That poor little girl would be in for a rude awakening.

That night dressed in dark clothes and soft soled shoes, his gloves, flashlight and tools stuffed in his pockets, Reed drove back to the Lake Calhoun area. He parked in a heavily wooded stretch of wet-land and darted through the shaded private yards to the back door of the Ciem residence. The first time he'd been inside the house, he'd seen the security system was first class, but not something he couldn't work out. There would be four minutes after opening the door to punch in the password, or a call went into the police department. He slipped on latex gloves and went to work.

Seconds flew by as he worked the lock, then the tumblers fell into place and he was inside. He checked his watch. Four minutes from now!   Most people used a nickname, kid's names, birthdays, or even a pet's name as their keyword. He'd memorized all the possible words he could think of. Now the test. Three minutes and thirty-seconds or he'd have to retrace his steps and get out. That first time he'd been in the Ciem house, he'd gotten a quick glance as Hilda had turned the alarm off, before she'd noticed his interest and stepped in front of the pad on the wall to shield her efforts. He was sure the password had started with the letter C and had five digits. He stood without moving and let his eyes adjust to the darkness. A sliver of moonlight crept under the shades, just enough for Reed to make out the kitchen. The house was cold and tidy except for dishes stacked in the sink. A faint smell of bacon lingered in the room. A   line   of   perspiration edged over his upper lip as he turned to the security pad and began. He had thirty-eight possible words. First of all, he tried various combinations of Carmen Ciem's name. Nothing. Okay, he looked at his watch, start at the top. All words or names containing five letters beginning with the letter C. Cabin, Carrie, cello, cigar, just some of the words he typed out on the pad, the keys silently accepting his efforts, but not accessing entry.

Damn! One minute had gone by. Celia, combs, Chris, Chloe. Bingo! The red flashing light died. Reed exhaled and smiled. Yes!

He knew the lay-out of the first floor of the house, but he wanted Tony Roman's bedroom. He climbed the marble stairway, ran his gloved hand along the railing to guide him in the dark only using his flashlight for a second at a time. At the top, pictures decorated the walls of a long hallway, and a table with a huge floral arrangement stood at the end. Reed opened doors, flashed the light into perfectly decorated guest rooms, a closet that held scented linens and then a set of double doors. He pushed them open, flashed his penlight around the room. Roman's bedroom.

A definite man's room with black leather furniture in a sitting area, with black and white accessories, a king-sized bed. Not a trace of his wife's presence left. Reed looked behind pictures, searched dresser drawers, checked under sweaters, underwear. The guy had learned style, he muttered. He lifted the mattress. Then knelt down and opened the drawer to a bedside table. It held the usual; Kleenex, inhalers, Dramamine. Aha--, a box of condoms. Reed stood up and opened a louvered door that led into a walk-in closet. Roman's clothes were lined up perfectly in groups of suits, sport jackets, shirts and slacks. A shoe rack covered one wall. A built in cupboard lined another. He flipped open the doors and behind stacks of terry towels he found what he was looking for; the safe. He expertly spun the dial, put his ear to the door, listened and caught the rhythm. A minute and a half. He was getting rusty, but safe cracking wasn't called for much in his line of work. He shook his head at how easy it was to be a guest in someone's home without their knowledge. A smile edged the corner of his mouth as he opened the door to the safe, flashed the light, and then stepped back.

The goddamn thing was empty!   Okay asshole, Reed mumbled, what are you hiding and where? The third floor? He'd seen a light up there just a few days ago. Back in the hallway, he found the door that led up a steep stairway. Not marble, like the grand one downstairs, but plain wood. Reed cautiously flashed his light around as he climbed and found it opened into a cavernous room. Discarded furniture shrouded in covers stood haphazardly among numerous boxes. Plastic bags covered clothes hung from exposed rafters. There were hundreds of places to hide something. Reed surveyed the area.

Damn, there wasn't time. But, if all else failed, he'd have to come back and patiently take the place apart.

His shoes whispered on the stairs as he went down, reset the alarm and was out the back door. His trusty tools worked the lock to the side door to the garage in seconds. As his eyes adjusted to the dark, slivers of moonlight reflected on the four cars, shined and ready to go; the Mercedes, Lincoln town car, Carmen's Mustang and Tony Roman's Prowler. Off to one side was a complete workout gym; top of the line equipment. Reed checked his watch. Ten minutes was the length of time he allowed himself to be inside anywhere, after that anything could happen. Starting now. He studied the room. Hilda had said, Roman spent his time in the garage 'tinkering with the cars and fine tuning his muscles.' From experience, Reed knew most people kept their valuables close by, in places where they spent a lot of their time. He opened drawers, shook containers, ran his hand inside tires stacked up in a corner. Opened glove boxes in the cars, slid his hand under seats. Nothing! Time was running out. He wiped his forehead in frustration.

Okay Roman, you're not that smart!

A tall red tool chest stood next to the Prowler, drawers open. Tools lay on the top. Reed opened each drawer, moved hammers, screwdrivers, and various tools and checked under rubber mats.

Aha--, there it was. A fat plastic covered manila envelope. He stuffed it under his shirt, and within seconds was back in the Corvette. The motor in his car purred softly as he rounded a corner just as a taxi turned into the street. Was it Hilda and Otto Sorenson back from their trip? Would they recognize his car?

Back at his motel, Reed spread the contents of the envelope out on his bed. Inside he found a birth certificate, a copy of the couple's marriage license, and a passport. Anthony Romanopilos was his name. Born in Chicago. Nothing Reed didn't know already. Then a small red packet fell out, inside was a key with the number 2020. Reed turned it over in his hand; obviously to a safe deposit box, or a locker. He picked up his cell phone and dialed a number.

-25-

Lindy gaped at the look on Shirlee's face when she told her that she worked at the Ashton mansion. The two women sat at the bar drinking brandied coffee in Shirlee's place. The cleaning crew had turned off the vacuum cleaners; put the barstools back down on the floor. The place stood clean and ready for the next day.

"Lili, that's scary!" Shirlee turned to her.

"Why?" Lindy asked anxiously.

"You don't know?"

Lindy leaned closer, her eyes large. "What?" she breathed.

"That place is haunted. It's full of ghosts!"

"Ghosts?" Lindy gaped at her new friend.

"Yes. It's been talked about for decades. They say that the daughter, Lili, poisoned her Mother. That they still live there!"

"No--." Lindy's breath caught.

"Nobody told you, huh?"

"Well no--," Lindy said again. But, she began thinking of that room that always gave her the creeps when she was near. About Sid's obvious refusal to answer her questions about it.

"I'd get out of there, if I were you Lili." Shirlee asked then, "Is that Sid still there? There were strange stories about him too, and rumors a while back that his last girl friend disappeared!"

Lindy drove through the streets of Newport and back to the mansion. She'd smiled at Shirlee's story about ghosts, about Anne and Lili Ashton still living there after being dead for years. What a lot of bunk! She didn't believe in that nonsense. As a kid, she remembered playing with friends, putting sheets over their heads and chasing each other around outside after dark. Just fun and make-believe. A childhood game.

But what about Sid? A sudden shiver shook her to her heels. She swung the silver Lexus through the tall gates that opened on to the grounds of the Ashton house, over the gravel drive to the pagoda that was her home. She opened windows to let the late night breezes in, undressed and got into bed. After the Margarita's and the brandy she'd drunk, she was tired. She lay under the covers and dozed. Then jumped up. She'd forgotten to check the mansion. It was way over-due. Maybe she wouldn't tonight, after all, who would know!

Damn, but she had promised. It was part of this darn job. She threw the covers off, found some clothes, slid into a pair of tacky moccasins and went outside. But, on the way she grabbed a metal nail file from her manicure bag.

The big house stood dark and silent as she went in. She checked the locks on the windows, turned lights off and on as she went through the hallways, peeked into the now familiar rooms. The antiques were all there, everything stood safe and secure until she passed by the door of that room. Shirlee had said it was Anne Ashton's sitting room. That same light shone again under the door. Being a little tipsy yet and with her usual curiosity, Lindy decided with a giggle this was the time to explore. She had to look in there, find out what the heck all this ridiculousness was about. She tried the door, but of course it was locked. She knelt down and took the nail file out of her pocket and got to work. Her bottom lip caught between her teeth as she concentrated.

Damn, this wasn't as easy as it looked on television. Her knees began to hurt, her head throbbed. Then the lock clicked. She stood up, put her hand on the door and pushed. It swung wide with a creaking groan. She gulped and her eyes grew large at what she saw.

The room was dark except for a bright light centered on a grouping of furniture. A table was set for tea and two women were sitting companionably, intent in a hushed conversation, dressed in afternoon gowns. Cups raised to their lips. Lindy stood in the doorway, frozen. After a moment she wet her lips and said a squeaky hello. The women didn't take notice and went on with their conversion. Lindy blinked her eyes.

Was she dreaming? She put her hand out and touched the door, ran her fingers over the boards. Everything was real. As her eyes returned to the scene before her, the light around the women became brighter, their voices raised in what sounded like an argument, but, still not loud enough for Lindy to understand. Then the younger of the two stood up and began to laugh wildly as the older one slid down off her chair and crumpled in a heap on the floor. The light became blinding for a second, and then began to fade taking with it the scene and the presence of the women. Lindy stood petrified, as the room darkened leaving only a faint odor of ashes. She turned and ran. Through the long hallways, the dark kitchen and out the door. She didn't take time to lockup, just ran like hell back to her small house and collapsed in a chair.

Good Lord, she gasped. Was it a dream, a hallucination, too many Margaritas? She sat huddled in a chair. Her face was pale; her blue eyes a pool of fright. She'd get help, call the police. She dialed 911.

A man's voice came on the line. "Emergency."

"Help," Lindy's voice quavered. "There's someone in the Ashton house."

"Are you hurt?" he asked.

"No--, I went in to check the place, and these two women were there."

"Do they live there?"

"Yes-- no, they used to."

"Take a breath now Miss. Was there a break in?"

"No."

"What exactly are you reporting?"

Lindy whispered, "I think they're ghosts!"

"Ghosts?"

"Yes!" Lindy swallowed over the lump of panic in her throat.

"Now Miss, take it easy now. Have you been drinking or taking drugs?"

"No--, well I did have something to drink. But I know what I saw!" Lindy replied, indignant at his tone of voice.

"Well Miss, I suggest you go to bed and sleep it off. You'll feel better in the morning. I'll send a squad car by just in case."

Lindy hung up the phone. Was it her imagination playing tricks?

Her hands trembled as she fumbled for a cigarette, didn't take time to put it in the fancy holder, but raised it to her lips and inhaled, hard. Those women had been the Ashtons. Mother and daughter. The same as in the pictures Lindy had studied earlier as she'd prepared for her job. She eyed her small living room uneasily. The curtains on the opened windows ruffled in the breeze as if being moved, and the crashing waves echoed mournfully from the ocean far below.

This is nuts, she whispered in a shaky voice and jumped up, grabbed her purse, ran to her car and sped through the tall gates. She drove towards the business district of Newport. Now the sidewalks were empty of tourists, all the shops closed. Everyone tucked warm and safe in their beds. And here she was again, wandering around alone in the middle of the night. Seeing ghosts yet, with only her trusty stuffed dog Pal, lying on the floor in the back of her silver Lexus. And Sid! He had known all along about the haunted room and hadn't told her. She shivered again. What had really happened to his girlfriend?

Lindy drove aimlessly. She looked at the clock in the dashboard. Four o'clock. Wasn't there anyone up and around at this time of the night in this damn town? At last, she found a cafe with bright flashing lights. Reggie's, it was called. A railroad car transformed into a diner. As Lindy ran in, the delicious smell of bacon frying on a grill greeted her. She scooted to the counter that lined the narrow space and perched on a red stool, but tucked her feet under the bar, suddenly aware of the dusty wool that stuck out of the edges of her favorite moccasins.

Well, who had time? She took another cigarette and this time put it in the elegant holder.

"Good morning Miss. Coffee?" A tall black man behind the counter greeted her.

"Yes, and anything you can scramble up."

As he placed a steaming cup of brew in front of her, he asked, "Are you up early or out late?"

"I guess both." Lindy blinked her eyes and shook her head. "You wouldn't believe it."

"Bad night?"

"One of the worst," she groaned.

"The weather man says a heavy rain is on the way later, probably be around for a day or so." He turned to the grill and began to break eggs, and turn sizzling bacon.

"Oh great, just what I need, a gray, depressing day." Lindy put a hand over her eyes, suddenly overcome with fatigue.

"Well, you can look at it that way," the cook said as he put silverware down on the counter in front of her, "but then again they always say things will look better after tomorrow's rain!"

She raised her head and stared at the man. After a few minutes he placed a plate of scrambled eggs in front of her. As she ate, the food began to steady her stomach, diminish the anxiety in her heart.

But suddenly, as the morning sun arose and streamed through the windows of Reggie's diner, Lindy stopped with the fork in mid-air and gaped in astonishment as a familiar face appeared in the rays and said in a faltering voice, "Lindy, come back, I need you!"

-26-

Earlier that same evening, Reed sat in an easy chair in the motel room, Tony Roman's papers spread out before him on the bed. He held the key up to the light and squinted at the numbers, as his cell phone buzzed in his ear. It was after midnight and was picked up on the second ring.

"Yah," the man answered. A wheelchair creaked.

"Bernard, sorry to call so late but I need you to look at something."

"What?"

"I've got a key. I need to find out what it belongs to and its location." Reed dropped it on the table. A pinging hollow noise vibrated in the room.

"Come on over," the computer whiz said putting the phone down without saying goodbye. Reed slipped on his leather jacket.

The parking lot around the motel was full, but not one light shone from the windows as he hurried to his car. The sky was black, and hard white stars shed a chilling glow over the town. A cold north wind blew across his face and down his neck, and he shrugged his shoulders against a sudden uneasiness. Within minutes, he was across town and knocked on the flimsy door of an apartment in downtown Minneapolis.

"Conners, I was just going out when you called." The abrasive manner of the guy was more than usual this early morning.

Reed stepped into the apartment. "Sorry Bernard, but I really need your help." Reed handed the key to the man and watched as he went over to his desk and began working on one of his elaborate computers. Reed's eyes roamed around the room as he waited.

One wall was filled with shelves loaded with books and magazines. The other three desks held computers, screens and monitors. The air was stale with cigarette smoke and grease from leftover pizza boxes. A lonely siren wailed somewhere in the distance. "Easy,"   the craggy voice of the invalid said as he wheeled his chair around and faced Reed. "Yup, it's from one of the airport lockers."

"The main one?"

"Nah, the charter one."

"Thanks buddy." Reed said and handed him a hundred dollar bill.

Snowflakes bounced off the windshield as he sped to the airport. He locked his gun in the glove box and hurried into the huge complex, the warm air a welcome relief from the below zero wind. He walked through the lobby, the security checkpoint, then downstairs to the baggage department and over to the lockers. He walked slowly, found locker number 2020, then sat down in a nearby row of seats and picked up a paper. He needed to take his time, check around just in case someone was watching.

What the hell, he muttered after a few minutes. He was one of the good guys! He walked over and put the key in the locker. The door swung open easily. He reached in and found a package about the size of a cigar box. Minutes later, back in the Corvette as he stopped at a light he opened the box and found a blue velvet drawstring bag nestled inside. With one hand on the steering wheel, he used the other to undo the tie. As the light changed and he stepped on the gas, gems spilled out over the leather seat. Rings, necklaces, bracelets, and earrings sparkled against the black leather upholstery. Diamonds, rubies and emeralds.

So, Roman had stolen Carmen Ciem's jewelry! Two bit hustler, Reed muttered. Goddamn, now he was getting close!

As he stopped for the next red light, he scooped the jewels back into the bag, but as he reached down to the floor to retrieve a ring, a deafening shot rang out. Reed's breath exploded. His foot slipped off the brake and the powerful car shot across the median into a barrier. Ripping metal, breaking glass, and then steaming water sprayed up over the radiator as the shiny black Corvette stopped instantly. The motor continued to roar, then was silent. It was two o'clock in the morning.

*****

"Hey buddy, good to see you. I've been waiting to talk to you," a familiar voice said. Reed blinked his eyes and tried to focus. Everything was white; his surroundings, his clothes, even the air. A weightless white haze seemed to envelope him in a state of suspension. Then a warm feeling of recognition came over him.

"Tanner?"

"Reed!" The two men stepped close, hugged and slapped each other on the back.

"Man, I'm glad to see you. I've missed you buddy." Reed said and stepped back.

Tanner looked the same, except most of the lines in his face were gone. But he was pissed.

"What the hell happened to you Reed? I went up to your spread last summer and you were gone!" Reed remembered Tanner had been shot in a small town, close to his ranch.

Tanner went on, "Christ, I couldn't believe your place. Everything overgrown, quiet like that. I looked all over hell for you!"

"Man, I'm sorry," Reed said. "It was sudden. I closed up and sold out in a couple of days to a neighbor and moved to the cabin. Needed a change."

"Thomas got me, shot me you know."

"And I got the asshole--twice!"

Reed studied the familiar face as Tanner spoke. "You know he killed Sierra, forced her car off the road."

"Yeah buddy, I figured it out. And the asshole confessed on his way to serve two life sentences." Reed smiled at his best friend.

"You got that case wrapped up?" Tanner asked.

"Yup, buddy, sewed up tight," Reed said.

"You know Lindy is the key to your new case, don't you?"

"How?" Reed whispered through parched lips. But Tanners face began to fade, his voice muffled. Reed reached out a hand in the white swirling haze. But it was too late; the wide expanse of white was empty. He tried to take a breath, but it hurt. Hurt like hell. He groaned then as machines clicked and hummed in the white hospital room, the days only marked by changing shifts and the rustling of the charts as doctors shook their heads.

*****

In Stillwater Minnesota, Sheriff Gil Finney's wife sat at a desk importantly manning the phone. Not that it rang that often in this quiet town nestled next to a river, but just in case something came in while Gil was taking his daily morning drive through his town.

Now she informed him, "Gilbert, I got a call from some old man saying you should check on a house. He said a dog has been barking and whining for days in there."

She tucked a strand of hair behind an ear and poured a cup of coffee for him.

"Aww- hell, where?" Gil lifted the cup to his lips and took a loud slurping swallow.

"Up the hill behind the depot."

"That rented place?"

"Yes Gilbert, that white house," she said impatiently.

"What's going on?"

"He said an old lady lives there alone. Hasn't seen her."

Gil ran a hand over his face. "Oh Lord, I got a report last week from some salesman saying she looked like she needed help." He took another drink of the coffee, set the cup down hard on the scarred desk top.

"Well, did you go and take a look?"

Damn, the woman bugged him sometimes. "Hell, I'd planned to, then got sidetracked by the city councils demands that kept me running and fetching all week. Damn!"

"Gilbert, I've told you, you need help here! Did you tell them that?"

"Yah, yah. Stay here, I'll go and look it over. Be back in thirty minutes."

"Hurry up then." Gil waved a dismissing hand in the air as he slammed the door. Always has to have the last word! He hoisted his suspenders over a huge pot-belly, jammed a hat over his rusty colored hair and groaned as he got in the tan and maroon car. The springs sagged to the left as he set his ample weight on the worn seats. Instead of that park by the water to snare big city tourists to his town, why couldn't they see he needed a new vehicle? He ground the gears as he backed out of the parking space next to the small building that held the town hall plus his office.

Damn, he mumbled again, that white house was a burr in his side. A rental that was nothing but trouble. Riff-raff coming and going over the years, he harrumphed. He stopped the car at the street and walked up to the door, stepping over snow drifts that reached to his knees. A dog whined like the neighbor said.

As he knocked on the door and waited, he looked around the neighborhood. A curtain moved at a window across the street. On his second knock, the dog's whine turned into a desperate howl. He walked around to the back and knocked. Nothing! Then braced a shoulder and rammed the door. As it flew open a huge dog bolted out knocking him down. The desperate animal ran around in circles in the snow, relieved himself, then sat down on his haunches and looked at Gil with soulful eyes. As Gil straightened and tried to get his wind back, a sickening stench hit him in the face. He bent over and retched and when his stomach was empty he finally managed to get to his feet and took a hesitant step into the kitchen.

Oh God, he mumbled with dread, found a handkerchief in his pocket and covered his nose. The room was a mess of broken dishes, chairs upturned with torn seats and stuffing scattered, rotting food, urine and feces. He walked into the living room, stepping carefully around the debris. Sweat poured down his florid face, dripped in his eyes. And there a woman lay on the floor, without going too close, he knew she was dead. Probably for days, he muttered. He hurried back outside and gulped fresh air and steadied himself and called a number on his cell phone.

"This here is Sheriff Finney," he told the undertaker at the local funeral home, "I've got a body."

"Where?"

"In the white house behind the depot." Then added, "It's been here awhile!"

By late afternoon, he had the gruesome pictures and fingerprints. But not one clue as to who this woman was.

He searched for mail, for anything that might give her name, but only found advertising fliers, letters to the occupant, and curiously, torn pictures from a catalog of women wearing winter coats. Not one piece of identity. Then as Gil had tossed the junk in boxes to search later, he saw a name written in a margin of a ragged newspaper, almost undistinguishable. He studied the scrawling words, held it to the lamp, and then exhaled as he made out the name.

Yes that's what it said, Carmen Ciem!

-27-

Carmen Ciem, Gil repeated. What the hell could she have to do with this? He shifted his weight. Was there a connection between that big case in Minneapolis and this dead little old lady?

Sheriff Gilbert Finney looked out the window at the familiar surroundings in Stillwater, Minnesota. Except for the eight years he spent at the Police Academy and on the force in Minneapolis, he'd spent his entire life here. As soon as he'd heard rumors that the sheriff in his home town was thinking of retiring, he'd camped on his doorstep. He had one thing in mind; to leave the loud, dirty city and get back home. His family was gone, and that, being the closest thing to belonging. He had no trouble getting elected to office as the chief law enforcement officer of the county. Keeper of peace and executor of court orders. After the fanfare, he settled into his new job. Young, enthusiastic and full of energy. Several years later, he married a local girl, bought an old Victorian house and waited to start a family. As years went by and no babies came along, his wife became embittered and Gil's only option was to slam the door on her tirades and spend more time in his office.

Gal-darn, he'd been at his job for years and he was good. He knew most everyone in town and took a personal interest in newcomers and saw that the tourists left happy. Never had, had a death that couldn't be accounted for. Until today. And, if he hadn't been pestered by the town's do-gooders all week, he wouldn't have forgotten that call that came in. His ruddy complexion turned darker at his thoughts. It would put a smudge on his perfect record. He had to make it good, he ruminated.

Carmen Ciem. He remembered her when he'd patrolled the neighborhood where she lived when he'd been on the force in Minneapolis way back. A young divorced woman with two kids, living in a poor part of town, working at numerous jobs to put a roof over their heads and food on the table. He'd seen her occasionally as she waited for bus connections. Her children had never gotten into trouble.

But what was the connection between her and this woman he'd found dead in his town?

As he sat at his desk with papers scattered in front of him, he went over the events of the day again to make absolutely sure he hadn't overlooked something. First, there had been no evidence of forced entry on any of the doors or windows where this woman had lived. Gil had slipped on gloves as he stepped into the ravaged living room where she lay. As he studied the body, no wounds or blood were evident. She was a small person, with gray hair clasped in a knot on top of her head. Wire framed glasses lay next to her. She was clad in red pedal pushers and a long white t-shirt. No signs of assault that he could see. As he had scanned the room, cushions from the couch were strewn on the floor, with foam rubber shredded and scattered. A scarred coffee table was overturned. In the small dark bedroom, quilts hung off the edge of the bed. Clothes were hung haphazardly on wire hangers in the closet. As he slid them across the bar, one shirt caught his attention. A bright turquoise shirt with the name, Tiger Lake Casino written in rhinestones. Under a pile of blankets on a shelf he'd found a purse. There, he'd thought as he'd pulled it out. But after he'd opened the shoulder bag, except for crumbs and lint, it was empty. He'd gone through the dresser drawers and checked under the mattress, but had found nothing.

In the bathroom, the medicine cabinet held a toothbrush and toothpaste. No drugs of any kind. The woman had nothing! No identification, no money. In the linen closet, he'd found boxes of jigsaw puzzles;

simple ones that a young child would use. On closer examination, the pieces were mixed and damaged. The cupboards in the kitchen were empty, except for used food cartons. The refrigerator and freezer? Frozen TV dinners. Gil had stuffed his gloved hands in his pockets and stood still; let the overall look of things register in his head. The dog had still sat outside on the porch, peering inside and whining. Wouldn't take a step into the house.

One thing about Gilbert Finney, he had a sharp mind and a good eye. And an uncanny instinct. It had been 9:30 in the morning, thirty minutes after Gil had gotten there, that he'd waited outside on the porch for the black hearse, driven by Green and his helper carrying the necessary equipment. They'd worked together closely for years, the funeral director acting as medical examiner when needed. Nothing got by the two men as they'd sat together, many times late into the night and put together the puzzle of a crime. "What's your take on this," Green asked Gil after they'd zipped up the body bag. Gil hoisted his suspenders, wiped sweat off his forehead again, even though a cold January wind blew through the house. It would take days before the smell dissipated from his pores.

"It's a mystery so far," he lamented.

"Okay, I'll check her out."

"I'll get in touch," Gil said as he fastened the door. "I'm going to take the dog to the vet and check around."

The neighborhood was old. Small clapboard two bedroom houses dating back to the 1930 and 40's, mostly inhabited by senior citizens or young families just starting out. Gil headed to the house directly across the street where he'd seen someone peering out a window behind a curtain when he first arrived.

"I'm Sheriff Gil Finney, are you the neighbor who called in?" He asked after knocking on the screen door.

"I know who you are," a balding elderly man said. He stood at the door dressed in a shiny blue suit, the jacket open to a red and black plaid flannel shirt.

"I'd like to ask you some questions."

"I knew something was wrong over there," the neighbor said, his face contorted. Gil stepped into the house, glanced around. "Do you know the woman's name?"

"Nope, never talked to her."

"Have you seen anyone around?" Gil asked patiently.

"Well--, some women come over sometimes, carrying groceries I think. Haven't seen them for a week."

"Well now," Gil stroked his mustache thoughtfully, "I don't suppose you knew who they were?"

"Nah".

"How long had she lived there?" The neighbor looked off in the distance to the house across the street.

"Don't rightly know. I can't keep up with those things; I've got better things to do."

"Well, did you ever get a look at the plates on the cars?"

"Nah--, I saw those cars a few times. A big one. Another small one too."

"Can you describe the women?" Gil asked then.

"Well," he exhaled and seemed to drift off. "They looked pretty old, but they were dressed swell."

"Can you tell me anything else?" Gil asked as he jotted the information down in his notebook.

"I'd say," the neighbor suddenly becoming talkative, "that woman over there was crazy having that dog around. I saw her one time trying to get out of the house and that damn thing wouldn't let her out the door. Growled, I could see she was scared of the mutt."

"Did you ever go over there and see if there was a problem?"

"Nah--," the neighbor said again, "Figured it was none of my business. People come and go."

"If you think of anything else, I'd appreciate a call." Gil stepped of the porch and continued his search down the street, but, the only thing he'd found out was that the woman left lights on all night and seldom opened the shades. Some hours later, back at the house, he'd gathered up all the papers he'd found and left. As he sat at his desk in his small office, he took a swig of his cold coffee.

Goddamn, he was tired! He ran a hand over his face, scratched his head, stood up and stretched his large torso. As he stepped in the door at his home, his wife stood up from the easy chair she'd been sitting in watching television, and with hands on hips ordered, "Gilbert, go directly to the laundry room and put your clothes in the washer and take a shower with that soap!" And after that, he guessed the guest room was ready for him. Then she added, "Gilbert, I told you to go over and check that house, remember?"

"Yah, yah," Gil said and clumped loudly over the highly waxed wooden floors she took so much pride in.

Early the next morning, he called the funeral home and got the report from Green.

"Couldn't find a thing wrong," the man reported. "Strong heart but something seemed odd. I'd say she was poisoned!"

"The hell you say," Gil mumbled under his breath. "I'm going down to Minneapolis today and look up someone I know in the Police department. I'll get back to you."

He held his foot down hard on the gas as he neared the cities, grumpy at the cars hugging his bumper, forcing him to go over the speed limit. With relief, he parked and walked a few blocks to the familiar brick building that housed the Police department. He adjusted his tan and maroon uniform over his ample body, pulled his cap down squarely on his head.

"Hey Murphy, still here I see," he greeted an old friend.

"Gil, long time! Have a seat. What brings you to our busy city?"

Gil settled his large frame on a metal folding chair. Took his official brimmed cap off.

"Well," he said in his usual unhurried voice, "I've got a Jane Doe and I found the name Carmen Ciem in her belongings. Remembered the case here."

"Yeah?" Murphy said with immediate interest.

"Wondered if there might be a connection." It wasn't often Gil needed help, but something had nagged him all night in his restless sleep. His town might be involved in a big way.

"That case is still unsolved," Murphy said as he shifted papers and files on his desk, then looked at Gil and shook his head. "Now all of a sudden, it's wide open. I've got a man in the hospital in a coma. He worked for the insurance company investigating the claim that covered the woman. Got shot up with a car load of her jewelry." Murphy exhaled.

Gil sat back on the uncomfortable chair as he went on. "I've got a man down there keeping an eye on him." Murphy ran a hand through his gray hair. "I know this guy, we've fished together."

"What's his name?" Gil asked curiously.

"Reed Conners!"

"Reed Conners?" Gil sat up, the metal chair creaked loudly. "Hell, I knew him years ago! Younger.

Just out of law school. Hung around with another guy, Tanner Burke." Gil scratched his head, thought a minute and continued, "Read in the paper Burke took a bullet, and Conners put this John Thomas guy away for good, a while back."

"The same!"

"The hell you say. A good man." Gil sat silent.

Murphy continued, "Christ, I don't know what to make of it, there must have been a couple million bucks worth of stones on him when he was shot!"

Gil chewed on this latest bit of information. Got up off the flimsy chair and adjusted his holster over his ample hips. "I'd like to take a look at Conners, see if he's awake yet, that's if it's okay with you?"

"Fine with me. I'll give the guard at his door a call."

-28-

Gil arrived at the hospital trauma center which sprawled over two blocks in downtown Minneapolis. The busy halls emanated an odor of sickness, and the sharp scent of disinfectants. His gun belt creaked against his thigh and his leather soled shoes gripped the shiny tiled floors as he walked down the plain impersonal hallways. No pictures graced the walls to give the place a homey look. A paging system alternated between calls for doctors and families of patients. After inquiring about directions to Reed Conner's room, he talked briefly to the guard stationed outside the door, and stepped into Room 607.

The drapes were open to cold bright sunshine. Pigeons sat on a nearby roof top. The man lay silent and pale, stretched out flat in a railed bed. Tubes and machines hummed and dripped. Gil pulled up a chair and sat, then took a long breath. So this was the Reed Conners he'd known when they'd both been young and fresh, so many years ago. Now, he too had aged and filled out his lanky youthful frame. The fair-skinned, freckled young man of long ago now had gray in his sandy hair. Lines deeply engraved in his face.

Gil swallowed hard as he surveyed the austere room and the sight of this helpless man caught in a tangle and not able to defend himself. He put his hand on Reed's still arm. "Reed Conners, I don't know if you remember me, I'm Sheriff Gilbert Finney. I heard you've been here for awhile. Now, I've got a problem and I need your help!" Half expecting Reed to open his eyes and begin to speak, Gil sat and watched for a reaction. After no change, he cleared his throat and wiped a hand over his face, thoughtfully smoothed his mustache that trailed over his upper lip. He'd heard that if you spoke to a comatose person, there was a possibility they could hear and understand, even though they didn't respond.

"Conners," he began again, "I've got a body I can't identify and I found the name, Carmen Ciem in her things. I looked up Murphy downtown at the Police Department here and he told me you've been working the Ciem case."

Gil studied Reed as he talked, and not a flicker of awakening crossed his face. He got up and opened the door and spoke to the guard.

"Has anyone been here to see this man?" he asked.

"Nope. I heard he doesn't have any family."

"Friends?" Gil frowned.

"Just a couple from out of town, but they couldn't stay long."

Christ! Even if he hadn't any family except his wife, he was sure plenty of concerned friends would come around to encourage him to get well. "I need to get a cup of coffee," he told the guard and took off down the hallway. His gruff exterior hid a soft heart. This could be my brother, if I had one, Gil lamented sorrowfully as he walked. It was late afternoon. It didn't sit right with Gilbert Finney to see one of his own shot up and being accused of something and unable to fight back.

He sat at a table in the hospital coffee shop, absently stroked his mustache, and put another spoonful of sugar in the coffee cup. This man needs help. And since there doesn't seem to be anybody else, I'll elect myself to stick around. A man needs someone to care if he doesn't make it, Gil lamented sorrowfully, besides I don't believe those suspicions! Gil took another loud slurp, put the cup down on the table top with a determined thump, and dialed a number on his cell phone, which connected him to his deputy back in Stillwater.

"I'll be here for a couple of days," he said, "I'll be in touch." He had just disconnected the call when the phone buzzed in his hand. "Sheriff Finney," he answered in his usual slow drawl.

"Gilbert? I heard your message," his wife said.

"Figured you would. I was planning to call. What is it?"

"I'm just checking to see if you've found out anything yet."

"For God's sake, I just got here."

"Well, where are you? I hear people."

Gil took an impatient breath. "I'm sitting here in the hospital café having some coffee."

"Well, I don't like being alone."

"Won't be long." Damn woman wouldn't let him alone, always nagging about something. He left after eating a sandwich and found his way through the weaving hallways, determined now to put life back in Reed's inert body. He put his cap on the foot of the bed, unbuckled his gun and holster and laid them on the floor and settled in. "Reed Conners, I'm here for the duration and by God, I'm not giving up!" Gil began to talk. He told Reed about his fishing trips, hunting for elk in Montana, his frustrations on his job, anything that came into his head, even his wife's constant carping. At midnight, he was exhausted, his voice hoarse. He raised his stiff body out of the chair, stood and stretched. "Buddy, even if I bored you, the least you could do is tell me to go to hell!" He tucked the blanket around Reed and said, "I'm going to get some shut-eye, but I'll be back in the morning."

He left the hospital and found a cheap motel. As he lay in the foreign bed, the streets outside hummed with activity; car horns honked, a city bus roared by, a siren screamed on the next street. After shifting and turning, trying to find a comfortable spot in the bed, Gil tossed the covers aside. The air was stuffy and dusty, the sheets smelled of bleach, and water dripped from the bathroom sink faucet sending out something like the ticking of time. He opened a window and inhaled, then shut it with a bang.

"Gal-darn, air is rotten!" he grumbled. His body was heavy with fatigue, but his mind was awake and alert. He hadn't talked that much about himself for a long time, maybe ever. He gave up the idea of a good night's sleep and stepped into the shower and let the hot water pierce his tired muscles. For once, his wife had done something right and sent along a bag with clean clothes and a toothbrush. He might as well go back to the hospital; after all if Conners woke up he wouldn't care if it was the middle of the night. He'd had enough sleep already.

The lights in the hospital hallways were low and nurses sat at desks huddled in sweaters, intent on paperwork. The guard at the door to 607 sat sleepily paging through a magazine.

"Anything new?" Gil asked. After a negative response from him, Gil stepped into the silent room.

"Well by God, I can see you need some more of my stories to liven you up." Gil settled in the same chair he'd spent hours in earlier and began to regale Reed with anything that came to mind. After a time, he wound up with the case again.

"Conners," he said, "years ago, when I was on the force in town here, I knew of this Carmen Ciem you've been investigating. She was alone with two kids. I'd see her with an older lady now and then." Gil scratched his chin, brushed at his mustache and stared off into space. A habit, his wife said he did just to annoy her.

Then he continued, "I've been thinking my Jane Doe could be the same woman. She didn't look like she was from around here. All her clothes were light weight summer, and her skin was lined and parched like she'd spent a lot of time in the south. And from the looks of things, it appears like she was being kept against her will. You had a suspicious death here, and now I've got one. What do you make of it?" Gil got up and walked around the room, stopped and peered closely at Reed.

"Conners, gal-darn it, open your eyes and let's get cracking. You can't just lay there; you're under suspicion for hoisting your client's rocks! You've got to defend yourself!"

Gil paced around the room, raised the blinds to let in the moonlight. He watched the pigeons lined up on the rooftop across the courtyard as they flew in formation to a nearby power line, sat for a few seconds, and then flew back emitting their soft song. His determination waned as he looked at the quiet man in the hospital bed. After all the things he had told Reed, he felt a close kinship to him. But his shoulders sagged at his inability to bring him out of this deep sleep.

Another cold spell, he supposed as he turned back to the window. His stomach rumbled. He needed food. This time real food, not any more of that hospital rabbit food. He'd go to that restaurant at the corner and have bacon and eggs. Pancakes, too. With butter! For once he'd eat what he wanted. He stood lost in thought imagining the taste of the delicious grease, as footsteps into the room brought his attention back to the moment.

-29-

Lindy gasped as the scene flashed before her eyes, and then sat astonished. The image she'd seen had only lasted for a few seconds, just as the rising morning sun pierced through the receding storm clouds.

She put her fork down carefully on the edge of the plate as her eyes darted around the small diner. After seeing ghosts in the mansion earlier, was she loosing her mind? She felt the color drain from her face as she remembered the time in Dallas when she'd lost her memory and had been hospitalized. Everything had vanished from her mind.

Could something be happening to her again? She sat in a daze at the counter in Reggie's Diner in

Newport, Rhode Island and tried to sort out the bizarre night. First, meeting Shirlee at the piano bar earlier, and her warning that the Ashton mansion was truly haunted. Then her own curiosity about that secret room in the house and breaking in, and finding what appeared to be the ghosts of Anne Ashton and her daughter Lilli involved in a murder scene.

Her hand shook as she lifted the coffee cup to her lips. She took little sips; let the warmth seep down her throat as she recalled the picture she'd just seen. The face and the words had been Reed's. His voice had been faint but she'd clearly heard him say, "Lindy come back. I need you!"

What the hell did that mean? Why did he need her? Why did he need her to come back? She hadn't allowed herself to think of him for awhile. But even in the years she had been happily married, memories of their love affair would surface from time to time. And, those same feelings had emerged again after the death of her husband, when she had been charged with arson and he'd worked to clear her.

Lindy's shoulder's sagged as she sat on the red plastic covered stool. The image had been real and clear as day. She couldn't discount it! This time, he was in some kind of trouble and he needed her!

She shivered as a chill spread down her back. Lord, if she went back it would mean she'd have to face the consequences! Well, maybe it was time. Not one to dwell too long on making a decision, Lindy put her coffee cup down with a clunk.

"That's it then, I'm going back!"

The black man turned from the grill where he was cooking mounds of maple flavored bacon, punctuated the air with the spatula he held and smiled showing brilliant white teeth.

"Good choice, pretty lady. Remember every rain shower gives us a clean slate!" Lindy   stood   up, returned his smile even though a corner of her lip quivered at her declaration. She left the diner and sped back to the Ashton mansion, threw her belongings in suitcases. Leaves crunched under the car tires as she left the estate. Sid would wonder what happened to her, but not for long. She couldn't care less, what had she seen in him anyway?

This time, she would be smarter about carrying all her cash and chancing the possibility of being robbed again like she had been in Dallas. She killed time until her bank opened where she sought out her advisor, told him she had been called out of town and needed traveler's checks. The remainder of her money would be safe right there until later.

As Lindy drove out of the beautiful resort town, cold weather had finally set in. Chilling winds cut through to the bone and she dressed in the warmest clothes she had. A long red turtleneck sweater that came down over her hips, a pair of black slacks and a black curly lamb vest. The dark roots in her hair were starting to show again and somewhere on the road she'd have to find a shop. Maybe she'd even go to red. She smiled as she got in her silver Lexus and set Pal on the seat beside her to keep her company. By now the stuffed dog seemed almost real.

She left the New England coast and headed west. Not sure exactly how to get to Minnesota, but she figured if she traveled in that direction, the roads would eventually lead her there. She did feel relief to be getting away from her bad experiences, then fear jabbed at her belly as she fully realized what she could be getting herself into.

It had been many months since her first house fire and weeks since she'd left Reed's bed and fled back to the south, weeks since she'd pictured herself a housewife with babies clinging to her knees, when he'd talked about them settling down together.

What do you think, big guy, am I going to be sorry? She glanced in the rear-view mirror as she turned and talked to her traveling companion. Her eyes widened at her reflection. My God, she looked ghastly! There were deep vertical lines knifing into her upper lips. Bags puffed under her eyes. Her foot hit the brake and she skidded to a stop off to the side of the highway.

Good Lord, she looked like an old woman. When had this happened, after all she was only forty-four years old. She fumbled in her purse for her compact and the magnified mirror. Remnants of yesterday's makeup and the loss of sleep last night had caused double damage. Cars zoomed by on the highway as she opened her case of make-up.

For God's sake, she had to fix up. She hastily went to work. Intent on applying mascara she jumped as a loud knock echoed on the car window. Her hand slipped smudging her eyelid when she saw a huge uniformed man standing by her car.

"What is the problem?" he asked.

"Huh?" she managed to squeak. A highway patrol! He motioned for her to roll down the window.

"Are you in trouble?" he asked again.

"No, no--," she glanced at the mess of makeup scattered on the car seat. The stuffed dog. What could she say, that she'd scared the hell out of herself when she'd looked in the mirror?

"I got something in my eye and had to stop." She wiped the spot of mascara off her eyelid with a Kleenex.

"Very well Miss, you know this is an emergency lane only, don't you?"

"Yes sir, thank you." Lindy smiled sweetly as he turned and walked back to his patrol car. She scooped the things back into the case and waved at him as he passed her car and left.

"Well mister," she mumbled, "this is an emergency and only a woman could understand!" In the next town, she'd get a manicure, a pedicure, and her hair done. Whatever it took. After all, she deserved it after all the things she had been through. And no matter the future, she had to look good. She drove through the day, through Massachusetts and into New York State, and by evening found a motel. Her body ached from the tension of the day. Her stomach hurt since she hadn't eaten since the middle of night at that diner in Rhode Island. She dropped her suitcases but didn't have the energy to find a restaurant, but she'd seen some machines in the hallway. She found cocoa, crackers and peanut butter, a bag of potato chips and hurried back to her room. As she sat cross-legged on her bed, she ate her dinner.

'Sure wish you could talk," she said through a mouthful of chips to black Pal, who sat slightly tipped on the edge of a chair.

Am I nuts going back? Here I am worn to a frazzle sitting in a hotel somewhere, God knows where, running back to Reed Conners because I saw his face and heard him utter some words in a flash of sunshine? Am I just lonely and wishing for love again? She spread peanut butter on a cracker with a wooden stick that came in the package. A wisp of cold air swept through the room from a nearby window. She shivered, and then tucked the bedspread around her shoulders.

Maybe she'd go into New York City, she'd never been there. And why hadn't she gotten two cups of cocoa to wash down the peanut butter that stuck to the roof of her mouth. Or was it her nerves that made swallowing hard.

What had Reed really meant when he said he needed her? Would he welcome her with open arms? And if he welcomed her back and wanted her to stay would she truly be content this time? After all, she'd gotten used to living as she wanted. Being her own boss. Had been extremely lucky when she'd honestly collected almost another million dollars from the fire that burned the house and antiques that she'd bought from Madam Fitzgerald for a dollar in Savannah, Georgia. For one dollar! She grinned. That seemed like such a long time ago, but had actually been only a few weeks. But what now? She glanced at the phone on the bedside table. She could make a call, simply talk to Reed and find out why he needed her before she traveled any further!

She scraped the last of the peanut butter out of the plastic container and sucked on the stick. Cracker crumbs lay in a puddle on the bed, sprinkled over her bare feet. She'd have to buy some socks, she thought absently.

But where could she call him at? His house was being rebuilt and he could be anywhere. Then she remembered his good friends and neighbors, Joe and Abby, a retired couple who lived next to him at his lake home. She picked up the phone, then dropped it back. Was she nuts? She wet a finger with her tongue and began picking up the crumbs on the spread and put them in her mouth as she contemplated.

Don't be stupid, a little voice rang in her head. What are you getting yourself into? But she had to know now before she traveled any further. She had to find out for sure if that scene had been real and if he really needed her, or if it was only a bizarre figment of her imagination she'd seen through tired eyes!

She reached for the telephone again, gripped it firmly and pushed the button for the long distance operator and got the number in northern Minnesota. Before she had time to reconsider, a woman's voice answered. Her throat closed and not a word came out.

"Hello," the woman said again.

"I'm trying to reach Reed Conners," she managed to say.

"Who's calling?" Static muffled the phone lines. For a moment Lindy was tongue-tied, she'd met Abby when she'd been there earlier, and was sure she wouldn't think favorably of her now. She changed her voice and said, "I used to do secretarial work for Reed for years before he moved."

"I see, and where was that?" The woman waited and wariness edged her voice. Lindy cringed. All she wanted was his phone number. "High Landing," she said. "My husband and I lived on the next ranch." She picked another crumb off her sweater as the fib rolled over her lips.

"I see, I guess it's all right then." The woman's voice broke for a moment. "There's been an awful accident, and Reed is doing poorly. My husband and I were down to Minneapolis yesterday morning."

Lindy's heart lurched. "He's been hurt?"

"Shot they said; he's in a coma."   Lindy felt the blood drain from her face. "I didn't get your name, please," the woman said, "in case--", but before Abby could finish her sentence Lindy hung up.

She sat on the bed huddled under the bedspread. My lord, it was true, Reed was hurt and in a coma. He could be dying!

With a strangled cry, she reached for the stuffed dog. Now without a doubt, the vision and cry for help from Reed she'd witnessed at the diner was real. She rocked back and forth on the bed holding the dog. Her mind spun. She'd heard or read it somewhere that a dying person could send a message. Her head began to throb as she tried desperately to remember. What had it been called? Telepathy, astral projection? Something like that. Something about sending a message through unnatural channels. She rocked and hugged the toy. It was true then, Reed was in desperate trouble and he needed her! She had no choice, regardless of the implications she had to go to him.

She grabbed her things and left the motel even though she hadn't gotten any rest. January winds swept snow over the highways and howled through the vents of Lindy's silver Lexus as she sped through the states, only stopping to sleep a few hours, shower and eat. Pennsylvania, Ohio, the tangled traffic in Chicago, and then the high snow banks bordering the roads in Wisconsin. At last, after almost three days on the road and in the middle of the night, Lindy arrived in Minneapolis. She found a place to stay and a phone book. She'd check every hospital in the city until she found Reed. On the fourth call an operator said, "Yes, they had a patient by the name of Reed Conners registered."

"How is he?" Lindy's voice faltered. Oh Lord, was she too late?

"Are you family?" the impersonal voice asked.

"No, but I'm--,"

"I'm sorry, that's the rule," but then the woman added solicitously, "he's holding his own."

Lindy put the phone down. Reed was still alive!

-30-

Lindy opened the door to Reed's room in the hospital trauma center and slipped in. She leaned against the frame and took a deep breath. It hadn't been easy to get in at this time of night. After being told only family was allowed, she'd dodged nurses and finally, when the guard left his post at the door for a moment, she'd had her chance. She gasped at the immense amount of machines attached to him that hummed and flashed and tiptoed to the bed, then drew in her breath sharply at his appearance, the man she'd left only a short time ago. His muscular body seemed smaller and his face, ashen. His hands lay still at his sides.

Tears ran down her face unchecked and she wiped them away with the back of her hand. Suddenly, all the pent-up tension of the last days came crashing down on her as she realized the severity of his condition. She began to cry, unaware of the man who stood quietly at the window in the shadowed corner of the room until he cleared his throat. She jumped in alarm and turned towards him.

"I'm Gil Finney," he said.

Her eyes widened at his uniform, then saw his gun and holster lying on the bedside table. She wanted to run.

"Is he going to die?" She finally managed to ask after a moment.

"Not if I can help it!" Gil stepped closer and peered into Reed's pale face. "There's been no change so that's good in a way. I didn't get your name." Gil looked at her expectantly. Warily, Lindy drew in her breath as she groped for an answer. Well, this was it.

"Lindy Lewis," she said and looked him in the eye.

Gil came over and stood by the side of Reed's bed protectively. "Who are you, Miss Lewis?"

Lindy gulped. "I'm an old friend. I just heard of his accident and came right away."

"I'd like to see your identification, please." Gil eyed her suspiciously. Lindy dug in her purse and gave him her driver's license. She drew in her breath to steady her nerves, knowing it was too late to turn back now.

"What's your connection with Reed Conners?" Gil stroked his mustache after he'd fired off the question.

Lindy wiped her eyes. "We were close in college. In love we thought. I met him several times lately and he helped me with a legal matter."

"How did you get past the guard?"

"A guard? I didn't see anyone." Lindy turned innocent eyes towards him.

"I'm warning him to keep an eye on you. I've got to leave for a few minutes. Talk to this guy, I think he can hear." Gil went out the door and the guard came in.

Lindy perched on the edge of a chair by Reed's bed and took his hand. Not knowing what to say, she studied the strong fingers that had smoothed her hair, stroked her body. She gently lifted his hand to her cheek.

"Reed," she whispered, "I got here as soon as I could. Can you hear me?" She sat in anticipation, waiting for his response. Would he be happy to see her? Minutes went by. "Reed, you've just got to wake up," she said He'd always been there when she needed him. How could she manage without him if something happened? He was the only one who understood her!

"Oh God, I'm sorry, I'm being selfish," she whispered and put her head down on the bed. Tears slipped from her tired eyes again as she clasped his hand. After a time, she fell into an exhausted sleep, her body bent over in the hard chair.

She awoke later as Gil Finney clasped her shoulder, called her name and said, "Miss Lewis, why don't you go and get some rest."

Lindy lifted bleary eyes to the uniformed man. "But I can't." she said, "I need to stay here."

Gil eyed her kindly. "I plan to stay right here, but you look like you could stand some sleep." His concern touched her.

"Well, maybe for just a few hours then!"

The sun was just beginning to brim over the horizon as she ran to her Lexus clutching her skimpy jacket, her bare feet frozen in backless sandals. She shivered as she turned the heat on and wondered when she'd have time to find a store to buy a coat and some warm woolly socks for this awful weather. Back at her motel room she crawled into bed, clothes and all, and slept soundlessly. She awoke hours later with a start.

Where the hell was she? Then remembered she was in Minneapolis and why she had come back. Running a shaky hand through her blond hair she groped for her watch. Oh Lord, it was late in the afternoon! She hurriedly showered and dressed, and within minutes, spun her car through downtown and to the hospital. Gil Finney was still sitting at the side of the bed talking to Reed, and he lay just as she had left him, but now his hair had been brushed and his face shaven. She leaned over and searched his face, then straightened and turned to Gil.

"Is there any change?" she asked anxiously.

"Nah," Gil answered and stood up, "He seems the same. Sit here," he said and got out of the one easy chair in the room. He went to the door and motioned to the guard just outside. "Talk to him Miss Lewis, I'll be back," he nodded his head and left.

Lindy stood hesitantly by Reed's bed, then bent over and touched his lips with hers. "Reed I'm here," she whispered then took his hand and sat down. "You've got to wake up and I'm going to stay right here until you do." She fussed with his blankets and then began to talk. "I'm so sorry I left you," she said, "but you see, at the time I just couldn't stay."

She gazed out the window as the sun began to fade in the afternoon sky. Pigeons cooed on the roof tops. The gray feathered birds lineup like a watchful army of protectors. Dozens of eyes seemed to peer intently at her through the window.

"Reed," she began again, "when I got your message I was sitting in a diner out on the east coast and just as clear as day I saw your face and heard you. So, here I am!"

Lindy took a deep breath but still wondered, what exactly had he meant when he'd said "Lindy, come back, I need you!" Had he meant he wanted her back because he still had feelings for her, or because he needed her to help him now in his struggle for his life?

She thought again now of their being together again, pictured them watching a snow storm by a warm fire in a cozy home and maybe, even those little ones later on. And, the longer she thought about a future together with Reed the more determined she became. Yes, this was what she really needed after all. And it would be safe! But first, she would have to make things right so she began to pour out more of her story.

"Reed, even when I was married you were sometimes in my thoughts. And listen to this, for some reason I felt sometime we'd get together again. Remember those years we lived together in college? We shouldn't have let our careers separate us." She picked at a cuticle, noticed a chipped nail, and then glanced out the window again. The damn pigeons were still there staring at her. Momentarily unnerved, she took a deep breath but plunged on, "You know, after my husband died I was terribly stressed. My precious house was falling apart and then I found those awful ants eating and chewing away at it. All I could think off was to burn them!" She shuddered and ran a hand through her hair then whispered, "Well, I did check my insurance papers. But, what else could I do?"

She glanced around the hospital room. She should buy him some flowers. There was nothing in the austere, impersonal place to brighten it up. Still determined to tell Reed everything, she went on, "You know Reed," she said, "my BMW was smashed in a storm, so I had to get a new car. It's a silver Lexus." She smoothed her skirt and fussed with the top. She was wearing one of the smart outfits she'd bought at Armani's in Boston. She looked good except for the dark roots that had grown out of control in her blond hair. She realized too that in her haste, she'd forgotten to wear the silver jewelry that really set of her dress.

"Reed," she began in earnest again, "you're not going to believe my incredible luck. After I left Minnesota I stayed in Savannah,Georgia, and one day I was driving around and ran across a house for sale. Just out of curiosity, I stopped and met the cutest little lady. Her name was Madam Fitsgerald and she sold that house to me for one dollar. One dollar!" Lindy reached for his hand. "Reed, it was so incredible," she said again and remembered the quaint two-storied place. "It was full of antiques, how I loved it!" She saddened but went on. "I only got to live there for a few weeks and it burned too! If it hadn't been for my friend Solly, I would have too." She stiffened as she remembered the horror of the flames, choking on the smoke. "This sweet lady I got the house from said she didn't need the money; she was going to travel with her boyfriend, look up an aunt who lived here in Minneapolis and stop at some casinos, then they were going to check into a nursing home. So, when the house burned, I got all the insurance money. Now I'm going to stay here and this time, I promise I will pay back that money to your company! Reed, can you hear me?" Lindy leaned over the bed and peered into his face.

"He may or may not, Miss Lewis, but I can." Lindy gaped at Gil Finney standing just inside the door. Lord, how long had he been there?　How much had he heard?

Gil walked over and stood on the opposite side of Reed's bed. "How you doing my friend. Listen here, it's Thursday evening, January 20th and we've got a lot of work to do." He took off his cap, and unbuckled his holster and laid it on the floor out of sight. Lindy's heart lurched. He was the Police!　And he must have heard everything!　He turned to Lindy. "Miss Lewis, describe this Madam Fitsgerald?"

"Madam Fitsgerald?" Lindy choked on a breath. Why on earth did he want to know about her?　Nausea threatened again but she managed to say, "She was such a sweet little lady."

"Describe her physical appearance please, Miss Lewis." Gil Finney's ruddy complexion had deepened and his drooping mustache bristled in the glow from the setting sun. He instantly recalled seeing a t-shirt in his Jane Doe's clothes closet that advertised a casino. Could there be a connection?

"Well--," Lindy put a hand over her chest defensively, her eyes widened at his sudden gruff voice. "You mean, how did she look?"

"Yes," Gil answered impatiently.　"I'm not questioning you about your legal problems; I just need to know what this woman looked like."

Lindy relaxed, well if that was all and said, "I think she was in her late seventies, wore her gray hair in a knot on top her head. Had the cutest granny glasses and dressed in Capri's and big shirts."

"You said she mentioned going on a trip?"

Lindy smiled as she remembered. "Yes, she said she was going to travel with her boyfriend. Look up some of his relatives, also an aunt of hers around here in Minneapolis. They were going to some casinos to have fun. And after the attorney had taken care of the legal things, she left in a taxi with her suitcases. Told me everything there was mine!"

"How long ago was that?"

Lindy hesitated. Had she told him too much? But she murmured warily, "Not long, a few months."

Gil was silent and stared off into space.

An automatic light came on just then and brightened the stark room as the sun began to fade into dusk, and suddenly startled speechless, Lindy and Gil gaped at the patient in the hospital bed as he whispered, "Tanner said you held the key to this mystery, Lindy!"

31-

With a startled cry Lindy stared at the man who had lain silent in the hospital bed and exclaimed, "Reed, you're awake!" She moved closer.

"By God, you're right." Gil cleared his throat and smiled.

"Goddamn, you people talk a lot," Reed whispered and his lips twisted in an attempted smile.

"I'll get the Doctor!" Gil said and hurried out the door. Now that Reed was awake, Lindy stood hesitantly, suddenly overcome with uncertainty. She searched his eyes as he surveyed his surroundings then focused on her; stared at her. The door burst open and a nurse hurried to his bedside followed by Gil.

"Hello Mr. Conners, the Doctor is on his way," she said in a business like manner and shooed them towards the door.

"We'll be outside." Gil put a hand on Lindy's elbow and guided her out of the room. "Well, little lady, we did it! We'll wait here and catch the Doc."

They collapsed in overstuffed chairs in a small area just down the hall. Lindy's heart beat furiously in her chest. What would happen now? She crossed her legs, momentarily pleased she'd dressed up, even worn nylons and her best high heels. Although her outfit didn't look as good as it could have without the silver jewelry. She turned her head toward Gil as she realized he was talking to her.

"Seems you're in a bit of trouble, Miss Lewis." Lindy drew in her breath, unsure of what to say. Her underarms were damp and her back muscles tensed, bringing back an old familiar ache. She leaned back into the chair.

"Well," Gil mused, "we'll get our boy on his feet and figure out that puzzle first." He bent down over his abundant belly, placed his hands on his knees, and then turned his gaze on her. "You've been gallivanting around the country on somebody else's money, Miss, well-- it should help that you showed up on your own." He put a hand on Lindy's arm and smiled encouragingly.

She liked him. Almost as soon as Lindy had met Gil, she'd felt a connection. They sat in the small room lost in their own thoughts and finally, after what seemed like hours the Doctor came out of Reed's room. They stood expectantly.

"Well, Mr. Conners has regained consciousness. His wound is healing nicely. I'd say he's out of danger."

Gil blew out a breath. Lindy wiped her eyes on her wrist. "You can go back in, but don't tire him out." With a nod, the Doctor hurried off.

As Lindy and Gil stepped back into room 607, the nurse held a glass of water to Reed's lips, encouraging him to drink and then adjusted his pillows.

"Don't tire him out," she repeated echoing the Doctor's warning. They stepped closer to Reed's bedside. Lindy's lips trembled in an uncertain smile. Gill ah-hemmed gruffly.

"I've got some phone calls to make, and seems to me you two have some talking to do." Lindy watched Gil Finney leave, suddenly alone with the weight of her actions, facing the man she'd run from. She took a deep breath. Reed tried to sit up, then winced and fell back.

"Goddamn," he muttered.

"Reed what happened? This is the second time you've been shot!" He exhaled weakly and then closed his eyes. Lindy touched his cheek, held his hand for a moment and sat down in a nearby chair. A dark shadow passed outside in front of the window and as she glanced out, the pigeons settled down on the rooftops again and began their soft lullaby with their eyes riveted on room 607.

Lord, now they were watching her too! Maybe she had told Reed too much, especially about that first fire that took her beautiful house here in Minnesota. She sat by his bedside as thoughts scurried though her head. He stirred then and opened his eyes.

"Lindy," he beckoned raising a hand. "Take Finney with you and go see Murphy downtown." His hand dropped to the covers. "Tell him everything about that fire. He's a good man and he'll figure things out!" The exertion caused him to close his eyes again.

Lindy tiptoed out of the room. "He's asleep," she said to Gil who was waiting and went on, "Mr. Finney, I want to talk to you, but could we get something to eat?"

"I was thinking the same thing. There's a place a few blocks from here. We'll take my car."

"But mine--."

"It'll be fine here." Gil Finney reassured her.

For a moment Lindy felt a stab of uneasiness as she stepped into the official vehicle. Another as they were seated in the restaurant facing each other. Her stomach rumbled and a wave of nerves washed over her. The place bustled with early evening diners.

"You look like you could use a big juicy steak, Miss Lewis. Gal-darn, you're not one of those women who live on lettuce, are you?" His eyes twinkled at her. Lindy gulped her water as he ordered for them both. Then Gil began to make small talk.

"How do folks live in this noisy town? I used to be on the force here, but then it was another time. Now there's too many people and cars!" He loaded his coffee with cream and sugar.

Lindy had been raised in the country on a farm, and although she'd lived in a quiet suburb after she married, she loved the bustle of large cities, the excitement of shopping in up-scale stores and the glamour of the best hotels. In her career days, she'd traveled through most of the large cities in the US.

Gil stirred his coffee thoughtfully and slurped a swallow. "I left this sprawling hell-hole years ago and live just far enough away."

"Do you mind if I smoke?" Lindy asked then.

"Fine with me, I have a cigar once in a while when my wife isn't around."

"You're married?" Lindy searched her purse and busied herself lighting her cigarette. Her hands trembled.

"Yep. That woman runs my life." He chuckled. "Well, she thinks she does and that makes her happy." Lindy sat leaning her chin on one hand as he talked, still wary, and soon the waiter brought their food. "Now dig in, you need to put some meat on your bones," Gill said, salt flying from the shaker as he covered his steak. Then he lavished butter and sour cream on a baked potato.

"I guess I haven't eaten much lately. I didn't want to lose travel time after I saw Reed and he asked me to come back." Lindy buttered a roll.

Gil's head snapped up. "You saw him and talked to him?"

"Yes--, no, not really." Lindy bit into the bread.

"What do you mean?" Gil eyes bore into hers. "Yes or no!"

"Well not exactly."   Lindy answered through a mouthful. Well, she might as well tell Gil everything. She chewed and swallowed, "I was sitting in an all-night diner out on the east coast and after a bizarre night and a bad storm, just as the sun came up, I saw his face in a flash of sunshine!"

"The hell you say!" Gil started to laugh then, but caught himself and sobered. He put his fork down and took a loud slurp of his coffee instead.

"I know it sounds weird, but I really did!" Lindy chewed another piece of steak. "It was real!   You know, I think its called mental-telepathy."

"Ahh--," Gil eyed her curiously. "What did he say?"

"He said, Lindy, come back I need you!"

"I see."

"He looked and sounded desperate!" Lindy leaned closer. "You see, he has been there for me a few times when I needed help and now he was in trouble!"

Gil took the last bite of his steak and wiped his plate clean with a piece of bread. Then he sat back and lit up a cigar. A cloud of blue smoke enveloped his head. "Well, all right now, why don't you start at the beginning Miss Lewis, what's this all about?"

Lindy's full stomach started to revolt. Gil reached over and touched her hand. "Maybe I can help; you don't look like a hardened criminal to me." He smiled kindly.

Stalling for time, Lindy reached for her purse, took out a compact and lipstick and intently lined her lips. She studied the lines that cut through her upper lip. With a resigned sigh she began her story.

"It was those darn ants. I remembered my Dad saying, 'you got to burn them!' He was always fighting those critters. They ate our fences. Got in the barn, and it finally fell down!"

"Ahh, hmm-." Gil blew out another cloud of smoke from the cigar he was enjoying after his dinner.

"So you see, I had no choice, I had to get rid of them!" And Lindy told Gil her story, only stopping as the waiter cleared the table and replenished their coffee. It felt good to unburden herself. Gil Finney was her friend, and Reed's, she reaffirmed herself. "So, when Reed pleaded with me to come back, I had to. He needed me! And since I hadn't returned the million dollars that the judge ordered when Reed cleared me of that mess, I'm probably considered a fugitive now!"

Gill nodded in thought. "Well, just hang in there. If this Jane Doe I have in the morgue checks out to be this Fitsgerald woman you met, this is very important to Reed's case."

"She's dead?" Lindy gaped at him.

"We're checking it out."

"She was so nice." Lindy repeated the circumstance of their brief meeting and the astounding results as Madam Fitsgerald had handed her keys to her home and all its contents. "She was so happy that day as she left to meet her boyfriend. What happened?"

"Too soon to tell. But when Reed gets better he'll sort it out." Lindy turned wary eyes to Gil.

"Reed told me to have you go with and see this Murphy at the Police station. Apparently I'm in double trouble now and that he would know what to do for me."

Gil was silent, and then bent over the table towards her. "Here's what we're going to do. I know this Murphy down at the department too, talked to him earlier. He's been working with Reed on a case. I'll give him a call."

"Tonight?" Lindy's face paled.

"We might as well get started." Gil took out his cell.

"But it's late! We could go tomorrow."

"Nah, Murphy said he'd be at his desk late tonight."

"But--," Lindy stammered.

"Ah, it won't be so bad being you're going to turn yourself in." Gil laid some bills on the table as he punched in some numbers on his phone.

Suddenly, all Lindy's good intentions vanished leaving her totally unnerved. She looked frantically towards the door, measured the steps and wondered, was there still time?

-32-

"Miss Lewis, do you really want to do that?"

Lindy turned to Gil with a sheepish look on her face when she realized he must have read her thoughts to run like hell from the restaurant and not turn herself in to the authorities.

"I thought you wanted to straighten things out with the police and the insurance company," he said. As he talked he adjusted his belt over his ample mid-section.

Lindy hesitated uncertain now, "I guess," she finally whispered, "I'm pretty scared though."

"Well, I can imagine, but I'll do what I can to help."

"You're being awfully nice to me, Mr. Finney. You don't even know me."

"Well," Gil ran a hand through his bushy mustache. With a faraway look in his eyes he mumbled, "Something about you and Reed reminds me of things, --long ago. Come on, let's get this over with!" He stood up and waited for Lindy to gather her things. "I know this Murphy Reed wants you to see. He seems like a good guy."

"But what about my car? Can you give me a ride back here later then?"

"Oh sure, but I'll call security too and tell them to keep an eye on it." They left the restaurant and drove downtown and Gil made his calls. Even though it was ten o'clock at night, the traffic was backed up, he grumbled, "Just our luck, looks like a hockey game just got over with."

Lindy's stomach churned as they waited for pedestrians to cross streets, cars and buses to edge their way along. She forced herself to take slow breaths. They finally parked by a large brick building and Gil guided her through the long hallways. Her high heels clicked on the polished tiles as they walked and finally stopped at an entrance that led into the Minneapolis Police Department.

"Here we are," Gil said as they stepped into a huge room filled with uniformed men and women. Even though it was late at night phones rang and people jostled. He held her arm as they threaded their way through a maze of desks and finally stopped in front of a separate cubicle.

"Murphy," Gil extended his hand, "thanks for seeing us."

"Mr. Finney, have a seat." They shook and Murphy indicated some straight back chairs. "Thanks for your call, glad to hear Conners came around."

Gil and Lindy sat down and faced him. "This is Miss Lewis." Gil Finney put a hand on Lindy's arm. "Now she met a woman that could have a connection with the Ciem case. Could be the Jane Doe I have in the morgue."

Murphy nodded at her. "Thanks for coming in," he said.

Gil cleared his throat and put his cap on his knee. "Also, it seems she's got herself in a bit of trouble. Go ahead, Miss Lewis tell him what you told me."

Lindy cringed at Murphy's inspection of her as he eyed her up and down. Her stomach threatened in earnest. Her face paled as she sagged further in her chair.

"I don't know--," she whispered. She looked at Gil helplessly.

"Go ahead, Miss Lewis, tell him about the ants," he urged.

Lindy clasped her arms protectively across her chest and swallowed hard. Lord was she nuts, sitting here in the Police Department!

"Well," she began, hesitating, "I had this beautiful house and I saw cracks in the walls and in the ceilings. Then when I looked up in the attic, it was full of carpenter ants!" She shivered at the memory and went on, "I had to get rid of them!" Murphy sat listening and occasionally tapped on his computer and Lindy talked for almost an hour. Her throat was parched, and her heart thundered in her chest when she finally finished her story.

"Okay Miss Lewis. Thank you." Murphy's chair scraped across the tiled floor as he stood up and motioned to Gil, "Would you take Miss Lewis to the next room, I'll need to do some paperwork first, then I'll get back to you. There's a coffee machine in there."

Lindy searched Murphy's face for some sign as she stood on wobbly legs and followed Gil, who patted her arm again. They settled in a small stuffy room with only some ragged magazines to read.

"I'm sure things will be just fine," Gil reaffirmed her time after time, "It takes time to finish all the red tape with that paperwork." But after several hours of waiting, they settled into just looking at the walls. Then suddenly the door burst open.

"You can't do this, it's my case!" Murphy yelled as two men dressed in suits, walked directly over to Lindy and said, "You're under arrest, Miss Lewis!"

Lindy jumped to her feet and suddenly found herself handcuffed, heard one of them mumble something about her rights.

"Hey, wait a minute," Murphy said, "I call the shots here!"

"Sorry we've got a warrant for the arrest of Miss Lewis."

Stone-faced Murphy asked. "On what charge?"

"We're FBI!" Apparently that was supposed to explain everything.

With the two men at her side, Lindy was rushed from the room. Her legs seemed to move automatically as she was led through another maze of rooms and hallways. Her mind was numb as she was photographed and fingerprinted. Hours later, as she heard the lock snap into place on the metal door that locked her in a jail cell, she realized her worst fear. Not only was she wanted for fraud, now she was charged with murder!

This time she couldn't get away!

-33-

Reed sat up in the hospital bed after Lindy and Gil Finney left. The room tilted and then straightened. He punched the call button.

"Would you get the Doctor?" he asked as a nurse came rushing in. He swung his legs over the edge of the bed and stood up just as the Doctor came in. "I need to get out of here," he said clutching the bedside for support.

"Mr. Conners, you've just been though a serious trauma. We've got to do some tests!"

"I don't have time." Reed said impatiently.

"You've got to take time. Mr. Conners, you've been in a coma for Gods sake. Now the bullet wound is healing nicely. But you have to rest!" The Doctor shook his head and closed his chart. "We'll see in a day or two."

"Goddamn," Reed muttered and felt a cold sweat break out as he lay down. He grimaced in pain. His mind was a jumble of questions. Then against his will, he fell asleep. He awoke later as a dinner tray was slid onto his bedside table, and he looked on hungrily as a nurse uncovered the bowls. "Chicken broth, Jell-O, and juice," she said.

"That's it?" Reed asked.

"Sorry, maybe you'll get something better tomorrow." She smiled solicitously.

As Reed was grousing, all the events came back clearly. This Gil Finney had said it was January 20th. That meant he'd lain there for five days. And where did this Finney come from? He'd had some stories to tell. And what had happened after he'd told Lindy to go downtown to see Murphy? When was that?

What the hell was going on? Who had shot him after he'd found Carmen Ciem's jewelry in the locker in the airport, and why was there a cop outside his door?

He grudgingly drank his meal, then collapsed back against his pillows and closed his eyes. He remembered seeing Tanner. He swallowed a lump of uneasiness as he realized that must mean he'd been close to cashing in!

His room was strangely quiet now. Even though he'd been somewhere between heaven and earth, he'd been aware of machines humming and clicking. Now all he heard was a bunch of pigeons squawking on the telephone wire outside as the sun began to go down. He sat up as Murphy and Gil Finney came in.

"It's about time you decided to rejoin the human race," Murphy said as he walked towards Reed's bed and put a hand on his arm. "Seriously buddy, you had me worried." Gil stood off to the side, a smile plastered on his face.

"Yeah well, I'm worried now!" Reed motioned towards the door. "What the hell is that cop doing out there?"

"Well, I had no choice; we found you shot up with a bag of jewels, man! It was for your protection too."

Pissed, Reed threw back the bed covers. "I'm under suspicion?"

"Relax Reed, standard procedure. I got rid of him but I need to know what happened!"

Reed's pale face turned even whiter. "You mean to say you think I was on the run with those stones?"

Murphy shook his head. "It didn't look good, my friend."

"Goddamn!" Reed swiped a hand over his face, exhaled loudly. "I found a key in Tony Roman's possessions. Traced it to a locker at the airport. I found a bag of what I believe was Carmen Ciem's jewelry and I was on my way in to the department. All I remember is sitting at a stoplight."

"Did you see anyone following you?"

"Nope. Nothing!"

Murphy eyed Reed. "You didn't break into the Ciem house did you?"

"Me?" Reed's lips tightened into a weak smile.

"I hope not." Murphy studied Reed's face then added, "I don't want to know." "There must have been a fortune in that bag. Where's it now?" Reed asked curiously.

"Safely locked away," Murphy said, then added," A good Samaritan saw you hit the wall, called it in on his cell phone and stayed with you until help got there. My guess is whoever was after you didn't dare stop and grab the bag of jewels."

Reed exhaled a ragged breath. "I don't believe this. Where the hell is my car?"

"Downtown. It's being checked out."

"How bad was it smashed?" Next to his house up north, Reed treasured his Corvette.

"Pretty bad! Do you want me to call Rudy's for you and have them start putting it back together? He's the best in the city."

Reed sat up on the edge of the bed. "Yeah, I know him. Okay, thanks." He nodded at Gil. "You took Lindy downtown last night?"

"Yup." Gil's face was downcast. Reed looked at Murphy expectantly.

"Well, how'd it go, can you straighten out that mess she's in again?"

Murphy shifted his weight. He shook his head. "Buddy, it's out of my hands!" Reed dropped back down to his pillow. "What do you mean it's out of your hands?"

"I mean," Murphy's face turned livid, "the Feds came in and arrested her and she's sitting in a cell. I've been at it for hours."

Reed's face paled as he stared at Murphy who said, "They've arrested her for a murder down in Hilton Head, South Carolina, and they are pretty interested again in that million dollar insurance case of yours."

Reed exhaled. "What's going on?"

"I don't know the details yet, but by God, I'll find out!" Murphy walked towards the door. "Take it easy buddy, I'll keep in touch." He nodded at Gil. "I should get the results of those fingerprints of your Jane Doe soon."

After Murphy left, Reed turned to Gil. "Finney, what the hell happened down there last night?" His jaw tightened.

Gil harrumphed, "Well, Miss Lewis talked to Murphy, he told us to wait while he made some calls, and then those two men came in and arrested her!"

Reed was silent. If the FBI was involved that meant real trouble. He punched the mattress, then winched. What the hell was going on now? His mind raced but he turned his attention to Gil and asked curiously, "You've been here for days, Finney, who the hell are you?"

Gil hoisted his suspenders. "Well--, I remembered you from back in your college days and it looked like

you needed some help. I remember Tanner Burke too."
Gil looked out into space and drifted for a moment,
then shook his head. "I heard about him catching that
bullet in the Thomas case."

Reed was silent as Gil went on. "When Miss Lewis
told me about her troubles, and mentioned that
Fitsgerald woman, I remembered reading about this
Carmen Ciem case you're working on. You see I ran
across her name in my Jane Doe's papers. There could
be a connection."

"Yeah?"   Reed lay back against the pillows.

Gil got up off the creaky chair. "Well, I've got to
make some calls. I'll be back." He clamped his cap
firmly on his head.

After Gil left, Reed's mind raced. Had he been a
complete fool to believe Lindy when she had said she
had clearly seen Mario D'Agustino kill that man out on
that boat?   No, he didn't think so. Regardless, she
didn't have a chance in hell up against the Federal
agents!

He struggled to get out of bed, steadied himself
against a wall. His legs felt like rubber as he sank into a
chair. He sat for a minute then forced himself to walk
to the closet for his clothes. His trousers hung next to
his jacket. No shirt. They'd probably thrown it away.
"Covered with blood," he mumbled as he stuffed the
hospital gown in his pants. He cringed as he tried to
bend over to put on socks, then tossed them aside and
slid his bare feet into his loafers.

No one paid any attention to him as he walked out of his room amidst the evening visiting hours and got into an elevator. On shaky legs, he stepped out an exit door and faced the brittle January wind.

Where in the hell were the taxicabs when you needed one? Up ahead a restaurant sign beckoned, just two blocks away. He pulled the collar up on his brown leather jacket and found his gloves in the pockets. Pain shot down his neck around the shoulder wound. He walked slowly, unsteadily, hoping no one would report a drunk on the street. The two blocks looked like two miles. When he got to the cafe he stumbled to a stool and gave a waitress some bills and asked her to find a taxi for him.

Back at his motel, he ordered a rental car and changed clothes, only sitting down when he felt the room began spin. Finally arriving at the jail, he clenched his teeth against the pain in his shoulder and said, "I'm an attorney, I want to see Lindy Lewis!"

-34-

Lindy sank down on the narrow cot in the jail cell. Her worst nightmare had come true! She'd been a fool to let her heart direct her actions after seeing Reed in that stupid vision, when he said he needed her and she had rushed back to Minneapolis. Then, taking his advice to see Murphy at the Police Department and that Murphy could get those bothersome fraud charges against her straightened out for good this time. She had told Murphy she had could pay the damn insurance company back their million dollars. But suddenly she'd been arrested for murder and tossed behind bars instead!

She touched the rough gray blanket, eyed the stale smelling flat pillow. My God she couldn't lay down on these awful bed clothes where all kinds of strangers had slept on them. She glanced at the floor and drew her feet up off the dingy concrete. She wasn't a real criminal. She was well dressed, well traveled, not like these low-life's that had spent time in here.

"Hey Blondie, what you in for?" a voice rasped. Lindy turned her gaze to the next cell where an African American woman lay sprawled on the cot. She didn't answer and averted her eyes. Pretended to be miles away, deep in thought. Good lord, a common criminal expecting conversation with her?

"Hey, you too good for this?" The black woman sat up and glared at her. "What's the matter, were you on the wrong street corner?"

Lindy sucked in her breath, put her arms around her chest and rocked back and forth and ignored her.

It seemed like days since she'd left Reed's hospital room, since she'd had dinner with Gil Finney. The jail was dimly lit with no windows or clocks anywhere. A cold draft swirled around on the floor. Lindy sat huddled and forlorn. A chill started between her shoulder blades, spread down her arms and body. She was tired, frightened and alone. Terribly alone.

She could be sitting somewhere in the sunny south on a beach by the ocean instead of this God-awful place. She wrinkled her nose, but finally took the blanket and wrapped it around herself as a foreboding began to chill her. She perched on the narrow hard bed and glanced around the darkened space, heard occasional groans and snoring vibrating through the bars. Her eyes were heavy and her body ached and finally she sagged down onto the cot and laid her head on the dingy pillow. She was beside herself with anxiety, but angry at herself for walking right into this nightmare. She huddled under the blanket and gave into the raw edge of hopelessness that blackened her senses and finally fell into an exhausted sleep.

Suddenly, in the twilight of a dream, a scene flashed through her thoughts. This time, the scattered bits and pieces she'd formerly seen and tried to figure out, paraded through her mind like a camera filming a rolling action scene; a seemingly familiar- looking woman stood by a railed balcony terrified, as a gray haired woman in a black uniform pointed a gun at her. And to Lindy's dismay, the cute little Madam Fitsgerald, whom she had gotten the house from in Savannah lay on the floor with her hands bound and her mouth taped. Lindy's eyes were riveted on the scene.

'"Hilda, no, you'll never get away with this,"' she heard the lady at the railing plead as she clutched a robe around herself. Now Lindy placed the identity of the threatened woman. She was the matriarch of that well- known world-wide cosmetic company. Carmen Ciem!

The sky was dark, with just a few brittle stars shining on the third floor balcony as Lindy watched the attacker in the black uniform hold the gun to

Carmen Ciem's head, force her to climb to the top of the railing. Then watched her wrestle for her life with the uniformed woman and finally was pushed over. Lindy gasped in her sleep.

"No--," she cried out, but everything had disappeared leaving only that same odor of ashes hovering in the air. She lay suspended in horror and confusion. Then awoke abruptly and sat up. She rubbed her eyes. Swallowed a sob.

What was happening to her? First, she'd seen ghosts in the Ashton mansion, then Reed's face and heard his plea to her to hurry back after that storm in Rhode Island, and now a stranger who had Madam Fitsgerald bound and gagged. And a woman who was pushed over a balcony to her death!

Lindy took a rasping breath and tried to calm her hysterical thoughts and focus on something real. Then keys jangled in the door and a uniformed guard said, "someone wants to see you."

Lord, now she remembered; she was behind bars, locked in a cell. She needed help!

She followed the guard to a room and was told to sit and wait. Surely they were going to release her. She fluffed her hair and straightened her dress.

The room was small and held a scarred table and two chairs. Again there were no windows, only a solid door and ugly green walls. Minutes went by, the silence only broken as footsteps passed outside the door. Lindy sat on a metal chair and tried to take small calming breaths to still nerves that suddenly began to jump in her chest. Just then keys jangled again and two men walked in. The same men who had handcuffed her earlier in the night! They were clad in severe blue suits with stern cold faces.

"Miss Lewis," the shorter of the two said, "my name is John Henry, and this is my partner Charles McGovern. We're FBI!"

Lindy stared at them.

John Henry went on, "You might as well make it easier on yourself and confess. We matched your prints with the ones we found in that yacht down in South Carolina. We've also got the gun you used to kill a man and your prints matched!"

The blood drained from Lindy's face. Agent John Henry continued with a sly look on his face. "We've been keeping an eye on you, Miss Lewis. We know about your house fire here in Minnesota, and the arson and fraud charge and your travels around the country. We also know about the second fire in Savannah, Georgia. We don't think you're innocent of that one either!"

Lindy's heart thumped in her chest. The room started to spin and turn black. She put her hands out to the edge of the table to steady herself. For Gods sake, they thought she had shot that man on Mario's damn yacht? Well, she might be guilty of some things, but not that! She'd clearly seen Mario shoot him when their boats had met in the night. Had seen Mario push the body into the ocean! Just lucky she'd clunked Mario over the head and gotten away or she'd have been in the water too.

But, Reed had cleared up her involvement weeks ago! This was getting worse by the minute and the extent of her predicament finally sank in.

Reed had set her up! She put a hand on her pounding forehead. This was too much for her brain to absorb. The visions, the nightmares, and now being imprisoned by the FBI. Her dulled attention swung to John Henry as he said, "Miss Lewis, the man you killed was an FBI agent!"

The room was silent as they let that sink in. Lindy's face paled as she remembered meeting that man in a restaurant in South Carolina, then realizing that he was following her, recognizing him when Mario had shot him. The pieces finally began to fall into place; they suspected her of being in the drug business with the D'Agustino brothers, and good Lord, they thought she had killed their agent!

"I want to call an attorney," she finally said, totally frazzled from the man's onslaught of threats.

"We know you killed our man Miss Lewis, and we found D'Agustino tied up in a stateroom. We figure you were going to make a big drug deal with Mario and his brother, but when our agent turned up and interrupted you, you shot him!" The ropey veins in John Henry's neck stood out as he leaned over. She turned away from his bad breath as he continued his tirade. "We know you knocked D'Agustino out and took the drugs. How much did you make on the street for them, a million? Two?" He continued to bark at her.

Lindy struggled to swallow over a lump of hysteria rising in her throat. The man wouldn't give her a minute to think. This went on hour after hour into the night as she was herded from room to room somewhere deep in the department, totally confusing her.

"Did you make enough on those drugs to keep up your lifestyle? Well, kiss it good-by, Miss Lewis, you'll never see it!" With a cunning look on his face, Agent John Henry said, "you're going to prison for a long, long time!"

35-

"Are you sure Miss Lewis got my message?" Reed asked impatiently as he waited in the lobby outside the jail. "It's been almost an hour, would you please call again?" He put a hand to his feverish head. He felt like hell.

The clerk spoke into the phone, and then hung up. "They say she's tied up."

"With what?" Reed asked curiously.

"Don't know." The man avoided Reed's eyes and shifted papers on his desk.

"Well, try again!"

"They got the message, Mr. Conners." The man got up and walked out of the room. Reed ran a hand over his clammy forehead. Was Lindy talking to the

Feds? Did she have enough sense to keep her mouth shut and demand an attorney? Reed glanced at his watch again. It was getting late. His stomach growled for real food as he retraced his steps back and forth across the worn linoleum.

Goddamn, his head hurt. He probably should have stayed in the hospital for another day, but what the hell could he do? After telling Lindy to turn herself in to Murphy and that he could straighten out the new charges against her, when the FBI had come into the picture that changed the scene drastically. He stopped his pacing as the clerk came back into the room and motioned him over.

"Mr. Conners, it seems we can't locate Miss Lewis."

"What do you mean, you can't locate her," Reed demanded, an impatient glare in his eyes.

"Just what I said, the guard got orders to take her to one of the conference rooms. She's not there, or in her cell."

"Well, I'm sure she hasn't broken out," Reed said sarcastically. "Find her!"

"We're checking, Mr. Conners."

Reed dialed Murphy's department on his cell-phone. He picked up on the first ring. "Murphy? Conners, what the hell is going on? Where's Lewis?"

"Christ, man," Murphy exhaled, "the chief has had me out on the streets and all I've got so far is that she's indisposed."

Reed kicked a chair, "What the hell does that mean?"

"My friend, it could mean the Feds are having a field day."

Reed's foot connected with the chair again and sent it screeching across the floor.

Murphy continued, "I know how those assholes work, they can run her around anywhere they want to in here to give themselves time."

"They can't do that. I'll tear this place apart," Reed shouted.

"Slow down Conners, you know they can and they will!"

"It's against the law; they can't bulldoze their way in here and take over."

"Sit tight. They'll come up for air soon," Murphy assured him. "Christ, I'm sorry man; it looked like your insurance company was going to take my offer. They were pissed, but how often do they get their money back? Then all hell broke out when the Feds entered the picture. How the hell they found out she was in my office, I don't know, but by God I intend to find out!"

Reed sucked in a breath and groaned as pain shot down his side.

Curiously Murphy asked, "Buddy, the hospital sprung you pretty fast."

"I left, lost enough time." Reed shuddered now as chills spread over his back.

"Jesus, that doesn't sound too smart!"

"Yeah?" Reed muttered.

"My phone is lit up like a Christmas tree. Don't worry, I'm on it."

Reed disconnected and put the phone in his pocket. He got to his feet and went back to the clerk at the desk. "Okay, you got ten minutes to find Lewis, if you don't I'm going to find myself a judge!"

-36-

"**Y**ou're in big trouble Miss Lewis!" Agent John Henry, the FBI man sitting across the table from her snarled.

Lindy slumped down in the hard metal chair and stared at the two men through dazed eyes. Their cold aggressive manner terrorized her. She'd hardly comprehended their words earlier when they'd arrested and handcuffed her, and read her her rights.

Who could she call to help her? For sure not Reed or Gil Finney. The two of them must have been together in this scheme to sabotage her. She swallowed over a sob as Agent Henry hurled accusations at her.

"Tell us how you burned your house; the first one. Did you hire a pro? How much did it cost? Did you play with matches when you were a kid? Have you always been a firebug?" Agent Henry's eyes bore into hers while the other man stood silently by leaning against the wall.

"How did you burn the house in Savannah, did you have an accomplice with that one too?"

Her eyes were riveted on the Agent as he spoke and saw tiny bits of saliva escape his full lips. Her thoughts became totally disoriented as he hurled charges at her; his hawk-like face became flushed. He was the cruelest looking man she'd seen since John Thomas.

"Were you going to buy more drugs from that insurance check after your second fire? Where's you stash?" The Agent's voice cracked. "We've got you for murder, fraud, arson, drug trafficking, just to name a few charges."

Lindy's heartbeat echoed in her ears. Her throat closed as she tried to gasp for air. Amid the turmoil, one thing remained clear, and that was the loss of Reed's support. Even though she'd treated him shabbily lately, she'd always felt he could be counted on if things got out of hand. Now, apparently, he'd tossed her to the wolves. That hurt. Her heart ached. Ever since college, through her career, even in her marriage, her feelings for him would surface occasionally. She hung her head and closed her eyes and tried to tune out the voice of her captors all the while desperately trying to think of what to do. Who could she call for help now?

"How long did you think you could get away with this? Were you checking out a new scheme on the east coast? What exactly did you and Sid have planned for the Ashton mansion out there? Torch that too?" Agent Henry hurled the questions at her.

Lindy swallowed hard. My God, they knew everything! No wonder she'd felt like someone was always behind her, following her. They had been!

"Where have you got the money hidden, same place as the drugs? What are you doing back here in Minnesota?" The man licked his lips. "What's your next move, Miss Lewis, rob a bank, kill someone?" Agent Henry's fist hit the table. She sank lower into the chair, her body shrinking as his voice barked, tossing more accusations at her. He jumped up from the table suddenly and paced around the room, then sat down again.

"Did you kill your husband? Is that when you started this cunning ploy to get rich? Talk to me Miss Lewis!" His face was distorted in an ugly grin as he growled.

Lindy shrank further as the man barked relentlessly at her, intimidating and stripping her totally of her spirit and her fearlessness. She huddled into herself as it went on and on, hour after hour. She was unaware of time, only the voice was a constant harangue.

"All right, lay off!" The second man who had stood by silently and watched the tactics of his partner yelled, "Get the hell out of here!"

A chair scraped over the floor and then a door slammed.

"I'm sorry Miss Lewis," Agent McGovern said then and came over and sat down on the vacated chair. He took his cell phone out of his pocket and spoke to someone. "Get something nourishing for Miss Lewis to eat. I need it now!"

Lindy straightened and tried to focus on the second man. He was older, had gray streaks in his short hair.

"Miss Lewis, we're not all bad guys. My partner gets carried away at times. Call me Charley." He smiled at Lindy. "I don't think you're all that bad either." He pushed his chair back and reached in his jacket pocket. "Mind if I have a cigarette?" He laid the pack and lighter on the table as he inhaled and blew smoke into the air. The room was suddenly quiet after John Henry left. "Take it easy now," he said and leaned back.

Then a knock echoed on the metal door and a container of food and a plastic cup of coffee were handed in. As the aroma permeated the air, Lindy's stomach growled. She eyed him warily as he opened the carton and laid out a ham sandwich, a pickle. She began to eat, oblivious to the fact that the January moon was waning and the city had been asleep for hours, and the sun was soon to rise. Unaware, that the reason she'd been piloted around the building through out the night was purposely to confuse and refrain her from seeking council.

But suddenly as John Henry had flung that last accusation at her, she became conscious of her situation. She finished eating and felt strength surge through her body. She helped herself to McGovern's pack of cigarettes and took her time lighting and inhaling it. Then she exclaimed, "How dare you accuse me of having a hand in my husband's death!" She spoke adamantly and stared the man down. "I want a lawyer, and my phone call!"

Agent McGovern smiled gently, "I'm sorry for what John Henry said; I know your husband's death was due to a catastrophic illness. Forget my partner, sometimes I can't stand him either, but I'm stuck with him." He blew out a seemingly disgusted breath.

Lindy inhaled the cigarette smoke, grateful for the nicotine as it surged through her veins and calmed her nerves. She studied Charley McGovern; there was something about him that she felt drawn to. His eyes did have a gentle look in them. Contrary to his partner, whose suit and shoes were top quality; this man's clothes were well-worn. His face was round with a deep dimple in his chin. His nails were bitten down to the quick. They could be about the same age, Lindy judged.

She smoked the cigarette and was silent.

"Miss Lewis, it's up to you if you want council, but if you've got nothing to hide, well, I can help you." He straightened his rumpled tie. She thought she saw a ketchup drip on it.

After the cruel harassing she'd been through with Agent John Henry, Charley's voice was gentle, his face kind and his eyes understanding. For God's sake, she was innocent of all those ridiculous charges! And she couldn't trust Reed anymore. She decided to put her faith in Charley McGovern! Even though he was a federal agent for some reason she felt a connection. She was sure he'd believe that she'd been an innocent bystander in the murder they were trying to pin on her. And she'd give the million dollars back to the damn insurance company and she'd move far away!

"Charley, do you promise to help me?" she asked then.

"I promise to do what I can, do you mind if I call you Lindy? " Charley McGovern asked.

She nodded and swallowed hard. "You've got to believe me; I'm innocent!" Her eyes darted to his face as she put a hand to her forehead and massaged the ache. "While I was in Dallas, I lost my memory for a few days and they said it was amnesia. Then, later I began to have nightmares, saw visions, then ghosts!" She pushed a strand of hair off her cheek and sighed.

Charley studied her actions. "I know something about your malaise, Lindy. Do you want to rest for awhile?"

God, she'd love to be back in her motel room and crawl between the covers and sleep. To wake up and be somewhere else! With her friend Mitzi Grover; they'd been having such a good time in Hilton Head until

Mario and his brother came into the picture. She took a breath and then suddenly became aware of her surroundings.

How many rooms had she been in? Two, ten? She had been shuffled doggedly around the building by the two men. The rooms had all been alike; cramped, dingy green walls, scarred table and chairs and no windows. Was it still tonight, or had she lost track of those as well? As she gazed around now in this room, she saw the walls were pink, even though it was a smoky pink. It had carpeting on the floor; a little worn, but at least it covered the cold concrete. Instead of the garish fluorescent lights, this room had small spots in the ceiling.

She realized now things had changed. They'd been playing the "good cop, bad cop" game. She glared at Charley and said, "I know what you two have been doing!"

"I'm sorry for that but listen Lindy, I can help you." Agent McGovern reached in his pocket and took out a recorder and laid it on the table. "We'll tape this, that way we won't have to repeat things, but don't worry Lindy, this is just between you and me."

Lindy forced herself to relax, even though she was bone-tired, emotionally drained, she just wanted it over. "What do you want to know?" she asked.

"Lindy, start at the beginning." Charley smiled at her. "I'm on your side, you can tell me anything!"

"Well," she answered still a little wary, "I worked for a hotel chain for years and traveled for the company."

"Where did you travel to?" Charley asked.

"The southern states mainly." She smiled to herself. "I met my husband and got married. Later on I gave up my career; you see, we bought this house!"

Seeing the sudden anxiety that covered her face then, Charley asked, "What was it about that house?"

She was silent and her eyes took on a far-off look as she remembered that afternoon.

They'd been out driving on a Sunday. It was a lovely spring day and the countryside was alive with budding trees, green grass and a warm sun. A blessed relief after a harsh northern winter. They'd left their small cramped apartment and halfheartedly looked at some newly built houses to buy sometime in the future, only to be left cold by the stark impersonal enclosures. They had just rounded a corner on the highway and had taken a gravel road out of curiosity, when they'd come upon a vista that took their breath away. The sun glinted off a stream that bubbled over rocks leading down from a grove of trees, and nestled in amongst the evergreens was the most wonderful two-storied house. A porch ran around three sides. Granted, it had stood forlorn and drastically in need of paint, shingles and most everything else. A clump of birch trees shaded the front entrance, wildflowers grew everywhere. A rusty, rooster weather-vane stood on the roof and swung in the breeze.

"Stop the car!" Lindy remembered saying excitedly as she had sat up and opened the window to get a better look. They had parked along the roadside and walked up. Her husband had opened the old wooden gate and they'd stood for a minute, awed by the serene setting and the romantic ambience of the place.

"Look at this," her husband had said, and lifted a weed covered sign up for her to see. Her eyes had widened in pleasure as she read, "For Sale." They'd gleefully peeked in windows, tried to open locked doors and finally found a spot in the yard and sat down to gaze at their find. Lindy was brought back to the present as Charley said, "Did you buy the house?"

"We bought it and settled in. I was in heaven. We worked for years redoing everything, room by room. I learned how to remove wallpaper, strip woodwork, take up floors and scrub decades of grime. We painted it white with black trim. I had flower gardens and lovely trees." She stopped talking and her shoulders sagged.

"Lindy, are you okay?" Charley asked after several seconds went by.

"No--.it was terrible! You see my husband got sick and died. It seemed that house got sick too, everything went wrong. The bills for repairs were endless. I tried to do a lot of the things myself, but couldn't keep up. The water pipes broke, the furnace quit, my lawn became full of damn weeds. Then I found the ants!" Lindy shuddered, "I didn't know what to do. They had infested the walls, ceilings and were eating my beautiful wood floors!" She blew out a breath and reached for another cigarette, then inhaled deeply.

"I'm so sorry Lindy, what did you do?" Charley asked concern on his face. She looked at him and suddenly giggled. Then put a hand over her mouth and whispered, "I'm sorry, I'm just so tired. It's not funny I know, but I burnt them!"

"You deliberately set you house on fire?"

Lindy sobered. "Oh no--," she gasped, "just the ants!"

-37-

Reed had been at the jail for several hours waiting patiently, as Murphy had advised. He knew he couldn't do a thing for Lindy unless she asked for him to be her council, but he had to find her first. Just then his cell-phone rang. Goddamn, who wanted him now?

"Reed Conners," he muttered.

"Where the hell are you? They said you left the hospital!" Reed moved the receiver away from his ear as he recognized the booming voice of Ed, his boss at First Federated Insurance Company.

"Conners, I just got back into town and read the report about you catching that bullet!"

"I heard you were out of town." Reed leaned his head back against the wall.

"I just talked to Murphy. He told me about you getting shot. Jesus, that was too close!"

"Yeah," Reed exhaled into the phone.

"You sound like hell. It wasn't very smart to walk out of the hospital. Where are you?"

Reed sat up in his chair. "I'm down here at the jail. The Feds have Lindy Lewis tucked away somewhere."

"That's what Murphy said. Christ, Conners, I want that money back but it's not your case!" Ed's voice vibrated in his ear.

"Yeah!" He repeated. Even though Lindy had put him though an endless amount of hell, he still felt a responsible tie to her. But he didn't say anything about that to Ed who went on, "Now as soon as you feel up to it, I want your report on the Carmen Ciem case. We need to wrap it up!"

"I'm getting close," Reed said and tried to cover his irritation.

"Good. Take it easy for awhile and let Mona know when you can come in. She'll know where to find me!" The phone clicked off.

Now, Reed was really pissed. Not only from this latest pressure from Ed, but he felt like hell; he was hungry and cold. He got up again and went to the desk.

"Any word on Lindy Lewis?"

"Like I told you before, all I know is she's not where she's supposed to be!" The man turned back to his computer and shook his head.

Reed swallowed a sarcastic barb. For Christ's sake, he'd punch this asshole out if he hung around any longer. He left the Police Department and picked up fast-food and went back to his motel room. After eating the cardboard tasting sandwich, he piled into bed and thankfully closed his eyes.

In the twilight of his slumber, he had decided one thing. He'd had enough! To hell with trying to help Lindy. To hell with the Ciem case. He was going to sleep until next week if he felt like it, resign from First Federated Insurance Company and go back home. He'd set out the fish house on his lake and enjoy the peace and serenity. His only challenge would be to catch that elusive walleye for his dinner.

-38-

"**D**o you admit to deliberately setting the fire that burned your house?" Agent Charles McGovern from the FBI asked Lindy as they sat in a conference room at the jail.

Lindy's breath came out in shallow little gasps. "Oh no!" she said innocently, "I was just going to burn the ants!"

"The fire got away from you?" Charley's eyes were noncommittal.

Lindy's fingernails dug into her hands as she clasped them in her lap. "I was cleaning house that day, and had been in the middle of painting a bedroom earlier when I saw them."

"The ants," Charley asked.

"Yes!" Lindy turned tear-filled eyes to him.

"Tell me about them," the agent lit another cigarette as he listened.

"Well--, I found them first in the attic and then everywhere, eating away at my beautiful house," Lindy said and sniffed. "I had paint, thinners and all those messy rags around and then suddenly the fire was everywhere!" Oh lord, for a minute she felt like she was back in grade school, sitting in the principle's office.

Charley was silent as he studied her face. "You collected a million dollars, what happened then, Lindy?"

Her eyes darkened. "I had to run for my life! I had met a man, John Thomas, and he tried to kill me. He was a swindler and wanted my money. Reed Conners caught him!"

"Tell me about this Reed Conners."

Lindy brushed her hair off her face again and put a strand behind her ear. Well, this was going better. "He's an attorney and an investigator. We met in college and we lived together for a time. I ran into him again in a casino up North. He was trailing this same John Thomas I was trying to escape from. I went to Dallas then.

Charley eyed Lindy curiously as he tried to keep up. "What did you do there?"

"I had to go to work!" She shook her head wearily.

Charley gave a short laugh. "Why, when you had all that money?"

Lindy leaned towards him as she said, "I had just gotten there and had stopped at a restaurant to eat. As I got out of my car I was mugged! In a matter of seconds, I was lying on the ground, and everything I had was gone!"

"Your car and everything?"

Lindy's eyes grew large. "And all my money!"

"You had a lot of cash with you?"

"Yes, I had it all, but it was hidden!"

"You were traveling with a million dollars in cash," Charley asked incredulously.

"Yes, well, I had it safely hidden; I'd sewn it into the car seat. The thief didn't know."

Charley looked at Lindy and shook his head. "And you got it back?"

"Well, I had to go to work for a few months, then I placed an ad in the Dallas newspaper offering a reward for my BMW, and I found it! The money was just where it was supposed to be!"

"Incredible," Charley said and almost smiled, then sobered. "Go on." he said.

Lindy relaxed and took a breath. "During that time, I dated a man named Dade Lampart. He gave me this huge diamond engagement ring, but I found out he was gay and just wanted to marry me to keep his inheritance." Her face saddened for a moment as she remembered the betrayal. She sat up straighter then and said defensively, "Well, I sold that big diamond and left Dallas, but that was after I'd been hospitalized there with amnesia."

"Really?" Charley blew smoke rings as he listened.

Lindy put her chin on her hand and sighed. "It was after that, that I started having these headaches along with awful dreams, seeing and hearing things." She went on to tell him that she had seen ghosts in the Ashton mansion, Reed Conner's face in a vision and heard his plea for her help.

Charley, the FBI agent sat fascinated as Lindy continued talking and then asked, "You met the D'Agustino brothers earlier in Hilton Head, South Carolina?"

Lindy's face fell. "Yes, I ran into my friend Mitzi there, and we met Mario and Andre. We all dated." Lindy shivered as a chill spread down her back.

Charley glanced at the tape recorder to make sure it was still running, then back to her. "Tell me about it."

Lindy took a deep breath. "One night Mario invited me to dinner out on his boat. It was a palace. We had wine." Lindy hesitated and her face flushed pink. "We were in the bedroom when we heard a boat come up to us. Mario went out to see who it was. When I heard angry voices, I peeked out a porthole. That's when I saw Mario shoot this man. Saw him push the body into the ocean and then our boat sped away." Lindy shifted in her chair, her back was stiff, her shoulders sore.

"Then what did you do Lindy?" Charley studied her actions intently.

She took a shuddering breath. "I wasn't sure, but I thought Mario had seen me at the window watching. And the man was someone I recognized. I was so scared, I had to do something! When he came back to the bedroom, I hit him with an ashtray and knocked him out. I tied him up too!" Lindy exhaled and her voice wavered. "I took his gun and held it on the man at the helm until we got back to Hilton Head. We'd been way out on the ocean somewhere. I threw the gun in the water as I ran off the boat!"

"We know Lindy, we found it and it has your fingerprints on it!" Charley said solemnly.

Lindy blanched. "You found it?"

"Yes, but go on." Charley's face was still impassive.

Oh God, that was a mistake. She should have gotten rid of it some other way!

She was exhausted. And, how many times did she have to tell this? First to Reed, then Gil Finney, Murphy and now the FBI. She took another breath and began again.

"I was terrified, and came back to Minneapolis to see Reed. I told him about what had happened and he got things straightened out. Well, then I left again and went to Savannah, Georgia." Charley waited for her to continue.

"I bought a house and then that one burned too!" Lindy's shoulders sagged. "Well, I went to the East coast and got a job at that mansion in Rhode Island. I met Sid, which was a mistake, but I was lonely. That's when I saw the ghosts, started to have visions and nightmares and my headaches got really bad!" Lindy put her head in her hands.

Charley sat quietly not saying a word, deep in thought. He jerked his thoughts back to the present and said, "Tell me about them, Lindy." He nodded at her and smiled gently.

Lindy swallowed a sob. "Just last night, and this nightmare is really strange! Remember that house I bought in Savannah? It was from a lady named Madam Fitsgerald? She told me she was going to a retirement home, but in my dream I saw her bound and gagged, and a woman holding a gun on another lady. That other lady was someone I recognized from magazines, Carmen Ciem. Then this gray-haired person, who wore a maid's uniform, pushed Carmen Ciem over the railing! I don't know what it means." Lindy's eyes teared. "I never get a good night's sleep anymore."

"Tell me more about this Lindy," Charley encouraged.

Lindy went on to describe the surroundings and the cold night. The woman who was killed and the person who murdered her. Also the woman she knew as Madam Fitsgerald, lying helpless on the balcony floor.

"Have you told anyone about these visions?" Charley asked as he ran a hand over his face.

"Who'd take me seriously?" Lindy gave a short painful laugh and lowered her eyes. "I think I'm loosing my mind, I don't know what to do!

"Well, I'll tell you what, I want you to rest now, and try not to worry." Charley stood up and pocketed the tape recorder. He walked over and banged on the door. "Miss Lewis needs some rest," he told a guard as the door swung open instantly. He put his hand on her shoulder and smiled kindly at her. Then nodded his head and said, "I think things will work out!"

The guard took Lindy's arm and steered her back through the hallways and finally to the cell she'd been in before. She'd followed in a trance, and mechanically put one foot in front of the other. Her lovely gray dress was wrinkled and the make-up that she'd applied so much earlier, caked and dried on her tear-stained face. By now, she didn't have an ounce of strength to think further. She lay her head down on the offensive pillow and pulled the dreadful blanket over herself.

-39-

Reed Conners jerked at the blankets on his bed as a grating noise shattered the peaceful silence in his motel room. He sat up, groped for the phone and awoke fast as Murphy said, "Conners, get down here, I just got word the Feds are going to slip Lewis out the back door! And get this; the insurance fraud case is wide open again!"

"Goddamn, stall them!" Reed threw the phone on the bed, splashed water on his face, dressed and was out the door in minutes ready again now to take them on.

It was just as he figured. The Feds had gotten to her. They needed her for their case coming up in South

Carolina next week; she would be their star witness in the Mario D'Agustino murder trial!

The Police Department hummed with activity; phones rang continually as uniformed men and women rushed in and out. He stopped in his tracks and turned curiously as a soft female voice murmured, "Hi handsome, what are you doing later?" Three girls smiled at him. All of them were dressed in leather and animal prints and their perfumed fragrance was a welcome relief in the stagnant atmosphere. He grinned and hurried on.

This time a clerk at the check-in desk motioned him to a conference room where he found Murphy and two strangers at a table in the middle of a heated discussion.

"Reed Conners," Murphy greeted him, "meet agents Charles McGovern and John Henry from the Federal Bureau." Then added, "Mr. Conners represented Lindy Lewis in that insurance fraud case!" Then turning to Reed went on, "I'll let agent Henry here, bring you up to date. Have a seat." Reed unzipped his leather jacket and sat down.

"Mr. Conners, we're taking Lindy Lewis back to South Carolina for the Mario D'Agustino trial. The man who was killed was one of our men!"

Reed jumped up.

Agent Henry, the taller of the two men added, "Her prints are on the gun that killed him!"

Reed faced the FBI men squarely. "I don't think so, those charges were dismissed and the case is closed!"

"Well, Mr. Conners, the case is wide open now!" John Henry said.

Reed's lips were a thin white line as he glared at agent Henry. Goddamn, this was one of the reasons he detested the egotism of the bureau. They always thought they had the upper hand and with their usual arrogant approach, used intimidation to get it.

Agent Henry broke in. "We're taking Miss Lewis with us now!"

"Not so fast gentlemen, I need five minutes." Reed left the room and raced down the hallway to the jail. Goddamn, Lindy would be a sitting duck not only from the drug world, but even the FBI. He rushed into the front office of the jail.

"Get me Lindy Lewis now," he yelled. Precious time went by as the guard wordlessly punched buttons on his phone.

"It'll be a few minutes," he said to Reed and turned away to read some papers. Reed began to pace as he waited. Regardless of the ache in his shoulder, the challenge of Lindy's prediction had gotten his adrenalin flowing. He liked a good fight. Years ago, when he'd been confronted by the FBI, he hadn't liked their attitude then and he didn't like it now.

The door opened and a guard stood aside as Lindy walked in looking lost and pathetic. Without wasting time he said, "Lindy, you need an attorney or else the FBI will bury you in some prison in the deep South and you'll never be heard of again!"

Lindy sucked in her breath, put a hand over her chest. "Why--? I told Charley McGovern everything. He told me not to worry."

"Yeah, wait and see. Did he tell you, that you have to appear in court next week in South Carolina as a witness for the prosecution in Mario's murder trial?"

Lindy was fully awake now. She gaped at him and whispered "No--."

"Lindy, listen to me, the FBI found the gun that was used to kill that man. That man was a federal agent, and it has your prints on it!" A vein pulsed in Reed's neck as he repeated what she had already heard from Agent Henry. "Right now Lindy, you are charged with murder! And more than likely," he shouted at her, "they'll pin drug dealing charges on you. For Christ's sake, you were playing around with one of the biggest drug lords known! Do you understand?"

Lindy whispered, "But he'll kill me!"

"Don't you understand; the Feds need you to make their case!"

Lindy hugged herself. "I don't believe this. Charley was so nice!"

"Lindy, goddamn it, can't you see they tricked you!" Reed pounded the table with his fist as they faced each other, still standing. "You don't have a choice, Lindy you need an attorney! You don't want to know what goes on in those Federal prisons!"

Stricken, Lindy realized she'd been deceived! But, could she trust Reed? After all, all this started when he told her to turn herself in to his good friend Murphy at the Police Department.

But, if what he said about the FBI was true. God, after she'd poured her heart out to Charley. She exhaled a deep breath. She had no choice, she had to trust Reed again She straightened, "Alright Reed, I want you as my attorney." Then declared, "And you better get me out of this!"

"Okay!" Reed shouted and banged on the door and then disappeared down a hallway, as a guard took Lindy by the arm again and led her back to her cell.

He grinned to himself as he opened the door into the conference room, and then sobered when he stepped in. He had them now and knew exactly what he wanted. Without losing a beat he said, "As Miss Lewis's council, gentlemen, here are the terms!" He took a seat, lit a cigarette and blow out a cloud of smoke.

Goddamn, how he loved this. He went on, "In exchange for Miss Lewis's testimony, we're requesting the bureau pay full restitution of one million dollars to the First Federated Insurance Company and all charges against Miss Lewis be dropped!"

"Impossible!" The two FBI men said in unison.

"Well, that's the deal!" Reed said confidently.

Agent Henry smirked. "Conners, you're out of your mind!"

"Yeah?" Reed smiled and shrugged his shoulders. "She could disappear and where would that leave you? Without her, you don't have a case!"

"She wouldn't get far, we've been with her all along," Agent Henry huffed.

"Are you willing to take that chance?" Reed asked coolly. These men pissed him off, especially dog-faced Henry. He continued, "You know as well as I, that we're talking about billions of dollars here from this bust. Tell your boss to dig down in the bureau's pockets!"

Reed walked to the door. He knew he had them. Although he didn't like the way Lindy had gotten the insurance money, but if his company was reimbursed, why should he care? He would soon be leaving this hell hole and going home! Maybe he'd write a book.

He turned in his tracks as Agent Charles McGovern said, "Give us a minute." The two men walked to the side of the room, stood in a huddle and whispered. Reed returned to Murphy at the table who had silently watched the heated exchange.

Murphy raised an eyebrow. "Think they'll go for it?"

Reed smiled, "Buddy, they don't have a choice!"

-40-

Reed and Murphy waited for the FBI men to rejoin them. The headquarters still vibrated with the conflicts between the revelers and the protectors of peace. The fluorescent lights were harsh and unflattering.

Reed inhaled deeply on his cigarette. "Got any coffee around here?" He sat back.

Murphy left the room and came back carrying two Styrofoam cups. After taking a swallow Reed mumbled, "What the hell is this made off, old tires?" He blew smoke rings and forced himself to appear nonchalant, but he'd have given anything to hear the conversation going on across the room. Agents Henry and McGovern were on their cell phones talking fast, nodding their heads. Henry's face was contorted in anger, McGoven's impassive.

Murphy spoke to Reed in a low voice. "I called ahead to a guy I know in the South Carolina Department. The brothers are both cooling their heels in lock-up. Their attorneys are scampering around."

Murphy had been with the Minneapolis Police for over twenty years, first on the street, then promoted to head of detectives. He pulled a lot of weight. He was a conservative man, both in his dress and his manner, and ran his department with an iron hand. He was well known around the city and respected by his men. His white shirt was crisp and his trouser creases sharp. He was a true Irish man; with black hair, fair skin and piercing blue eyes. His six foot frame matched Reed's, and like him, Murphy loved the challenge of a good fight, especially now, after discovering a leak that had brought the FBI into his department.

"Got the number of the guy you know down there?" Reed took out a notepad and nodded towards Murphy.

Murphy took off his suit jacket and hung it on a coat rack as he said, "He's good. He's got good connections too." He reached inside his coat pocket and flipped the pages of a dog-eared leather bound book. "Here's his phone number, and also the name of a lawyer, a friend of a friend. From what I've heard, he's a high powered attorney."

"Great, I'll need someone with a South Carolina license." Reed jotted down the name and number.

"Hey Conners, what's the real story with Lindy Lewis?" Murphy asked as they stood together, "Is she really as innocent as she claims?"

Reed took a swallow of the coffee. Murphy continued, "She said you've known each other since college?"

"Yeah, we knew each other in those hungry, carefree days."

"When she came in and told me her story, I believed her about the shooting. The fire though, nah, she did it to collect the bucks."

"Yeah?" Reed was noncommittal.

"What's your story, Conners? Still got the hots for her?"

Reed raised his hands and shrugged. "It's been years since college."

"How'd that happen that she showed up a few days ago?"

Reed swiped a hand over a cheek and frowned at Murphy's question. He shifted in his seat, "She said she saw me in a vision, and that I was in trouble. All I can remember is her bitching at me to come out of that black hole I was stuck in."

Murphy shook his head. "Christ man, she probably saved your life considering the shape you were in."

"Could be." Reed checked his watch and glanced at the two men still huddled in the corner. He tried to read their lips, judge their actions by the expressions on their faces, but like the persona of their trade, their facade was unreadable.

Reed's stomach recoiled after another swallow of the terrible coffee. Even though the circumstances were critical, his mind wandered. He needed food; bacon, eggs and hash browns, smothered in onions.

When was the last time he'd had a good meal? Christ, last week? Thirty minutes had gone by. He crushed out the cigarette and asked, "Murph, you want to come up north for the fishing opener? Second weekend in May, you know."

"Hey, I've got some time coming." Murphy rolled his eyes, "But I've got to get the okay from the wife."

"Bring her along."

Murphy laughed. "Nah, her idea of fishing is a blue sky and getting a tan."

"That's a woman for you, just can't understand the seriousness of the business." From the corner of Reed's eyes, he saw the two men put their phones away, exchange a few words and start over to where he and Murphy stood. He kept his expression flat. Agent Henry unbuttoned his Brooks Brothers blue suit jacket and ran a hand down his silk tie. The ceiling light flashed off his gold cuff links and Rolex watch. His small eyes pierced through the distance as he looked over. Agent McGovern had a worried look. His blue suit was a cheaper version. Agent Henry cleared his throat.

"We need Lindy Lewis in South Carolina the first of the week."

Reed waited. A few seconds went by. "And?" he asked.

"That's it, Conners! You really expect us to fix the charges against Lewis for ripping off the insurance company, then pay the money back? Outrageous!" Agent Henry had a smug look on his face.

Reed lit another cigarette, blew some smoke rings and calmly proclaimed, "Gentlemen, my terms or no deal!"

Agent Henry smirked. "I've got a subpoena for her to appear!"

"So--, what if she doesn't show up!" Reed loved the power he had over the situation.

Henry's face turned red as he stomped over to the window and stared out. McGovern hadn't said a word.

Reed held his silence for a few seconds, then added, "Sure you can subpoena Miss Lewis to appear, but you can't rely on her testimony. She's proven time and again, she can't be trusted. You willing to take that chance?"

He knew it was their ploy to play hardball. He was pisssd and when Reed got really provoked, he never gave an inch. His pallor flushed to pink as his blood hurdled though his veins. "And, she could plead the fifth! Not that I'd encourage her, of course." He had the bastards now. Let them worry about that! Without Lindy, their case wouldn't hold water.

Agent Henry stared at Reed. His Adam's apple jerked in his throat as he fidgeted with his shirt cuffs, adjusted his collar. His back was ramrod straight as he walked away. Reed threw his hands up. "Well, times up. I've got things to do!" He walked to the door and was about to step out when Agent McGovern spoke up. "Mr. Conners, get your boss at First Federated Insurance on the phone for me please!"

Reed stopped in his exit, hid a grin and turned. "It's pretty early, he won't be happy!"

Agent McGovern's round face was still impassive. Reed dialed the number that could be used in emergencies. After four rings Ed answered. "This better be good," his voice boomed.

"Ed? Conners here, I'm with the boys from the bureau and it seems they're ready to make a deal on the Lewis case." He went on to bring Ed up to date.

"Christ, put those assholes on. I want my company's money back!" Ed growled and Reed handed the phone to McGovern. McGovern walked away and stood next to Henry, and talked in a low voice. Murphy nodded to Reed and winked.

"Who's going to win the Super bowl?" he asked.

Reed grinned. "Our team will annihilate those Easterners."

"Want to put some money on it?" Murphy laughed.

"How much do you want to loose?" Reed and Murphy bantered back and forth, seemingly unconcerned about the conversation going on in the far side of the room. After another ten minutes, Agent McGovern handed Reed his cell phone back. His face was grim. Agent Henry stalked out the door.

"Conners, you drive a hard bargain. However, I've come up with a number the insurance company will settle for, if they drop the charges. I'm going over to see Ed."

"Thanks McGovern, under those conditions, I can assure you my client will be in South Carolina in time to appear in court." Reed extended his hand

"Conners, got another minute?" Agent McGovern said, "I'd like you and Murphy to listen to something." Reed looked at him expecting another snag in their arrangement. "There's something you'll want to hear."

Reed looked at McGovern curiously as the agent took a tape recorder from his pocket, set it on a table and turned it on. The men were silent as they listened to Lindy Lewis talk about her travels, her involvements and finally her nightmares and visions.

After it was over Agent McGovern explained, "Miss Lewis has what's known as mental telepathy. Some would call it psychic, clairvoyance, or a sixth sense. I've studied this for years." He continued, "She had a clear picture of that murder I heard your working on, Conners. I'd say it's worth looking into."

When Reed had been in the coma, he remembered bits and pieces of her conversation and her telling about seeing him in a vision, and having strange dreams.

Could any of it be true?   He turned to Murphy who was gathering papers. "What do you think? Do you believe any of this?"

Murphy had an intrigued look on his face. "Jesus, I've used psychics a few times, and I'm always flabbergasted when they're on the mark." He was quiet for a minute. "Conners, when Lewis came in to see me, I got this strange feeling about her." He shook his head, "I can't put my finger on it."

Reed sat deep in thought, then said, "You know, the only connection is this woman Lindy bought the house from in Savannah, Mrs. Fitsgerald."   He got up and walked around the room. "Yet, she described the Ciem house perfectly, and the people involved in the murder scene she claimed she had seen in one of her visions

Murphy went on, "One thing I know for sure Conners, at this point, we can't afford not to take everything seriously!"

"Would you be willing to take a chance on something?" Reed leaned closer and continued, "I've had a gut feeling all along that the housekeeper, Hilda Sorenson was involved in Ciem's death, somehow. I just hadn't gotten far enough in the case when I caught that bullet."

Murphy sat back in his chair. "Reed, you found Ciem's jewelry in the airport locker, the key in Tony Roman's things. You think they were working together?"

"No--I don't think so. Roman's not smart enough. The impression I got from them was of forced tolerance." Reed swiped his hair off his forehead. "According to Ciem's will, if she died from natural causes, her kids got the ten million dollar life insurance, the Sorenson's, the house. And an aunt, one million and the rest of her wealth would go to her old college. Roman wasn't listed. But Murphy, one thing, I didn't get to check was the reason there was a one hundred thousand dollar withdrawal from the Sorenson bank account!"

Murphy's voice rose. "Oh shit, when?"

"Just a few days before I got shot! I know a guy over at their bank and he owes me a favor. Goddamn, Murph, we need to get into their apartment!" Murphy listened as Reed went on. "Can you get a warrant? We need some concrete evidence and I think we'll find some there!" Reed's lips tightened as a spasm of pain burned down the side of his neck and shoulder.

"Reed, you okay? Christ man, you look like hell. Are you up for this?" Murphy put his coffee down and looked at him with concern.

Reed exhaled, "I've been better. What do you think? How long would it take to get a warrant?"

Murphy was silent for a minute "Okay, good idea, I'll need an hour!"

Reed walked out to his rented car, found a diner and had breakfast, but he still felt like hell after eating. He rejoined Murphy, who waved the warrant in the air and said, "Four of my best men will meet us there. Called them in for special duty."

They headed their cars towards the Calhoun area. The twin lions stood guarding the pink stucco house as before. Reed punched the doorbell as Murphy stood at his side. On the third ring, Hilda Sorenson opened the door.

"You!" She put a hand on her chest and stepped back. "I thought you were dead!"

"Nope, I'm alive and well!" Reed put a foot in the room as she tried to shut the door.

"But the news said--." Hilda was attired in a fashionable silk dress. Her lacquered up-swept hair looked freshly done. "But, I thought--." She looked at Reed warily.

Actually, the Police Department had purposely kept Reed's condition quiet. "Hilda, I'm sure you remember Mr. Murphy, chief of detectives from the Police Department!" She drew herself up as he smiled innocently. "Got any of those doughnuts left?" Reed asked as he and Murphy stepped in and walked through the house towards the kitchen. Hilda followed.

"What do you want?" she hissed.

"Well, how about some coffee to go with the doughnuts?" Reed pulled out a chair at the table and sat down, his eyes coolly going over Hilda's actions. Murphy watched with interest. The back door opened and Otto came in. His overall covered in snow. "Take those clothes off, Otto, I don't want my floors messed up," Hilda said, and then put a hand over her mouth. She turned away and busied herself in a cupboard. Otto grumbled and stepped out of his overall and hung it in a closet.

"Conners, isn't it?" He turned towards the detective. "Murphy, we haven't heard anything from you lately." He took a chair and sat down. Hilda's face was flushed, her actions agitated as she set coffee cups on the table, one spilling over the edge. She stood and looked at the liquid sliding towards the edge of the table, unmoving. Otto looked at her curiously as it dripped over the edge. Reed and Murphy made small talk as they waited for the search party to arrive. With a righteous look on her face, Hilda said, "Tony's back, but we don't see much of him. Comes and goes in the middle of night, usually has company until all hours. Not that we keep track."

"Oh Hilda, you've been keeping an eye on him," Otto said.

Reed glanced around the kitchen with its rich wood cupboards and floors. The top of the line appliances and the beautiful china they were using. Remembered the opulence of the rest of the house. He studied Hilda's appearance and her actions, apparently she thought she was the lady of the house already. Reed took out a cigarette and blew perfect smoke rings, then said, "Get Tony Roman!"

Hilda came out of her daze. "Well, it's about time!" She went to the intercom.

"Mr. Roman, Mr. Conners and that Murphy from the Police Department are here. They want to see you!" Reed watched her face go from anxious to triumphant. Ten minutes later, Tony Roman walked into the kitchen. He had the typical Sylvester Stallone look; Tanned, bulging muscles and an arrogant stance. His belligerent attempt at bravado failed when he tried to sound tough as he said, "If you guys can't get this case wrapped up, I want someone who can!"

"We're getting there," Reed answered. Stalling for time he asked, "Roman, what's it like to work with those Hollywood stars?" And Tony Roman, ego driven, didn't hesitate to bring up his own importance in the trade. At last, the doorbell chimed and Hilda went to answer it with a pinched look on her thin lips. She came back in the room followed by four uniformed Policemen. Murphy stood up and reached into his jacket pocket.

"Folks, I have a warrant to search this property, signed by a Judge!" Hilda's intake of breath echoed and Otto looked confused. Tony Roman muttered obscenities. Murphy continued saying to the four new arrivals, "Gentlemen, I want you to start in the apartment over the garage." He turned back to the group at the table, "This may take some time so I suggest you three stay put. Johnson here, will keep you company!"

*****

"We're taking you in, Mrs. Sorenson, you're under arrest for attempted murder," Murphy said several hours later, slipping handcuffs over her wrists, after the search of their apartment revealed a gun. The same caliber as the one that had been used to shoot Reed. They'd also found a slip of paper with the name and the written directions to the airport locker where Reed had found Carmen Ciem's jewels. Hilda glared at him defiantly as he read her her rights. Otto's eyes bulged, his jaw went slack.

"Take her." Murphy ordered his men and they walked her out. Tony Roman sat at the table. Reed looked at Otto and said, "Sorry about this." Turning to Tony he said, "Take care of him." He zipped his leather jacket and walked out with Murphy.

"Let's let her sit for awhile and cool her heels," he said as he stood by Murphy's unmarked car. He blew out a ragged breath.

"Take it easy Conners, you look pretty wasted." Murphy got in and started his car.

"Well, I figure in about a week, I'll be back up north where the world is normal. By the way Murph, can you keep Lewis safe in lock-up until we're ready to take off for the airport? I need time to wrap up things here!"

He got in his car and reminded himself to call the garage and see how long it would take to put his Corvette together. It was a Thursday morning, a few weeks into January. The trial for Mario D'Agustino started the next week. As he drove, he dialed phone numbers and connected with the attorney in South Carolina and explained the situation. The man was explicit about the state laws and offered to be on hand when Reed got there. Back at his motel room, Reed tried to relax. Several hours later, he went back to Murphy's office, "You think Hilda Sorenson is ready to talk?" he asked.

The same clerk sat at the desk as Reed and Murphy walked into the jail. Reed held his tongue as Murphy did the talking. As they waited in a conference room for her, Reed said, "Murphy, let me have the first go around with her. After all, the woman shot me!"

An officer brought Hilda Sorenson in. Now, her carefully lacquered hair was askew, her silk dress wrinkled. A wide run in her nylon edged its way down her leg to her shoe.

"Hello Hilda, have a seat. How are the accommodations?" Reed pulled out a chair and sat down across from her.

Hilda's cold look chilled the room. "What do you want?"

"I want to know why you killed Carmen Ciem, Hilda?"

"I didn't!" She glared at him belligerently.

Reed said calmly, "I've got a witness that'll swear in court that she saw you push Carmen Ciem over the balcony."

"Who?" Hilda's face distorted in anger as she glared at him.

"You'll see! Hilda, we also know it was you who shot me after I found Mrs. Ciem's jewels." Reed got up and walked around the room. Hilda's eyes followed his steps. Then Reed stopped and pointed a finger in her face and dropped the bomb.

"That nice old lady you kept prisoner in Stillwater is dead Hilda, and you'll be charged with that murder too!"

Hilda blew out a huff.

"How were you planning to get rid of Tony Roman?" Reed continued walking in circles around the table as Hilda clutched the arms on the chair. Then he stopped in front of her again and glared at her, "You'll never see the light of day again. It's over Hilda!" He watched for some sign; a sudden plea in her eyes, tears, an apology, anything but only saw defiance as she said, "I want to call an attorney!"

"You better get a good one, even the best in the country couldn't get you off!" Reed shot back at her. He took one last stab at getting her to talk and said, "Hilda, make it easier on yourself. Talk to me!"

"Get out!" She stood up and yelled and waved her arms. Now, she looked like a crazed old woman. Her dress hung haphazardly on her bony frame. Her eyes flashed wildly.

Reed asked patiently, "Hilda, don't you know you'll spend the rest of your life in prison?"

"You'll never prove anything!" Hilda flung back. She sat down and was silent for a moment. Then suddenly, her face went deathly white and she clasped her chest. She began to gasp for air and slumped in the chair.

"Goddamn Murphy," Reed yelled, "she's having a heart attack!" They eased her onto the floor and felt for a pulse. Her eyes rolled back in her head as she gasped for a breath. "Hilda, take it easy." He chaffed her hands as he kneeled by her side.

"The paramedics are on the way," Murphy said, putting his cell in his pocket just as the door burst open and a guard rushed in. Reed watched in trepidation as he and Murphy immediately began CPR.

Oh Christ, had he killed her with his deliberate accusations? Maybe, he'd been completely mistaken! But they'd found the gun under the floorboard in her bedroom!

He swiped at perspiration on his forehead and sat back on his heels as he watched. Murphy was on the phone again. Then, Hilda started to move and opened her eyes. The guard giving the CPR stepped aside. Hilda stared at Reed.

Grabbing at a last straw, Reed bent down close to her and asked, "Hilda, do you want to confess?" Hate flashed in her eyes again.

He repeated, "Hilda, did you kill Carmen Ciem?"

She closed her eyes and was silent. Moments went by, as she struggled to breath. Then her face crumbled and she whispered, "Yes, I did it!" Gasping she said, "I was tired of waiting on that woman. I wanted my house!" The room was silent as the men watched her. She opened her eyes again, and whispered, "Otto didn't know." Then she was still.

Reed stood up on shaky legs. "You heard it," he said to Murphy, who nodded his head. Just then the doors burst open and the paramedics arrived. After long minutes of extensive ministering, they shook their heads and turned to Reed and Murphy, who stood off to the side in the room.

"Sorry, we did all we could. She's gone."

-41-

After the guard brought Lindy back to her cell after meeting Reed, she sat on the narrow cot, paralyzed with fear. He'd said she had to appear in court in South Carolina, and testify for the FBI, that she'd seen Mario D'Agustino commit murder! She drew a strangled breath. She couldn't do it! She'd never forget the look in his eyes, when he'd killed the man that turned out to be a Federal agent. In a matter of those few seconds, her feelings had exploded into stark terror!

The lights in the jail were dim, the place eerily quiet. She'd only slept for short periods and was totally disoriented, had lost track of days and time. She put a hand over her chest and felt the frantic beat of her heart. How she longed to go back to the time in her life when she'd been completely happy and safe. To the time before her husband got sick.

Her jumbled thoughts drifted and she remembered the joy of fixing up that old manor they'd found and making it a home. She sat up suddenly with an alarmed look on her face. She'd completely forgotten about the antique soup tureen that she'd gotten from her Mother that had been in the family for decades. She slumped as she realized sadly, like so many things, it was gone too.

Lindy clutched the blanket closer around herself. She'd finally slipped on the formless coverall the matron had presented her with. But she wondered, was she supposed to sleep in it?

So much had happened in her life since those happy days. She remembered back to that time her husband had gotten the bad news that changed their lives. He would always grumble about having to take time off from work to sit and wait, and freeze in his underwear in the Doctor's office for his yearly check-ups. She remembered the day he'd called her from work and said, "'I need to go back to the clinic, there's a spot on my x-ray and they want to do a ct-scan. It's nothing honey, I'll be home for supper.'"

As Lindy heard the words, a trickle of fear edged itself into her heart, but she kept her voice light as she said, "I made your favorite."

"Chili and fresh bread?" he asked.

"You guessed it, sweetie. See you soon." Lindy hung up the phone, checked the kettle on the stove and began to pace. She watched the clock. An hour went by, then another and finally as the sky began to darken, he walked in the door. One look at his stricken face and she knew the outcome of the test even before he slumped down in the nearest chair.

'"I've got cancer, honey!"' he had said in whisper. She remembered her strangled cry of alarm as she ran to his side. She never could remember if they had eaten the chili that night. Eight months later, Lindy watched as they lowered his body into the ground. During those months, she'd spent hours reading labels in grocery stores and learned to cook nourishing foods. Encouraged vitamins and expounded on the necessity of positive thinking. But, the challenge fell flat. He became angry, silent and withdrawn. In the end, she was ridden with guilt for being the survivor.

Lindy turned her stiff body to the side and stared at the wall of the jail. Her glance caught on a small heart scratched into the cement surface and etched in the middle, the initials MM loves BL. She wondered; had these strangers felt the same bleak abyss of fear creeping closer threatening to engulf them?

She slid further under the scratchy blanket as silent tears fell and soaked into the stale pillow. She felt total despair.

What had happened to everyone? Where was Reed? Or that nice Gil Finney?

Never again would she depend on a man for her safety and happiness. Especially Reed! His betrayal really hurt. He'd always been the one person she felt she could count on.

A sob caught in her throat, but, be damned if she would cry anymore. She'd shed enough tears for a lifetime. When they came to get her she'd serve her time in prison and then go far away!

*****

Reed took a shaky breath as the coroner left with Hilda Sorenson's body. Goddamn, never in his life had he felt so responsible for a death, although he'd been involved in John Thomas's demise that man had fired his gun point blank at him and he'd had to defend himself.

"Conners," Murphy said, "you got a confession from her. Jesus, that woman was a cold hearted killer."

"Yeah," Reed rubbed his forehead and sighed, "I've got to notify Otto, her husband. This will probably kill him too."

"Reed, we'll take it from here. I'll personally go and see Otto." Murphy shot him a worried look. "Take off man and get some rest."

"I can't really until we get back from South Carolina."

"You're leaving soon?"

"Soon as I wrap this up." Reed started for the door then turned, "Hey Murph, can you keep a special eye on Lindy till we take off?"

"Don't worry; we'll keep her safe!"

Hours later, he left the Police Department and went back to his motel to catch some sleep. He was depressed. He couldn't get the picture of Hilda's pathetic body out of his mind as the medical team had worked on her. All her defiance and arrogance had left her as she had lain there grasping for life.

After a restless night he went back to Murphy's office for a final wrap. Gil Finney, the Sheriff from Stillwater sat in one of the straight backed chairs.

"I was just about to call you, Reed, get this," Murphy said, "Finney's Jane Doe turned out to be Jean Fitsgerald, an aunt of Carmen Ciem's. We identified her from dental records."

Gil Finney leaned over his ample middle as he said, "After the news came out that the maid, Hilda Sorenson murdered Mrs. Ciem, a woman walked into my office and admitted to being involved. Turns out she was a friend of Hilda and was in on the plot, then got worried and wanted out." Gil ran a hand over his mustache. "Hilda bribed her with a hundred thousand dollars!"

"Well, that explains the withdrawal from their bank." Reed lit a cigarette as Gil went on.

"You see, she said Mrs. Fitsgerald was on a trip with her boyfriend up to this part of the country and she had stopped in at the Ciem house and walked in on the murder scene. The woman admitted they were slowly poisoning Fitsgerald hoping to make it look like a natural death. They had a killer dog there to guard her."

Reed massaged his headache. Much to his relief, the pain had just about subsided.

"Reed, listen to this," Murphy added, "Tony Roman suspected Hilda was stealing Mrs. Ciem's jewelry and purposely hid them in that locker at the airport."

Reed sat up in the chair as Murphy went on. "I've met with Ciem's attorney, also Ed over at First Federated Insurance and given them the details." Murphy grinned, "Jesus Conners, you saved your company millions now that they don't have to pay out the insurance since Ciem's death was not from natural causes. It looks like the kids and her college will work out a deal. Roman might get a little something."

Reed shook his head. "Thanks for winding this up for me guys, now just so the D'Agustino trial goes okay." He turned to Gil Finney, "Did Murphy bring you up on Lindy's problem?"

"Yep," Gil harrumphed. "Poor girl didn't know what the hell was going on with herself, but I knew she was alright. You take good care of her now."

"Thanks again for your help Gil," Reed said and shook his hand. "Murph, I'll be in touch.

Reed went back to his motel, checked reservations and packed his things and hurried back down to the jail to pick up Lindy. He felt guilty for keeping her locked up and not telling her about the deal he'd worked out with the FBI. Of course she wouldn't be officially cleared until she'd testified for the Federal Bureau.

*****

Lindy was startled out of her haze as the matron brought her clothes and told her she had been released. Her face was devoid of makeup and her blonde hair in drastic need of attention as she walked out of the detention area and found Reed waiting for her. She looked at him warily, and then exploded in anger.

"What the hell is going on?" She glared at him.

"Lets get out of here and I'll bring you up to date," Reed said as he hurried her out of the Police Department. Out on the street as they walked to his car he said, "Lindy, I'm sorry you had to stay so long in there but we needed to keep you safe!" Which was partly true, he didn't dare tell her it was also because he hadn't trusted her not to run again, while he needed time to clear up the Carmen Ciem case. But, now he saw the rage in her eyes as she stared straight ahead. Felt the tension in the confined space of the car after they got in.

"We're going to your motel to get your things, and then we've got flight reservations to South Carolina."

Lindy clasped her arms protectively around herself as Reed turned the car into the busy downtown traffic. Her heart lept in her throat. With a strangled cry she whispered, "Reed no—I can't. I can't testify. Mario will kill me!"

"Lindy, you'll be safe. You'll be with me!"

"Oh really, with your help I've been behind bars!" She huffed and turned her face away and stared out the side window in the car.

"Listen to me," Reed said taking his eyes off the busy traffic and glancing at her, "Lindy, a lot has happened! All you have to do is tell the court what you saw on that boat and Mario will go to prison for life!"

Lindy shrank back against the car seat. Her heart thumped. They expected her to tell the court she'd seen Mario shoot that man? No way, he'd be right there in the same room! She clutched her coat tighter around herself against the chill.

"Lindy," Reed said again, "The FBI has released you into my custody and after you've testified for them in court, you'll be free!"

Her eyes widened as she turned to him. "Free? What do you mean, free?"

"The charges against you will be dropped!"

"Dropped?" Lindy echoed.

"Yes Lindy, and listen, I worked out a deal with the FBI; in exchange for your testimony they will also pay back my company, First Federated Insurance, the money they lost on your claim." Reed repeated, "Do you understand, the FBI will repay the million dollars back to the insurance company, Lindy!"

She sucked in her breath as she finally comprehended Reed's announcement. Then, an incredulous look spread over her face as her thoughts whirled.

"You will be cleared Lindy, and if you have any money left, it's yours

"What? I --," her voice faded away.

"I know you figured I just left you sitting in jail without a thought." She stared at Reed as he sat calmly driving through the hair-raising traffic, dodging in and out of the commotion, his sandy hair curly and unruly and wearing that same familiar cologne.

He glanced at her again briefly, "I figured I owed you Lindy! You not only kicked my butt out of that coma I was in, but, one of those nightmares you'd had helped us solve a big case!"

She gaped at him as her thoughts tumbled. My God, besides being free of all those outrageous charges that had forced her to fly around the country, she would still have her money! She thought of all those zero's in her account in Newport, Rhode Island.

For the first time in ages, her eyes lit up. "Reed, I can't believe this!" Impulsively, she scooted over on the car seat and kissed him on his cheek. "Reed," she said again after a few minutes, "this is wonderful!" Then she busied herself with her makeup; applied lipstick and mascara.

The traffic had thinned out as they left the downtown area and Reed checked the time and leaned back, he steered the car with his left hand and threw his right arm over the back of the seat. "I figure you'll need some time to rest before our flight leaves for South Carolina," he said glancing at her.

Lindy threw the door open back at her motel and saw things were just as she had left it days earlier, somewhat askew but safe. Reed carried a package under his arm as he had followed along and now raised it in the air after closing the door and said, " Lindy, I figured you needed something to celebrate with so I brought you this!" He pulled a bottle of champagne out of the bag.

She looked at him, momentarily startled then managed to smile.

And even though they had to use water glasses for the lovely bubbles it tasted glorious. It didn't take long for the elixir to soften her determined resolves to go solo and soon the walls of the room hummed again with the age-old sexual tension between them.

The last days had been agony for Lindy and now as they lay together on the bed, she exclaimed, "I'm not letting you go until you cry for help!"

"Oh, make me," Reed groaned as he spread-eagled himself out, put his hands behind his head and grinned.

When Lindy climbed on him and unbuttoned his shirt, when she ran her tongue over a nipple and added just a nip, the man groaned again.

When she tugged at his belt, he knew he was in trouble and watched helplessly as she straddled him.

And, for a titillating space of time, they balanced the scales of justice and cascaded down the hills of ecstasy.

"Well, what do you think about testifying now," Reed asked as *Tomorrow's Rain* fell gently on the motel roof.

Lindy sat up, then fluffed her hair and said without hesitation, "Just watch me put that drug-dealing jerk away for good!"

The End

Watch for SUNSETS coming soon!

TO ORDER COPIES OF THIS BOOK

ON-LINE

Go to www:
Mystery Novels- Lyn Miller LaCoursiere
Or by email--lindylewis1@msn.com

While you're there check out

300 pages........$12.99

Book 1 of Series

***Coming Soon--*Sunsets**

Make sure to include your name, address
with city, state & zip code.
Add $2.50 for postage on each book.